ADVANCE PRAISE FOR *THE SHEPHERD'S VOICE*
By *Robin Lee Hatcher*

"*The Shepherd's Voice* richly demonstrates Ms. Hatcher's unique ability to weave a compelling story enriched by the beauty and power of God's redemptive love."

—LORI COPELAND, BEST-SELLING AUTHOR

"In *The Shepherd's Voice,* Robin Lee Hatcher entertains us with interesting characters and a moving story line. Along the way she skillfully leads us in to a deeper awareness of God's providence, guidance, and love."

— RANDY ALCORN, BEST-SELLING AUTHOR

PRAISE FOR *THE FORGIVING HOUR*
By *Robin Lee Hatcher*

"Wholesome and heartwarming, Robin Lee Hatcher delivers."

—DEBBIE MACOMBER, BEST-SELLING AUTHOR

"Break out the tissues. I loved *The Forgiving Hour* and so will you. Robin Lee Hatcher shows God's grace and mercy in bringing healing into the most painful of circumstances. This book cuts through the darkness of betrayal and brings in the healing light of Jesus Christ."

—FRANCINE RIVERS, BEST-SELLING AUTHOR

"Veteran historical romance writer Hatcher uses her well-honed skills to craft a compelling story of betrayal and forgiveness that will leave her readers both emotionally drained and spiritually satisfied."

—LIBRARY JOURNAL

"*The Forgiving Hour* is more than inspirational...it is compelling drama that keeps the pages turning. As a lover of historicals, I am hooked on contemporary inspirationals because of Robin Lee Hatcher's superior writing talent!"

—ROSANNE BITTNER, BEST-SELLING AUTHOR

"Hatcher's entertaining story uses biblical principles to show how 'real' people can survive, and truly recover from, the devastation of adultery. The book contains wisdom and enough heart to make it worthwhile reading for every woman, including those who've experienced or caused adultery's pain."

—CBA MARKETPLACE

"GOLD MEDAL–4 1/2 STARS. Popular historical author Robin Lee Hatcher debuts on the inspirational scene with an amazing book— clearly blazing her own way and setting her own fine standards with a life-changing book that readers will read over and over again."

—ROMANTIC TIMES

"A story of hope in the darkest hour, of betrayal and healing, of destruction and building, this book will make you evaluate your life and your relationship with God."

—BEAVER HERALD-DEMOCRAT

"Powerful...anointed...a riveting look at broken relationships and how lives can be brought to refinement by the hand and the heart of the Father."

—DEBORAH BEDFORD, BEST-SELLING AUTHOR

"*The Forgiving Hour's* subtitle, 'A Searing Tale of Love, Betrayal and Forgiveness,' describes the depth and meaning with which Hatcher writes."

—CHRISTIAN RETAILING

The SHEPHERD'S VOICE

The SHEPHERD'S VOICE

※ A NOVEL ※

ROBIN LEE HATCHER

WaterBrook
PRESS

10/01

THE SHEPHERD'S VOICE
PUBLISHED BY WATERBROOK PRESS
2375 Telstar Drive, Suite 160
Colorado Springs, Colorado 80920
A division of Random House, Inc.

Scriptures are taken from the *King James Version* of the Bible and the *American Sandard Version.*

The characters and events in this book are fictional, and any resemblance to actual persons or events is coincidental.

ISBN 1-57856-152-3

Library of Congress Cataloging-in-Publication Data
Hatcher, Robin Lee.
    The shepherd's voice / Robin Lee Hatcher.
        p. cm.
    ISBN 1-57856-152-3
        1. Ex-prisoners—Fiction. 2. Sheep ranchers—Fiction. 3. Fathers and sons—
Fiction. 4. Idaho—Fiction. I. Title
    PS3558.A73574 S54 2000
    813'.54—dc21

                                                            00-035930

Printed in the United States of America
2000

10 9 8 7 6 5 4 3 2

TO THE GOOD SHEPHERD,
MY LORD AND KING,

Who took me from where I was,
brought me to where I am,
and, praise the Lord, isn't finished with me yet.
May the stories I write please You, Jesus,
for if they don't, they are without merit of any kind.

COME HOME

Wandering child,
I am here.
I am near.
I speak.
Do you listen?

Arms open wide,
I wait.
I call.
I woo.
I weep.

No matter how far you run,
How high you climb,
How low you sink,
I do not change,
Nor does My love for you.

Return today.
Heed the Shepherd's voice.
Come home, My child.
Come home.

— R. L. H.

CHAPTER ONE

July 1934

Gabe Talmadge felt the backside of his navel rubbing against his spine. An interesting sensation, he thought before losing consciousness.

He ran from the darkness. He always ran, and it always followed. There was no escaping it. There never would be. The darkness would always be with him, hovering nearby, waiting to encompass him, enfold him, devour him. It would be easy to let it overtake him, to allow it to...

"Are you hurt?"

The soft, feminine voice came from a great distance.

"Mister?"

A hand slipped beneath his head. A small hand, with a touch as gentle as the voice.

"Can you hear me?"

Gabe opened his eyes. A shadowy form leaned forward, the bright light of midday glaring behind the woman, blinding him.

"Here. Take a drink."

His head was lifted slightly, and something cool touched his lips. Water trickled down his chin. Covering the woman's hand with his own, Gabe steadied the canteen, then drank deeply.

"Easy. Not too fast."

His thirst momentarily slaked, he closed his eyes. "Thanks."

"We should get you into the shade. It's powerful hot today. Can you stand?"

"Yes," he answered, although he wasn't as confident as he tried to sound.

Holding his arm, she helped him sit up. "Don't hurry. Take your time."

He thought he could feel the earth turning on its axis, and he gritted his teeth against the sensation.

"Ready?" his angel of mercy asked.

He opened his eyes a second time. "Ready." As he rose to his feet, the woman slipped beneath his arm, close against his side, taking his weight upon herself. It was humiliating to be this weak. His mind raged against it, as it had raged against countless degradations in the past, but rage changed nothing, then or now.

He glanced down. He could see little besides a floppy-brimmed straw hat above a narrow set of shoulders.

"We're going over there." She pointed with her free arm toward a good-sized birch tree. "Careful. We'll go slow. Take your time. Not too fast."

He could have told her not to worry—he was unable to do anything fast.

Except fall to the ground in a dead faint…

Which he promptly did.

Well, Lord. What do I do with him now?

Akira Macauley rolled the stranger onto his back. It was difficult to judge his age, given the shaggy black beard covering gaunt cheeks. There were holes in the bottoms of his boots, and the knees of his trousers were threadbare. Both he and his clothes needed a good washing, but Akira guessed cleanliness didn't mean much when one was going hungry.

I hope this hobo's not the one You sent, Lord. He's nothing but a rack of bones. I could make better use of a man who knows sheep, if that wouldn't be too much to ask.

With a shake of her head, she said aloud, "He'll be even less use if he dies."

She stood, grabbed hold of both his wrists, then walked backward, dragging him toward the shade. Despite his rawboned appearance, he weighed enough to make the going hard. Sweat rolled down her spine.

The stranger groaned.

"We're nearly there," she said.

Reaching the cool shadows beneath a leafy green tree, Akira lowered his arms with a sigh of relief.

He groaned again as his eyelids fluttered and eventually opened.

She dropped to her knees beside him and leaned forward, waiting for his vision to clear. When she thought he could see her, she said, "Give yourself a moment. You're weaker than a newborn lamb." She glanced over her shoulder and pointed at the canteen where she'd left it. "Cam, fetch."

Her collie, who'd patiently observed all the goings-on from a short distance, jumped up and raced to obey her mistress's command.

Akira returned her attention to the stranger. "When was the last time you ate something?"

"I'm not sure."

"Days?"

He nodded.

How'd he get so lost, Lord? He's a long way from the rails. And any man who could get that turned around would serve me no purpose. I'd spend all my time looking for him in the hills. You must see I'm right about that. Surely You've got a better way of answering my prayers than sending a shepherd who can't find his way.

Cam delivered the canteen, and Akira offered it to the stranger. "Thanks."

With her help, he sat up, then opened the canteen and lifted it to his mouth. He took small gulps this time, washing the water around inside his mouth before swallowing. Finally he lowered the canteen and met her watchful gaze.

Something twisted in her belly, a reaction to the stark emptiness in his brown eyes. She didn't think she'd seen anything so sad in all her born days.

Dear Jesus, he's lost in more ways than one, isn't he?

"How far am I from Ransom?" His voice sounded utterly hopeless.

Still reeling from what she'd seen in his eyes, she couldn't think clearly enough to answer him.

"I'm on the right road, aren't I? For Ransom?"

She swallowed. "Yes. You're on the right road. Ransom's a bit more than fifteen miles to the north." She frowned. "But if you're looking for work at the lumbermill you needn't bother. There's no work to be had."

He turned his head, judging the short distance to the tree, then slowly inched himself closer to it, stopping when he could rest his back against the trunk. He closed his eyes again.

"No work at the mill," he whispered.

"No."

"But it's still there?"

"The mill? Yes, it's still there."

Silence fell between them. He kept his eyes closed, and she kept hers trained on him.

There's no work for him in these parts. He'll turn around and go back the way he came. As well he should. Look at him.

YEA, LOOK AT HIM.

But, Lord...

FOR I WAS HUNGRY, AND YE GAVE ME TO EAT; I WAS THIRSTY, AND YE GAVE ME DRINK; I WAS A STRANGER, AND YE TOOK ME IN.

"What's your name?" he asked, breaking into her silent conversation with the Lord.

"Akira. Akira Macauley."

He opened one eye. "Akira?"

"It's Scottish. Means anchor. My grandfather wanted me to have a strong name so I wouldn't be afraid of life, so I'd have a reminder of where to find my Anchor. He placed great store in the meaning of names, my grandfather."

"Mmm." The stranger's eyelid closed.

"And your name?"

"You can call me Gabe."

"Gabe. Short for Gabriel?" She smiled. "Gabriel—a strong man of God."

Eyes wide open now, he gave her a look that was anything but friendly.

"That's the meaning of your name," she explained.

"You're mistaken, Miss Macauley. That's the last thing my name could mean."

She knew she wasn't mistaken, but something in his dark countenance warned her not to argue.

"I'll fetch my horse and take you to my place. Get you something to eat." She stood, brushing the grass and dirt from the knees of her overalls.

"You don't have to bother. I've troubled you enough. I can get to Ransom on my own."

Lord, I have a feeling the trouble's yet to begin. Why is that?

She turned toward the road. "Mister, you couldn't make it fifteen yards, let alone fifteen miles."

With a shake of her head, she strode away, away from the stranger whose brown eyes were filled with indescribable pain, away from the man who denied the meaning of his name.

Gabe watched her go, her dark red braids swaying against her back, her collie trotting at her heels. Her stride was long and easy, a sign of a person accustomed to walking great distances. She was slender as a reed, but her build was deceiving; she possessed enough brawn to drag a grown man from the road to this tree.

Akira. She was as strange as her name, more than likely.

A strong man of God, she'd called him.

If he'd had the energy, he would have laughed aloud.

But he had no energy, no strength, no courage, no hope. So he closed his eyes and allowed the threatening darkness to move toward him once again.

When he next awakened, Gabe was no longer lying beneath the birch tree. He was in a room. In a bed. Between two *sheets!* He ran his fingers over the soft fabric.

What a luxury something so simple could be, he thought. Amazing.

Sounds from the next room reached his ears. He rolled his head on the pillow, searching until he found the entrance. He couldn't see anyone, for the door was only slightly ajar. Delicious odors wafted to him through the opening, causing his mouth to water.

He raised himself on his elbows. The room swam before his eyes, but this time he kept a tenuous grip on consciousness.

The door swung open, revealing Akira, a tray in her hand. "Ah, you're awake."

"Yeah."

"I'd begun to wonder."

He glanced around the room, then back at her. "How long was I out?"

"A few hours."

"Did you bring me here all by yourself?"

"No." She smiled; her voice softened. "I always have help when I need it."

Gabe couldn't say why, but there was something about her answer that irritated him. He wanted to lash out, which made no sense at all. Not even to him. Maybe because he wasn't used to being treated with kindness.

"I brought you something to eat."

"Smells good." The words came grudgingly.

She approached. "It's only chicken broth. You'd best see if you can handle that first." Reaching the bedside, she stopped.

He stared at her in silence, noting the smattering of freckles that spilled across her nose and high cheekbones, the blue-green color of her eyes, the fullness of her mouth, the hot-ember high-lights in her dark hair.

She was pretty, he realized. He wondered why he hadn't noticed it when she first came to his rescue. Maybe because he hadn't really looked at her. Or maybe he'd long ago stopped notic-ing anything that was good or pretty. Maybe it was because he only saw what he expected to see—the dark side of this world, the evil of one man to another.

"Can you sit up more?" she asked, that ever-present gentleness in her voice.

He scowled. "You're awfully trusting, bringing me into your home." With effort, he straightened, leaning his back against the headboard. "You don't know anything about me. Maybe I'll rob you blind."

The gentle smile she'd worn faded from her lips. "I don't believe so. Besides, you're welcome to whatever I have that you need."

"Maybe I'm a dangerous man."

"The Lord is the strength of my life. Whom shall I fear?"

Whom should she fear? He could tell her.

He heard the cell door slamming shut. Cold steel against cold steel. Cold, like his heart.

He heard it slamming again…

And again…

And again.

Oh yes. He could tell her whom she should fear.

She set the tray on his lap. "If you tolerate this broth, I'll serve you something more substantial later." She closed her eyes, bowed her head, and blessed the food in a low voice.

But Gabe wasn't listening to her prayer. All he could hear was the slamming of that cold steel door.

Hudson Talmadge stood as straight and tall at the age of sixty-five as he had when he was in his twenties. An imposing man with granite-gray hair and beard and piercing blue eyes, he used his physical appearance to his advantage, ruling his empire with an iron fist. He brooked no questioning of his authority and was unashamedly merciless.

Mercy, in his opinion, was a sign of weakness, and Hudson was not a weak man.

"You'll be gone from the house by tomorrow," he said as he stared out his second-story office window.

"But, Mr. Talmadge, the boy meant no harm. He—"

"You heard what I said, Wickham. By tomorrow. You and your family."

Charlie Wickham was silent awhile before saying, "We've nowhere to go, sir, and my wife's health isn't good."

"That isn't my problem." Hudson turned. "The house you live in is company owned, and you and your boy are no longer employed by the mill."

"I've worked for you for nearly fifteen years, Mr. Talmadge."

"And now you don't."

Charlie Wickham obviously saw the futility of arguing—his shoulders sagged as he turned away. "We'll be out by tomorrow. Just as you say." He departed, cloaked in an air of despair. His eighteen-year-old son, Mark, followed after him.

"See that you are," Hudson said before the door closed again.

Hudson turned toward the window, his gaze rising toward the pine-covered slopes of Talmadge Peak.

He felt no spark of remorse over what had transpired moments before. Young Mark Wickham had cost the mill a day's production with his carelessness, allowing the engine on the number-three saw to run low on oil. Granted, production wasn't as important now as it had been in the prosperous twenties. There was little building going on and few orders for Talmadge lumber. But Hudson never tolerated foolish behavior. If it cost him a penny, it cost him too much. The Depression couldn't last forever. One day this country would recover, and when it did, he planned to be even wealthier than before.

The squawk of the intercommunication system broke into his thoughts. "Mrs. Talmadge is here to see you, sir."

He frowned. He disliked Pauline coming to the mill. It was bad enough he had to spend his evenings in her company.

He returned to his desk, pressed a button, and said, "Send her in."

A few moments later, the door opened, and his wife, the third Mrs. Hudson J. Talmadge, entered his office. An attractive woman in her midthirties, buxom and dark-haired, she was impeccably dressed, as befit her station as wife of the town's patriarch.

"What is it you want, Pauline?" There had never been any pretense of devotion between them, although at one time they had at least been congenial. Now even that was gone.

Hudson had married the former Miss Hinnenkamp to provide a Talmadge heir; she had married him for his money. He'd kept his part of the bargain, but after seven years of marriage, she'd failed to keep hers. Twice she'd miscarried early in pregnancy. Twice she'd been delivered of stillborn girls. After the birth of the second daughter, the doctor had warned that another pregnancy could endanger Pauline's life. She'd locked Hudson out of her bedroom from that day on.

He couldn't honestly say he cared.

"Only a moment of your time, Hudson," she answered him, drawing his attention as she settled onto one of the chairs opposite him, opened her handbag, and withdrew an envelope. "We've been invited to a ball at the senator's house in Boise. I assumed you would want to know."

He took the invitation. "A ball." He hated those things, but he knew he would have to go. Plenty of deals were made in smoking rooms, and the senator had promised to help him with his land acquisitions.

"It's in two weeks," Pauline continued. "If you don't mind, I'd like to go early so I can visit my parents."

"Why would I mind?"

She smiled with false sweetness. "I knew that's how you would feel. I'll have Eugene drive me down in the morning. That will give me time to shop for a new evening gown."

"Another gown?"

"Would you have me appear as if we hadn't any money? The women will notice if I wear something they've seen before, and they in turn will tell their husbands."

He scowled. Unlike most people, he'd done well since the crash of twenty-nine. When people had been forced to sell off their land and businesses, Hudson had been there to buy them out. Paying as little as possible, of course.

He was a powerful, wealthy man, but he had greater ambitions still to achieve. He'd learned that perceptions were as important as reality.

"Fine. Buy whatever you need."

She stood. "I will." Without another word, she left his office.

Hudson sank onto his desk chair, leaned back, closed his eyes. Then he muttered a curse. Whatever mistakes he'd made in his life, Pauline was definitely one of them.

Akira worked the pump handle until water gushed from the spigot.

Lord, the weather's been cruel, and this drought's been hard. If it be Your will, I'm asking that this well not dry up.

She glanced toward the house.

And, Lord, about Gabe. That man's got a terrible hurt inside him. I know You've got Your reasons for sending him here, but I can't say I understand what they are. He was hungry and thirsty, and I fed him and gave him something to drink. He's a stranger, and I took him in. But now what, Lord? Is there more I'm to do?

She moved the bucket, then gave the handle one more vigorous push. She cupped her hands beneath the flow of water and splashed her face with the cool liquid.

Maybe later, she thought, after the sunset, she'd go down to the creek. It was running low, but there was enough water to get good and wet all over.

She dried her face on her shirt sleeve. As she straightened and turned, bucket in hand, her gaze swept over the surroundings.

Sheep grazed peacefully in the gently rolling valley, a valley sheltered by pine- and aspen-covered mountains. Purple wildflowers bloomed in defiance of this season of drought, laughing at the clear, cloudless skies.

A feeling of joy welled in her heart as she gazed at the valley the Macauleys had called home for three generations. She set down the bucket, raised her hands toward the sky, and began to twirl about in circles while singing, making up the melody as she went along.

"Make a joyful noise unto the Lord, all ye lands. Serve the Lord with gladness: come before His presence with singing."

It didn't matter to her that she could barely carry a tune in a basket. She was glad to praise Him with her joyful noise.

"Know ye that the Lord He is God: it is He that hath made us, and not we ourselves; we are his people, and the sheep of His pasture."

She closed her eyes, twirled with more abandon, sang louder.

"Enter into His gates with thanksgiving, and into His courts with praise: be thankful unto Him, and bless His name. For the Lord is good; His mercy is everlasting; and His truth endureth to all generations."

She fell to the ground, dizzy from spinning. She hugged her arms over her chest and reveled in the sense of well-being.

"*Ach!* Have ye lost yer senses, lass?"

Akira opened her eyes to see Brodie Lachlan's slow approach. He struggled with his crutches on the uneven ground, obviously hating every awkward step.

"No, I haven't." She sat up.

"Ye looked it."

Brodie was pure Scot, from the top of his head, ablaze with carrot-red hair, to the tip of his boots. He'd come to work for Akira's grandfather Fergus Macauley a few months after getting off the boat in 1901. He'd long since ceased to be an employee. Now he was family to Akira. In many ways, closer to her than her own mother.

"How's your leg?" she asked as he drew closer.

"Fair enough."

"Are you hungry? There's chicken soup on the stove."

"Nay, lass. I've had my supper."

"Did you find someone to help move the sheep?"

Shaking his head, he sank onto a large, granite boulder near the pump. "None I'd have. Any man worth his salt who's in need of work has left Ransom. Those who remain aren't to be trusted." He rubbed his thigh with one hand, adding with a sigh, "Besides, there's none that know sheep. Farmers and loggers, the lot of them."

"You can teach anybody what they need to know." She glanced toward the house. "Perhaps I found someone. I gave aid to a stranger today. He was on his way to Ransom, looking for mill-work. He was so weak from hunger, he fainted."

"From the look on yer face, I'd guess the stranger ye speak of is in the house. Am I right?"

She nodded.

"Ye're too trustin', Akira."

"I trust in the Lord. He told me to bring Gabe home."

The Scotsman arched an eyebrow. "Gabe who?"

"He didn't tell me his last name."

Brodie rose from the rock, slipping the crutches beneath his arms. "I'll have a look at this stranger of yours, if ye don't mind."

She smiled as she stood. There was no point arguing with him, and well she knew it. He would do what he pleased. If there was a more stubborn race of people than the Scots, Akira had yet to meet them. And she should know, being herself one of God's most stubborn children.

When Gabe saw the tall, beefy, full-bearded man standing in the doorway to the bedroom, leaning on a pair of crutches, he assumed he was about to be tossed out on his ear.

"My name's Brodie Lachlan, and who might ye be?" He entered the bedroom, moving slowly but steadily.

Gabe didn't answer.

"Did ye not hear me, lad?" Despite his injured right leg, he looked plenty able to do Gabe harm.

"I heard."

"And is it a secret?"

Gabe knew the sound of disdain. He'd lived with it for most of his life, first from his father, then from the prison guards, and finally from strangers who didn't want to look at another hungry beggar.

Brodie arrived at the bed, demanding an answer by his sheer presence.

"My name's Gabe."

Brodie squinted his hazel eyes and pressed his lips together in an unyielding line. It was obvious he wasn't satisfied with only a first name.

"Talmadge," Gabe added reluctantly.

A soft gasp from the doorway alerted him to Akira's presence.

"Gabe Talmadge?" Brodie said in a low voice. His eyes narrowed even more. "We'd heard ye were dead."

Gabe closed his eyes. "I was."

Maybe I still am.

CHAPTER TWO

"See that he's out of here tomorrow, Akira. Ye'll regret it if ye don't."
The door closed behind Brodie, his parting words lingering in the air.

Gabriel Talmadge.

Akira glanced toward the bedroom.

Hudson Talmadge's son.

Of all the people in the world who could have collapsed on the road for her to find, why did it have to be him?

"I'm trying to understand what You're doing, Lord," she whispered, "but it's far from clear at the moment."

She crossed the cozy parlor and eased open the door. A sliver of lamplight spilled past her into the darkened bedroom.

Gabe Talmadge had been convicted of killing his brother fourteen years before. A person couldn't live long in this county without knowing the Talmadge family history, including that tragic tidbit.

Maybe I'm a dangerous man. She shivered as the memory of Gabe's words replayed in her mind. *Was* he dangerous?

"I'm not asleep, Miss Macauley."

She jumped, startled by his voice.

"You might as well bring in the lamp and say what you came to say."

"I only meant to look in on you." It wasn't a lie, but it seemed one.

"But you'd just as soon I didn't stay in your house, right?"

Akira sighed softly. "I don't know, Mr. Talmadge."

"Gabe." He sat up. "If you'll bring me my shirt and trousers, I'll be on my way."

She pushed the door all the way open, then turned and reached for the kerosene lamp on the nearby table. "I washed your clothes. They're hanging on the line."

"They'll be dry enough by now."

"Mr. Talmadge, you don't—"

"I thank you for your kindness."

She held up the lamp, casting a golden light over the bed and the man in it. "You needn't leave tonight."

"I think I should." He looked toward the window. "And so does Mr. Lachlan."

Akira heard the hopelessness in his voice. She could almost see the vast wasteland of his heart. A lump formed in her throat, and tears welled in her eyes.

She lowered the lamp. "I can't force you to stay. You're free to do as you please. But the bed is yours for the night, and in the morning, there'll be a breakfast of eggs, ham, and biscuits with gravy. I imagine you'd also like to shave and bathe before seeing your father."

He visibly flinched.

"Go back to sleep, Mr. Talmadge." She turned toward the doorway. "You'll be thinking clearer in the morning."

When Gabe next opened his eyes, he discovered the bedroom was bright with lemon-colored sunshine. He couldn't believe he'd slept that hard or that long. He'd planned to be out of Akira's house and on his way before sunrise.

He sat up, glancing toward the door as he did so. It was shut tight, but there was no closing out the smell of ham frying in a skillet. His stomach growled in anticipation.

He tossed off the sheet and blanket and sat up. That's when he noticed not only his trousers and shirt—washed, pressed, and draped across the back of a chair—but also some clean underclothes. On the nearby stand were a wash basin, a porcelain pitcher filled with water, a washcloth, and a bar of soap.

Subtle, Miss Macauley wasn't.

Gabe rose slowly from the bed, testing his legs to make certain of their support before taking his first step. Convinced he would stay upright, he stripped off the undershirt and drawers he'd worn for longer than he cared to think about and washed himself, starting with his hair and working downward by inches.

It was one of those things most folks gave no thought to, the ability to bathe whenever they wanted. It was something he hadn't taken for granted for years.

As he dressed a short while later, he wondered where Akira had come by the men's undergarments. They couldn't belong to Brodie Lachlan, a man whose waistline was easily twice the size as Gabe's. Then he decided it didn't matter. He wouldn't look a gift horse in the mouth.

Pride took a backseat to practicality in times such as these.

A soft rapping on the door preceded Akira's voice. "Mr. Talmadge? Your breakfast is ready."

Barefooted, he strode across the room and opened the door.

She smiled when she saw him. "You found everything."

"Yeah. Thanks." He rubbed his jaw with the fingers of his right hand. "Except for a razor."

"I figured you'd want hot water for that. Why don't you eat first?" She motioned toward the table. "The biscuits and gravy are ready."

As if on cue, his stomach growled again.

Akira laughed.

The sound—sparkling, pure, and feminine—was so unexpected, Gabe took a step back. He needed to distance himself from a sound so joyful, so good. It seemed to shed unwelcome light into the dark corners of his soul, corners better left hidden.

She sobered at once. "Is something wrong?"

He shook his head and wished she would stop looking at him in that curious way of hers. She was too innocent, too trusting.

"Sit down and eat, Mr. Talmadge." She turned and walked to the stove where she filled a plate with food.

He said nothing as he obeyed. Silent obedience, he'd learned from painful experience, was usually the best route to take.

Akira carried his plate to the table and set it before him, then settled onto the chair to his right. He knew she was looking at him, but he didn't meet her gaze. Finally, she bowed her head and prayed softly over the food. As soon as she finished, Gabe picked up his fork and began eating, one mouthful right after another. That was something else he'd learned over the years. Eat fast before someone whisked the food away.

Akira didn't whisk it away nor did she speak while he ate. He was thankful for that.

After he'd polished off the last bite of biscuit, he glanced up. The look in her greenish-blue eyes was gentle. It wasn't pity; it was simple kindness. But he wasn't used to kindness.

"There's more if you'd like it, Mr. Talmadge."

"I'd rather you'd called me Gabe."

"All right. Would you like more to eat, Gabe?"

"No. Thanks, ma'am."

She laughed again. "And I'd rather you *didn't* call me ma'am."

He gave her an abrupt nod of assent, refusing to return her smile, then stood. "I'd best be on my way."

"I'll hitch up the team and drive you into Ransom."

He was tempted to refuse, but something told him she

wouldn't give an inch about this. "Fine. We'll go as soon as I shave, if that's all right with you."

Akira allowed the horses to set their own pace, which wasn't a particularly swift one. The first half-hour passed without conversation. She didn't mind. She was used to silence and the company of her own thoughts.

She pondered many things as they traveled, most of them about the man seated beside her. She wondered what captivity had done to Gabe Talmadge. She couldn't imagine the horror of being locked up for years, unable to go where she wanted whenever she wanted, unable to lie in the grass or stroke the silky coat of her dog or swim in the creek in the moonlight.

Why, of all people, had God brought the son of Hudson Talmadge into her home?

She glanced up at the cloudless blue sky. "Will You give me an answer to *that* question?" she asked softly.

"What?"

She looked at Gabe. "Sorry. I was inquiring of the Almighty."

He frowned as his gaze moved to the road before them.

Without his beard, she could see a slight resemblance to the elder Talmadge. She supposed Gabe was in his early thirties, though he appeared older with his hollow cheeks and the deep lines etched around his eyes.

"How long has it been since you've seen your father?" she asked.

The muscles in his jaw flexed, and a pained expression flashed briefly across his face. Then it was gone.

"I'm sorry. I had no right to ask."

He met her gaze. "Fourteen years."

"Fourteen?" She couldn't disguise her surprise. "But didn't he come to visit you when you—"

"Fourteen years."

How could that be? she wondered. How could a father abandon his son that way? No matter what Gabe had done, he was still Hudson's son.

"He doesn't know I'm coming," Gabe said, providing an answer to an unformed question.

"He must expect you, now that you're out—" She stopped abruptly.

"You can say it, Miss Macauley…now that I'm out of prison."

"I'm sorry."

"No need to be. It's a fact." He stared into the distance. "Actually, I was released four years ago. I didn't return then, and Hud has no reason to expect me now."

Hud? A curious thing to call his own father. *Why doesn't he expect you?* She pressed her lips together to keep from saying or asking something she shouldn't.

"Have you lived in the area long, Miss Macauley?"

"Nine years, not counting a brief spell right after my father passed on."

"Then I trust the gossips have done their job."

"I don't listen to gossips." She shrugged for emphasis, even though he wasn't looking at her. "Besides, I seldom go to town, and when I do, all anyone wants to talk about these days is the economy and the drought and whether or not I've decided to sell my land."

"Sell?"

She slapped the reins across the team's backsides. "Giddyap there," she called. Then she answered Gabe's one-word question with a bit of history. "My grandfather left me Dundreggan when he passed on to his reward. I won't sell it."

"Dun what?"

"Dundreggan Ranch."

"Dundreggan." Gabe gave her the closest thing to a smile she'd seen from him. "Your voice changed when you said it. You sounded like Lachlan."

"Aye, laddie," she replied with a cocky toss of her head, laying on a thick accent.

He chuckled.

Akira suspected it was a sound he'd not made in a long while, perhaps not for years.

A nicker from one of the horses drew her gaze to the road. Ahead of them, an old Ford truck, its bed piled high with household items, was stopped. Two men leaned over the engine. As the

Macauley wagon drew closer, Akira recognized the weary-looking woman in the cab of the truck as Nora Wickham. Akira's heart sank. She didn't have to ask what had happened. Charlie and Mark Wickham must have been let go from the mill, and the family was leaving Ransom in search of work. It had happened to many before them and would more than likely happen to others in the future.

She pulled on the reins, stopping the team as they came alongside the truck. "Morning, Mrs. Wickham."

Nora acknowledged the greeting with a nod; she didn't look well enough to do more than that. Akira had heard she'd been ill again.

She glanced toward Charlie. "Morning, Mr. Wickham."

"Miss Macauley." He looked at Gabe, but when no introduction was given, he returned his gaze to Akira.

"Is there something I can do to help?" she asked with a glance at the open hood.

"No. We've about got it fixed."

"Where will you go?"

"Oregon. We're hoping there's millwork to be found there." He looked at his wife, seated in the cab, her eyes closed. Worry lines carved deep ridges in his forehead.

ASK HIM.

The whisper in Akira's heart was familiar, the meaning clear. She didn't hesitate to obey.

"Mr. Wickham, I'm in need of a couple of hands to help with the sheep. Would you consider working for me?"

His expression was one of surprise. "Well, I—"

"You'd have a house of your own. It's small but sound. The pay won't be much, but there'll be plenty of good food." She looked beyond him to his son. "I could use Mark's help, too, if he's willing."

"I don't know anything about sheep, Miss Macauley," Charlie said, despair in his voice. "I've been a logger or a mill hand all my life. Lumber's all I know."

"Brodie Lachlan can show you the ropes." She paused, then added, "You'd be doing us a favor if you'd agree. You probably heard Mr. Lachlan had an accident. He's on the mend, but it's past time our band of sheep was taken to summer grazing. Mr. Lachlan can't manage them alone. Not while he's still using his crutches."

Another glance at his wife, and Charlie Wickham made up his mind. He nodded. "All right, Miss Macauley. We'd be pleased to work for you. God bless you."

"Just head on up to the ranch. Mr. Lachlan will show you where to settle." She adjusted the reins in her hands. "I'll talk to you more when I get back."

In the four years since his release from prison, Gabe had seen countless families like the Wickhams, suddenly homeless, all their worldly possessions piled into automobiles or trucks or wagons. He'd slept under bridges and in abandoned buildings with those once proud men, men who had left their homes so their wives and children could go on the dole instead of starving alongside them.

He was sorry to see it had happened to Charlie Wickham. Gabe had worked in the mill with him for a short while back in 1919. A lifetime ago. He'd liked Charlie, too, because Charlie had treated him fairly. Better than he'd deserved.

Akira clucked to the horses and smacked their rumps with the reins. The wagon jerked forward.

Gabe glanced over his shoulder.

"He didn't recognize you," Akira said.

"No." He straightened. "I was just a kid the last time he saw me. And I've changed a lot since then."

"Well, you have been gone a long time."

"Yeah." He wondered if he should have come back at all.

As if reading his mind, she asked, "Why'd you return now?"

He closed his eyes, remembering one particular night in a shantytown near Seattle. A cold and damp night that chilled a man to the bones.

A preacher had walked along the pathway that meandered between the shacks, speaking to any and all who would listen. He'd had one of those voices peculiar to men of the cloth, the sort that carried across a crowd and above the sounds of hurting humanity. The preacher's words had reached Gabe's unwilling ears; try as he might, he hadn't been able to block them out.

"And he went and joined himself to one of the citizens of that country; and he sent him into his fields to feed swine. And he would fain have filled his belly with the husks that the swine did eat: and no man gave unto him. But when he came to himself he said, How many hired servants of my father's have bread enough and to spare, and I perish here with hunger! I will arise and go to my father…"

There'd been a time, after Gabe's release from prison, when pride had kept him away from Ransom. But cold and hunger had a way of stripping a man of his pride—and everything else besides. So when he heard the preacher telling the story of the Prodigal Son, he'd made up his mind to return. The worst that could happen was that the old man would throw him out.

And maybe, just maybe, things would be different between them this time.

"Gabe," Akira said, drawing him back to the present.

"Hmm?"

"It's going to be all right. I've got a feeling about it."

"A feeling," he muttered, thinking how naive she was.

"In good time, you'll see I'm right, Gabriel Talmadge."

"Because you've got a feeling?"

Her smile was tinged with sadness. He could tell she'd wanted him to believe and was disappointed when he didn't.

The remainder of the journey to town was made in silence.

Ransom was Hudson Talmadge's town. He owned almost every square inch of it, from the Logger's Café on the west side to the Ransom Dry-Goods Store on the east side, from the First Ransom Bank at the north end to the Talmadge Home for Orphans at the south end. If a person wanted work in this county, it usually depended upon Hudson's good graces—of which he had few.

Akira cast a surreptitious glance toward Gabe seated beside her in the wagon. Perhaps, she thought, Hudson was the way he was—mean and twisted—because he'd lost all three of his sons, in one way or another. Maybe he would change for the better now that Gabe had returned.

Could this be the way You plan to heal this valley? Could this be the way You redeem Hudson Talmadge? Do you mean to use Gabe for that purpose?

When the Macauley wagon turned north, leaving the town behind them, Gabe saw the mansion on the hillside and knew it had to be his father's. Hudson would never allow anyone to have a greater house than his own.

"When did he build that?" he asked Akira.

There was a moment's silence before she answered, "Right before he married again."

Ah, yes. His stepmother. The third Mrs. Talmadge.

"What's she like?"

"Mrs. Talmadge? I don't know. I've never had the pleasure of her acquaintance." Akira sounded amused.

He turned from studying the Talmadge mansion to look at Akira, wondering what she found funny.

"Women like Pauline Talmadge have little to do with the likes of someone like me. A simple shepherdess."

"Then I suspect she's the poorer because of it."

At his words a blush climbed the back of Akira's neck, spilling into bright patches on her cheeks. Her gaze darted away from his.

Gabe might have said more, might have tried to explain what her kindness meant to him, only the lumberyard came into view at that precise moment. Memories assaulted him, none of them pleasant. A cold hand squeezed his heart. Dread iced his veins.

"Stop the wagon, Miss Macauley."

She did so.

"I'll go the rest of the way on foot."

"Are you sure? I don't mind—"

"I'm sure." He gripped the side with one hand, then dropped to the ground.

This is a mistake, he thought. *I never should've come back.*

But something forced him to put one foot in front of another, propelling him forward, toward the Talmadge Mill.

And toward the man who'd sent him to prison fourteen years before.

CHAPTER THREE

Hudson watched the man walking toward the lumberyard.

Another tramp looking for work.

And unless he was mistaken, Akira Macauley had brought him.

His eyes narrowed. There weren't many men who dared stand up to Hudson Talmadge. That his plans continued to be thwarted by a mere female galled him beyond measure.

They were his curse, the weaker sex. They'd always been his curse. Akira Macauley. Jane Sebastian. His wives—first Clarice, then Harriet, and finally Pauline.

He clenched his jaw as he turned away from the window and sat behind his desk.

He had one thing for which to be glad this morning. Pauline was on her way to Boise. For the next two weeks, Hudson would have the house to himself. He wouldn't be forced to participate in small talk over supper or listen to his wife's constant yammering.

A light rap sounded at the door a second before it opened and his secretary, Rupert Carruthers, slipped through the opening. A wiry, bookish sort with a boyish face that belied his true age, Rupert had worked for Hudson since they were young men in Minnesota.

"Sir"—Rupert never failed to be formal, despite the years they'd been together—"there's someone to see you."

"What's the matter, Carruthers?" Hudson snapped. "I don't have time to talk to every hobo who comes looking for work. Handle him as you've handled the others."

"But—"

"You heard me."

"You don't understand." Rupert lowered his voice. "It's Gabe."

Hudson rocked back in his chair. "Gabe?"

The secretary nodded, peering at his employer through the glasses perched on the end of his birdlike nose.

Hudson stood. "He's *here?*"

"Yes sir."

Like a bad penny, returned.

"Sir?"

Hudson sat down again, then cleared his throat. "Send him in." He swiveled his chair toward the window, leaving his back to the door.

Odd, it wasn't memories of Gabe he recalled at that moment. Nor was it Max, his firstborn son. It was Clarice, his first wife, Max and Gabe's mother.

As clearly as if it were yesterday, he remembered the first time he'd seen her, walking into the bank in Chicago on a sunny Wednesday morning. She'd been a girl of seventeen, come to visit her father, the president of the bank. Hudson had been twenty-eight, a cowboy from Texas by way of Montana, with all the rough edges still intact. He'd thought Clarice Wainwright the most beautiful girl he'd ever laid eyes on.

He'd soon discovered her beauty was more than physical; hers was a beauty of the heart and soul. There'd been a peace about Clarice that soothed something inside Hudson whenever she was near. He supposed he'd loved her. All he'd known then was he had to have her, had to possess her, had to make her his, had to keep her with him so he could share her peace. He would have kidnapped her if he'd been forced to, but he hadn't been. She'd willingly married him, and he'd taken her to Minnesota where he'd bought his first lumbermill.

Their son Max had been born before their second anniversary. By the time Gabe arrived, three years later, Hudson's peace had been shattered, and with Clarice's death, he'd lost all hope of finding it again.

Behind him, the office door closed. He took a deep breath and turned his chair around.

His father hadn't changed much, which was strangely comforting.

"Well, well," Hudson said. "So you've come back."

"Yes."

"I wondered when you would."

"Did you?" Gabe couldn't keep the hint of surprise from his voice. He'd doubted Hudson thought of him at all.

His father's gaze raked over him. Gabe endured the stare without flinching.

"Sit down," Hudson ordered at last.

He did.

"Why'd you come?"

He met his father's gaze. "I need employment and a place to stay. There isn't much work for any man these days, let alone an ex-con."

"And you thought I'd give you a job? And a home?"

"I hoped you would."

"Why should I?"

Gabe's chest was tight, making it hard to breathe, harder still to speak. "Because I'm your son."

"You heard your little brother died, didn't you?" Hudson stood. His eyes were like ice, his words filled with venom. "You figured I was getting old and there'd be no more sons for me after Leon. You thought you'd return, like a dog to its vomit, to inherit what I've built." He turned away and stepped to the window. "Get out. You'll get nothing from me."

Into the sudden silence came the same hate-filled voice, speaking from across the years: *You killed your mother when you were born, and now you've killed your brother. May you rot in prison.* Until a few minutes ago, those had been the last words his father had spoken to him.

He should have known nothing would change.

Gabe rose from the chair, turned, and left the office. He kept his gaze lowered, staring at the floor so he didn't have to make eye contact with Rupert or anyone else. He didn't know where he would go or what he would do. It didn't much matter. There'd been a time, when he'd first been sent to prison, that he'd asked God to kill him, to take pity and strike him dead. But he'd stopped asking long ago.

Just like Hudson, God wanted nothing to do with Gabe.

When Akira saw Jane Sebastian coming out of the small Ransom Methodist Episcopal Church at the edge of town, she drew the team to a halt. "Good morning."

The heavyset woman, a spinster-lady in her fifties with rosy cheeks and thinning gray hair, smiled as she returned the greeting. "Good morning, Akira. What brings you to Ransom?"

"An errand at the mill."

A cloud momentarily covered the sun, casting a shadow across the earth, not unlike the shadow that passed across Jane's face.

"Mr. Talmadge's son has returned," Akira added.

Jane pressed a hand to her heart. "Gabe? He's here? In Ransom?"

Akira nodded. "That's why I was out at the mill. I drove him there. He went to see his father."

"Oh, sweet God in heaven." The woman's softly spoken words could not be mistaken for anything but a prayer.

"What is it?"

"He won't find a welcome there. Or absolution."

Akira twisted on the wagon seat, staring back toward the mill.

"There's no mercy in the man's heart and no love for that boy."

"But he's his son."

"And it was Hudson Talmadge's own testimony that sent Gabe to prison. He would've seen him dead if he'd had his druthers."

"Surely you're mistaken."

"I'm not mistaken. I raised the boy, and I know the wickedness of the man who sired him."

Akira faced Jane again. "You *raised* him?"

"For twelve years. From the day he was born." Jane approached the wagon with determined steps, pausing only long enough to drop the basket she carried into the bed of the wagon. Then she grasped the seat and hauled herself up beside Akira. "Will you take me to him, please?"

"Of course."

It took Akira only a few moments to turn the wagon around and head up the road toward the mill a second time. All the while, questions whirled in her mind, and it took great resolve not to ask them. Curiosity was part of her nature, but she knew how quickly curiosity led to idle gossip. She was determined *not* to gossip about Gabe.

It was Jane who broke the silence. "He was a delightful young-ster, so eager to please. He had a good heart, and he always did his best." Her voice lowered. "But Gabe's best was never good enough for Mr. Talmadge."

"Why?"

"Why?" Jane harrumphed. "There's no cause for it. At least none a reasonable person can understand. The man has the devil's own heart, pure and simple. He wanted nothing more than to make Gabe rue the day he was born. It was always that way, from the very beginning."

Akira had seen how the elder Talmadge mistreated his employees, so she harbored no illusions about Hudson's nature. But she found it hard to believe he could be so cruel to his own son.

Jane's hand grasped Akira's forearm. "There he is. Stop the wagon." Her voice broke.

Gabe walked with his head slung forward, his gaze on the ground before him. He hadn't heard the wagon's approach, or if he had, he'd ignored the sounds.

Akira glanced toward Jane. Tears were running down the older woman's cheeks, unchecked. Akira looked ahead again.

What's the truth about him, Lord?

The question had barely formed when he glanced up, saw the wagon, stopped walking.

"Gabe," Jane whispered.

He showed one of his rare smiles, a brief curve of the mouth as heartbreaking as Jane's tears. Then he strode forward. When he reached the wagon, he stretched out an arm. "Miss Jane." They clasped hands.

"I'd nearly lost hope of seeing you again, dear boy. God was good to bring you back."

He didn't reply.

"Your father turned you out." It wasn't a question.

"Yes." He didn't sound surprised.

"What will you do now?" Jane asked, her tone gentle.

"I'll move on. Nobody in Ransom will give me work, even if they had it to give. They wouldn't dare. You know it, same as me." Gabe withdrew his hand, turned his back to the wagon. "Hud's won, Miss Jane. We knew he would."

"I'll give you work," Akira said. "If you want it."

Gabe's shoulders rose and fell, indicating the drawing in of a deep breath and the supervening, silent release. Then he faced her. "You have no idea what you're saying, Miss Macauley."

"I've got plenty of work at Dundreggan."

"You hired two men this morning."

"Yes, I did."

"Miss Macauley—"

"The Lord brought you here for a purpose, Mr. Talmadge. There's a reason He caused our paths to cross."

At one time, Gabe might have believed the same thing. But that was long, long ago. Before he'd listened to his father. Before he'd wandered far from the truth.

"I doubt that," he said. "God has better things to do than care about my comings and goings. He's washed His hands of me."

"No!" Akira exclaimed. "God doesn't wash His hands of people. His love is everlasting."

He frowned. "You'll only bring trouble on yourself if you try to help me. Ask Miss Jane what happened to her on account of me."

"I'm not afraid." Akira stiffened her back, defiantly lifted her chin. Her blue-green eyes swirled with emotion.

"And the wolf shall dwell with the lamb," he quipped.

The corners of her mouth curved in a smile.

It wasn't the response for which he'd hoped. He'd meant his words as a warning. He'd meant for her to understand he was like the wolf. The wolf could devour the lamb, and Gabe's presence could destroy Akira.

Jane spoke into the lengthening silence. "Stay, Gabe. Stop running."

Stop running. Stand still and let the darkness overtake him. It was what he deserved. The end result was inevitable. Did it matter *where* it happened? Wasn't Ransom, Idaho, as good a place as any?

Chapter Four

The cabin was only one room, but it had a stove for heating and cooking, a comfortable mattress on the bed, and a sturdy table with two wooden chairs. Cobwebs swung from the ceiling, wispy reminders of disuse. Dirty windows, bare of curtains, muted the daylight entering through the glass. A pile of dried leaves and pine needles were heaped in a corner, as if swept there and then forgotten.

"No one's used these quarters in years," Akira said from the doorway.

Gabe turned. He could have told her it seemed a palace after the places he'd lived. "It'll do fine."

"I'll bring you a broom, bedding, pots and pans and such." She pointed with an outstretched arm. "There's a pump between this cabin and the one the Wickhams are using. The outhouse is behind their place." A small frown puckered her brow. "Can't think of anything else you need to know right off. 'Cept supper will be about five o'clock."

"I don't expect you to cook for me, Miss Macauley."

An amused twinkle lit her eyes. "And you shouldn't. But tonight we'll all eat together—you, me, the Wickhams, and Brodie."

Why are you doing this? he wondered as she gave him another smile.

"I'll get you the broom. This room's not going to clean itself." With that, she turned and left.

Suddenly weary, Gabe settled onto one of the chairs, unmindful of the accumulation of dust on the seat.

He gazed around the interior. The room was spacious. Almost too spacious. Even four years after leaving prison, he still wasn't used to unrestricted movement. He often found himself waiting for an angry voice to ring in his ears or a strong hand to clamp onto his shoulder.

You heard your little brother died, didn't you?

Gabe winced at the intrusion in his mind.

You figured I was getting old and there'd be no more sons for me after Leon. You thought you'd return, like a dog to its vomit, to inherit what I've built.

It was no less than Gabe had expected from Hudson. The words shouldn't have stung. Yet they did.

Get out. You'll get nothing from me.

He closed his eyes, rubbed his face with his hands. A man learned a lot of tricks while locked in an eight-foot cell. One was how to turn off his thoughts, to silence the voices in his head.

"So ye've come back."

Gabe looked up to find Brodie Lachlan standing in the doorway.

"Ye'll work and work hard as long as ye're here. Ye'll do as ye're told or move along." The Scotsman pointed at him. "And if ye ever hurt the wee lass, I'll break ye in two with my bare hands. Have we an understandin'?"

Gabe nodded.

"Good." Brodie turned on his crutches and disappeared from view.

Do as he was told? That was easy. That was what he was used to. It was the freedom to choose that confused him.

"It's not a sick body troubling him, Lord," Akira said as she leaned a broom against the kitchen table. "It's a crushed spirit, and Your word says no one can bear that."

She stacked a pot and a frying pan on the table beside some dishes.

"I suppose that's why You sent him. So his spirit can mend. I know Your purpose prevails, no matter what plans we make. I'd be pleased if You'd tell me what I'm to do beyond giving him work and a place to stay."

She paused, glanced upward, then closed her eyes.

"And, Lord, I could use some help in having generous thoughts toward Hudson Talmadge. You say I'm to love my enemies, but that's harder to do than I ever thought it would be."

She felt a stab of longing for her grandfather. She could use some of his wisdom about now. Fergus Macauley had been a shrewd judge of character, a man of uncommon discernment. He'd been strong but gentle, and he had a faith to move mountains. She'd learned so much from him. But not enough. Not nearly enough.

"Ye've done it now, haven't ye, lass?"

She opened her eyes to find Brodie staring at her, his large frame filling the doorway.

"He's a Talmadge. He'll only bring more hardship upon ye."

"Did you know him as a boy?"

"I knew *of* him." The tone of his voice said more than his words. "He's from bad seed, that one."

Her chest tightened. Sudden tears stung her eyes. "I don't believe that, Brodie."

"Ye've no knowledge of men and the evil they do, lass. Ye're like a lamb for the slaughter."

She remembered Gabe saying much the same thing.

And the wolf shall dwell with the lamb.

She'd smiled at the time. She was fairly certain he hadn't known he was quoting from the book of Isaiah, but *she'd* known. She'd known and understood it was God telling her she was doing the right thing.

"Brodie, the Shepherd protects His lambs. I'm not afraid."

"Ye haven't the sense to be afraid."

She laughed softly. "Thank you."

"*Ach!*" He glared at her a few moments more, then left.

"The wolf shall *dwell* with the lamb, my friend," she whispered. "Not devour it."

Hudson rose from his chair. "Are you certain?"

"Yes sir," Rupert answered. "Quite certain. I followed them all the way back to the Macauley woman's ranch."

Hudson flicked his wrist, indicating he wanted to be left alone. Rupert was swift to obey the gesture.

The instant the door closed, his fury erupted "Blast her!" He hurled a paperweight across the room and bellowed a lengthy string of curses.

Wasn't it bad enough Clarice's spurious offspring carried the Talmadge name? Now Gabe had joined forces with Akira Macauley. As if to spite him.

Well, they didn't know with whom they were dealing. They wouldn't outfox Hudson Talmadge. He would destroy them. He would destroy them both.

Clarice's image flashed momentarily in his mind. *You know it isn't true, Hudson. I've never wronged you. Never. I love you.*

He cursed again, kicked over his desk chair, then strode out of his office.

Pity the first person who looked at him wrong.

There was something to be said for hard work. Especially when there was no one standing over his back threatening to do him bodily harm if he didn't move fast enough or talk right or commit any number of other infractions.

Gabe stood back and studied the cabin from wood floor to rafters. It had taken him the better part of the day, but he was satisfied with the results. The room was as clean as it could get.

It'll make a good home. He released a mirthless grunt at the passing thought. He didn't have a home. Had never had a home, if truth be known. This was a stopping place, a temporary sanctuary.

He carried the bucket of dirty scrub water outside and emptied it into the grass behind the outhouse. Then he went to the pump where he stripped off his shirt, gave the handle a few quick jerks, and stuck his head beneath the running water. It was icy cold, causing his breath to catch. When he straightened, he shoved his wet hair away from his face. It needed to be trimmed. He'd have to ask Akira for a pair of scissors.

Tossing his sweat-stained shirt over his shoulder, he picked up the bucket, refilled it with fresh water, and returned to his cabin.

He had one more clean shirt, thanks to the generosity of his new employer. He would wash up and put it on before joining her and the others for supper. Once he was out with the sheep, he didn't suppose it would matter if he had a clean change of clothing. But today it mattered.

There'd been a time when Gabe had a wardrobe full of clothes, drawers full of white shirts that had been washed and starched and pressed by servants.

He hesitated before glancing at his reflection in the small mirror on the wall. A haggard-looking man stared back at him. A man who appeared much older than his thirty-two years. Was there any sign of the kid he'd been? Of the spoiled youth, lashing out at the world, longing for something he couldn't have?

No, there wasn't. That boy was as dead as both of his brothers.

The clanging of the dinner bell pulled him away from the mirror—and his thoughts. It was just as well. He'd been on the verge of recalling things best left hidden in the darkest corners of his memory.

With a quick rake of fingers through shaggy, damp hair, he strode out of the cabin and toward the main house. He kept his head and eyes raised. In prison, he'd learned to walk with his gaze lowered. A man was less apt to get into trouble that way. But there was a desire in his heart to appear confident now.

And he would need confidence tonight, judging by the look of Brodie Lachlan. The Scotsman stood inside the open doorway, his arms crossed over his chest, his scowl as dark as a moonless night in the forest.

"There you are," Akira said, drawing Gabe's gaze to the opposite side of the room. Her smile was welcoming; Brodie's frown was not. "Come and meet the Wickhams." She motioned toward a chair at the table.

He moved past the Scotsman, half expecting a blow to the back of his head.

"Mr. Wickham," Akira continued, "you remember Gabe Talmadge."

Gabe noticed there was no flicker of surprise in Charlie's expression, and he knew the man had been forewarned.

"I do." Charlie held out a hand. "Good to see you again. Sorry I didn't recognize you earlier today."

Gabe had little choice but to shake the proffered hand.

Charlie glanced to his right. "This is my wife, Nora." Then he looked to his left. "And this is my son, Mark."

"Pleasure," Gabe mumbled with nods toward both.

Akira interrupted the awkward silence that followed by pulling out a chair from the table and saying, "Sit down, everyone, before supper gets cold."

Akira wasn't much good at the art of polite conversation. Even when she'd lived in San Francisco with her mother and stepfather, who had entertained frequently, she hadn't excelled at it. But tonight she was thankful for what little she'd learned from her mother's tutelage.

"Mrs. Wickham, I couldn't help but notice the beautiful needlepoint you were working on earlier this afternoon. Did you design the pattern yourself?"

"Yes, I did. Thank you."

"Perhaps you could show it to me later."

"If you'd like."

"I would. Of course, I'm all thumbs with a needle, but I do take pleasure in pretty things. My mother had high hopes for me. I failed her miserably." She smiled and shrugged her shoulders. "She never understood my love for Dundreggan."

"I didn't know your mother," Nora said, "but I understand she lived here for a time."

"Yes. After my father died, Mother and I came to live with Grandfather. When she married my stepfather four years later, we moved to California. But I was never happy there." Akira looked across the table at Brodie. "You remember the day Mother and I first arrived at Dundreggan. I was so afraid. My whole world had been turned upside down."

"*Ach!* I remember it, lass. A wee thing ye were. Six years old and pretty as a mountain bluebird. Eyes as big as saucers."

"That's because I'd never seen anyone with hair the color of yours."

Brodie glanced around the table before saying, "Afraid or not, she was filled with mischief, this one, and headstrong, to boot. Fergus doted on her, and 'tis me who's had to pay for it, now that he's gone to his reward."

"I learned all my most stubborn traits from you, Brodie," she retorted with a saucy toss of her head.

He grinned. "Aye, that ye did."

Somehow Akira was able to keep the conversation going in a similar lighthearted vein throughout the remainder of the meal. It wasn't until dessert had been served that she brought up the subject they'd all had in the back of their minds.

She looked first at Charlie. "It's time we talked about work."

"Yes." He pushed his plate away from him with one hand. "I've been wondering about it."

"I've given this much thought." She avoided Brodie's gaze. "I've decided to send you and Mark with Mr. Lachlan and the band of sheep. He can't get around the mountainsides on his bad leg, but he can ride in the sheepherder's wagon and will be nearby when you need advice or instruction. There's no one who knows more about sheep than he does."

Despite her better judgment, she glanced at her longtime friend. Brodie was frowning, as she'd known he would be. She raised her chin, hoping he wouldn't argue in front of the others. She couldn't avoid the confrontation forever, but she'd just as soon delay it awhile.

"And what about Mr. Talmadge?" Brodie asked, a thin edge in his voice.

"He'll stay and help me run the farm."

Brodie shifted his gaze toward Gabe. "Have ye done much farming, Mr. Talmadge?"

"Not much." His voice was totally without inflection.

Although she didn't attempt to explain, Akira had several sound reasons for her decision. First, the Wickhams were more apt to remain in the valley beyond this summer. Nora wasn't a strong woman and travel would be difficult for her. Their roots were in Ransom. Training Charlie and Mark to be Dundreggan shepherds made good sense.

She glanced toward Gabe, reminded of another reason for her decision. He needed rest and nourishment to build his strength. She doubted he would last a week in the mountains with Brodie. The big Scotsman would drive him too hard. She knew Brodie didn't like or trust Gabe.

But I do. For some reason, I do.

Gabe looked up, caught her watching him. A spark of something—rebellion? frustration? gratitude?—flashed in his eyes. Then the look was gone; the carefully composed mask dropped back into place.

She wanted to help him. More than anything she'd wanted in a long time, she wanted to help this man. And God wanted her to help him. She was certain of it. It was no accident she'd chanced upon him yesterday, and whatever the Lord's purpose, she meant to see it through.

Akira turned her gaze upon Brodie. "It's decided, then. You three will leave with the sheep by the end of the week."

"Aye," the Scotsman answered gruffly. "It'll be as ye wish."

CHAPTER FIVE

The next days passed in a flurry of activity. The wagon was stocked with supplies. The sheep were driven from the low-lying grazing lands to fenced pastures closer to the ranch house. Brodie worked with Charlie and Mark, teaching them the different voice and hand commands they would use with the dogs.

Gabe felt useless. All his offers to help were rebuffed, both by Brodie and Akira.

"You must give yourself time to regain your strength," she told him. "You need rest and plenty of good food if you're to be of use to me."

She was right, but it grated on his nerves nonetheless.

On Friday, he awakened before dawn. Try as he might, he couldn't go back to sleep. He got out of bed, slipped on his shirt and trousers, then made a trip to the outhouse. On his way back to the cabin, he heard something that caused him to pause.

It was Akira, speaking softly to her collie. Although the morning sky was the color of slate, the sunrise nothing more than a dim promise on the horizon, he was able to see her clearly enough as she made her way toward the lower pasture.

He followed her.

A crazy thing to do.

It was Cam who gave away his presence. The dog stopped suddenly, turned on the path, and growled a warning.

"Who's there?" Akira demanded.

"It's me."

"Gabe?"

He saw her place her hand on the dog's head, heard her whisper, "All right, Cam. Stand down."

Taking that as his cue, Gabe moved forward. "Sorry if I frightened you."

"You didn't."

"If you'd rather, I can go back."

"No. You're welcome to join us." She turned and continued along the trail. "I find it peaceful out here in the mornings. A good place to pray and meditate." She stopped again. "Did you hear that? A meadowlark. I love their sweet song. It's so joyful."

He hadn't heard it. Maybe because he'd stopped listening for joyful sounds.

She looked up, her face clearer to him now as the sky lightened. "We've a busy day ahead of us."

"The drive begins."

"Yes."

"Tell me what it's like," he said, wanting to keep her talking.

He didn't care what she said. He simply enjoyed the sound of her voice.

"What what's like?"

He had to think a moment. "The life of a sheep rancher," he answered at last.

"It's a hard and simple one." She smiled. "Is that a contradiction?" She didn't wait for him to answer her question. "In the winter, we keep the sheep nearby where we can feed them hay. The first lambs usually drop in mid-February, depending when the bucks were put with the ewes. In the spring, usually by the middle of March in these parts, we turn the band out to forage on the new growth, moving them to higher elevations as grasses and shrubs mature. The sheep shearers are usually at Dundreggan by May. They shear on the range, wherever the sheep are at the time, before the band moves to summer grazing in the high meadows." She pointed to the northeast. "Up there."

"And the Wickhams and Lachlan will stay in the mountains until they're brought back down? Living in that cramped sheepherder's wagon the whole time?"

She nodded. "Shepherds have to always be with the sheep, looking out for coyotes and bobcats and bear. So they take their home with them. The wagon sleeps two comfortably, three in a pinch, and unless the weather's bad, they can sleep under the wagon if they want. They've got their Dutch oven for cooking, and wool blankets and wood stove to keep them warm on cool nights. There's plenty of mutton on the hoof and plenty of fresh water to drink and a heaven full of stars to watch over them at night. It isn't as bad as it looks."

He couldn't help grinning at her. "I'll bet you make it sound better than it is."

Akira laughed softly, then gestured toward the ewes and lambs dotting the pastureland. "My grandfather was participating in the development of this new breed. The Targhees are a cross of Rambouillet, Lincoln, and Corriedale bloodlines. They're named for the national forest over near the Dubois Sheep Experiment Station. Grandfather believed in them so much. He held the popular view that the ideal breed is three-quarters fine wool and one-quarter long wool."

Gabe hadn't a clue what she was talking about.

"The Targhees you see here are third generation. I wish Grandfather could have seen them."

"How long has he been gone?"

"He died in '30. Sometimes it seems only yesterday." Her voice lowered. "And sometimes it seems like forever." She released a wistful sigh. "He understood me. We were so alike, he and I. Much to my mother's dismay."

"Why's that?"

Before answering, Akira sank to the ground, ignoring the dew clinging to the grass.

Gabe followed suit.

"Mother hoped I would become a proper lady." She drew her

knees toward her chest and hugged them with her arms. "She certainly did everything in her power to mold and shape me. But I
failed her miserably."

I disagree.

Akira looked at him as if he'd spoken the words aloud. Her
smile was as soft as the morning light, as sweet as the song of the
meadowlark.

Sweet. So sweet.

He didn't belong near her. Brodie Lachlan was right about that.

Akira turned her face toward the sky. "I tried to be what she
wanted, but my efforts only frustrated us both. Then I realized I'm
supposed to be who God made me to be. The Bible says, 'Who art
thou that repliest against God? Shall the thing formed say to Him
that formed it, Why didst Thou make me thus?' Now I'm content
to follow His plan for me and not someone else's."

Why didst Thou make me thus?

Gabe closed his eyes, swallowing hard as he fought the rising
sense of despair.

Why didst Thou make me thus?

Wasn't that what he'd asked God for years?

"Gabriel…"

He kept his eyes closed.

"Don't run from the One who loves you most."

"It isn't that simple, Miss Macauley."

"You're mistaken. It's even more simple than it sounds."

He stood. "I turned my back on God years ago."

She stood too. "But He never turned His back on you. He's waiting with open arms."

Gabe saw the childlike trust in her eyes, and it angered him. There was a part of him that wanted to shake her belief at its foundation. There was a part of him that wanted to make her see the evil lurking in his soul.

Instead, he turned on his heel and strode away.

Jane Sebastian pulled a bolt from the shelf, then unrolled a length of the diagonally striped cotton fabric on the shop counter. It was exactly the shade of blue she'd had in mind for a new dress.

"There Talmadge goes in his fancy new Duesenberg."

"I heard he paid over ten thousand dollars for it."

"Ten *thousand* dollars? No!"

"Yes. Can you imagine such a thing? And my Henry's working only two days a week at the mill. That's the best Talmadge says he can do in these hard times." She snorted. "Hard times for who, I'd like to know. Not him."

Jane didn't have to look to recognize the voices of the two women who stood gossiping near the front window of Ransom Dry Goods. She'd known them both for the better part of the last ten years. Irene Hirsch was the widow of the town's physician, who'd died the previous year. Dr. Otto Hirsch's passing had left a hole in the community that wasn't apt to be filled anytime soon. The other woman—Henry's wife—was Lilybet Teague.

"Did you know his son's returned?" Irene asked, her tone of voice indicating the importance of this juicy tidbit.

"No. You don't say."

"I do, indeed. He was seen earlier this week at the mill."

"But I never heard a word about it."

"Lilybet, have you known me to be wrong about such things? I'm telling you, he was there, and his father threw him out."

Jane ground her teeth. She had no tolerance for rumor-mongers.

"Wouldn't you do the same?" In a hushed voice, Lilybet added, "After all, he's a murderer."

"That's not true!" Jane exclaimed, unable to keep silent. She spun around to face the two women, trying hard to tamp her anger, doing her best to remember that a soft answer turned away wrath. "Gabriel didn't murder his brother. Max's death was an accident. A tragic accident."

Irene Hirsch's cheeks flushed with indignation. "He was found guilty by the jury."

"He was found guilty by his father," Jane retorted. "The jury did as they were told."

Lilybet Teague sputtered something unintelligible, then walked to the door, pulled it open, and left the store. Irene followed right behind.

How Jane wished she could throttle those two troublemakers! They hadn't a charitable bone in their bodies.

"Don't let them get under your skin," Dorothea Baker said into the ensuing silence.

Ashamed of her thoughts, Jane turned to look at the woman who managed the dry-goods store.

Dorothea moved to the opposite side of the counter. "You've never changed your mind, have you? About Gabe's innocence."

"Never." She shook her head. "He loved his brother."

"But he admitted his guilt."

"Strange how no one remembers what really happened that night." Jane rolled the fabric back onto the bolt, then returned it to the shelf. "Not even Gabe."

Heavy-hearted, she left the store, her desire for a new dress forgotten.

Macauley sheep had been following the same trail to summer pastures for many years, although normally this portion of the trek was taken in late May or early June.

Akira helped with the drive for the first couple of hours, loving the legion of sounds and the seeming chaos that accompanied the start of the journey—the tinkling bells on the lead sheep, the doleful cries of lost lambs seeking their mothers, the ewes bleating in reply, the dogs barking at stragglers, and the piercing whistles of the shepherds.

Her grandfather used to say Akira liked all new beginnings. She supposed he'd been right about that.

She also took pleasure in the way Charlie and Mark were proving themselves to be capable shepherds. Mark was adept with the dogs, and Charlie got along well with Brodie, a true blessing given the crusty nature of the Scotsman.

Now if she could only get Brodie to quit fretting over Gabe Talmadge, everything would be just about perfect.

"Ye're too trusting, Akira," he grumbled for the umpteenth time.

Riding her horse next to the sheepherder's wagon, she pretended she couldn't hear him.

He wasn't fooled. "Ye heard me, lass."

She grinned, still not looking at him.

"Ye're twenty-six years old, Akira, and ye're acquainted with the things of nature, with the making of new life. Ye ken what I'm sayin', lass? Ye must know how it is between men and women. Isn't right for ye to be alone with the likes o' him. Isn't safe. He's a dangerous man."

She drew back on the reins, stopping her horse. Brodie did likewise.

"You're wrong about him. He's not dangerous. Don't ask me how I know. I simply know."

"Ye weren't here when it happened. Ye weren't here for the trial."

"No, thank God."

Brodie shook his head. "Yer grandfather would—"

"He would do precisely what I'm doing," she interrupted. "He would give the man a chance for a new start. Guilty or not, he wouldn't hold the past against Gabe."

The Scotsman—his face flushed and his eyes dark with frustration—looked as if he were about to burst a blood vessel. To save him from such a fate, Akira chose a hasty retreat, waving to Brodie as she rode away.

"See you in a few weeks," she called over her shoulder.

As the sounds faded into the distance, Akira let her thoughts drift to that morning, to those few minutes when she and Gabe had sat in the grass and talked. Or rather, she'd talked. He'd said very little—as usual.

Lord, why are You, me, and Jane Sebastian the only ones who believe in him? Why only the three of us?

She worried her lower lip between her teeth.

Sometimes I think just looking at him could break my heart.

CHAPTER SIX

Hudson sank deep into the leather-upholstered chair. Smoke from his cigar coiled upward, joining the bluish haze that filled the wood-paneled room of the club. He didn't speak. He let his frown tell the senator's man exactly what he thought of the information imparted to him.

Keith Delaney cleared his throat in obvious discomfort. "Senator Fortier hasn't given up, of course."

"Of course."

"He's working hard to make this happen."

Hudson puffed on his cigar.

"I assure you, Mr. Talmadge, the senator *is* doing everything he can legally do."

Hudson clenched his teeth to remain silent, but inside he seethed. By heavens! He hadn't contributed all that money to Quincey Fortier's election coffers only to be told the man couldn't help because something wasn't *legal*.

"Well." Delaney cleared his throat again, then stood. "I look forward to seeing you at the ball, sir."

Hudson nodded in response, not bothering to rise or speak as the senator's harbinger of bad news set his hat on his head, turned, and walked away. But once Keith Delaney was gone, Hudson muttered a string of curses beneath his breath, wishing he could bellow them instead, wanting to give full vent to the rage that stormed inside him. But he wouldn't. Not here, surrounded by important men of business and industry. He would never be so foolish. He hadn't built his fortune by careless behavior, no matter what the provocation.

Provocation. He certainly had plenty of *that!* Beginning with Pauline, who had nearly bought out the stores in Boise in one week's time, and ending with Gabe's unexpected return to Ransom.

And of all people, it had to be Akira Macauley who took him in. Were the fates mocking him?

He needed to own the Macauley lands if his plans for the valley were to succeed. But she'd refused to sell Dundreggan, no matter the price he offered. For more than two years, she'd stubbornly turned him down. Even his less-than-subtle threats hadn't swayed her.

Hudson blew smoke rings toward the ceiling, imagining Gabe on that sheep ranch.

Was it possible Hudson could make use of this turn of events? he wondered. Akira Macauley had taken an interest in Gabe. Whether it was an act of charity or something else didn't concern him at the moment. What mattered was that Gabe was living there and possibly could glean information that Hudson couldn't.

Hmm.

Yes, he would definitely have to give this matter more thought.

A three-quarter moon dangled above the mountains as night settled over the valley. The air was warm. Too warm for sleep.

Gabe sat on the stoop of his cabin, gazing at the star-strewn heavens. So vast. So wide. So never ending. He remembered the countless times he'd gazed at a patch of night sky through a tiny window across from his second-story cell. If he closed his eyes, that was how he still envisioned it. Small and square and never quite clear. Four years of freedom hadn't changed the surprise he felt at being able to move about at night, unrestricted, to be able to look up and see the breadth of the heavens from horizon to horizon.

His gaze shifted toward the main house. No light shone through the open windows. He wondered if Akira was asleep.

Why did she let me stay?

It had been a week since Akira found Gabe on the road south of Dundreggan, a week since she'd given him a place to call his own. Supposedly he was working for her, but thus far he'd spent his days in idleness. She hadn't bothered to tell him what his duties would be. But then, he hadn't asked. He'd learned in prison to wait until someone issued orders. It was a tough habit to break.

He leaned the back of his head against the doorjamb and closed his eyes.

There'd been times, since his release, when he'd wished himself back inside the familiar walls of the penitentiary. At least there he'd known what to expect. Nothing about the outside world was familiar to him anymore. His life before prison seemed nothing but a dream, a life that had happened to someone else. And what he'd experienced since getting out had been no life at all.

He opened his eyes and gazed upward again.

What do You want from me?

There was no answer to his silent question.

He didn't expect one.

He certainly didn't deserve one.

The blow to the side of Gabe's head knocked him to the floor.

"Get up!" his father shouted as he leaned over and grabbed his arm, yanking him back to his feet. "Never let me hear you talking that rubbish again. Do you hear me, boy?"

Tears streaked his cheeks. "I hear. I hear." He hated himself for cowering, hated himself for crying like a baby. A twelve-year-old wasn't supposed to cry.

"As long as you carry my name, you'll remember what I said. God's a fable. He's for women and those weaklings who can't stand on their own two feet."

"But my mother believed and—"

Hudson struck him again, rattling his teeth. The pain shot from his jaw right to the top of his head. He tasted blood on his tongue.

"Mr. Talmadge! Stop!"

Gabe heard Miss Jane's voice as if from a great distance. He turned toward the door. Through the blur of tears, he saw her enter his father's library.

"What are you doing?" she demanded.

Miss Jane was the only person Gabe knew who didn't fear his father.

"Whatever it is," Hudson answered, "it's none of your concern. You're fired. Get out of this house."

"But, sir, I—"

"I said, get out! I told you not to push religion on these boys, but you wouldn't listen."

Instinctively, Gabe stepped toward Miss Jane, the woman who had raised him, the woman who'd loved him, but his father grabbed him by the arm a second time and jerked him back.

"Tell her," Hudson growled.

"Tell her what?"

"Tell her you don't believe in God."

He stared at his father, not knowing what to do.

Hudson backhanded him. "Say it, or so help me, I'll beat it out of you!"

"Gabe," Miss Jane whispered.

He didn't know what she wanted him to do, but it didn't matter. He had to obey his father.

"I don't believe," Gabe choked out, dying a little as he said it. "I don't believe in God."

Hudson shoved him into a chair, then turned toward Miss Jane. "There. You've heard it. Now go. Get out and don't ever come back to this house."

All Gabe had wanted was to share the joy he'd felt the moment he'd asked Jesus to come live in his heart. All he'd wanted was to tell his father about a God who loved him and wanted the best for His children. He'd wanted his father to feel the same joy—and then maybe learn to love Gabe the way he loved Max.

But instead Miss Jane was being sent away, and Gabe had denied God's existence…and now his father hated him more than before.

How had it all gone so wrong?

Gabe swallowed the lump in his throat. He was surprised the twenty-year-old memory still had the power to hurt.

Twenty years.

Somewhere along the way, he'd figured out his father was unable to love him. Gabe had come to understand that no matter what he did, Hudson would *never* love him.

Yet he'd returned to Ransom, still hoping.

Hope. It was both a blessing and a curse to a man in prison. Apparently the same was true outside the walls. Better not to hope.

"Gabriel?"

He looked up, surprised to find Akira standing before him. "What do you want?" he asked, his voice raspy with emotion.

"God sent me to tell you that you can never escape His spirit. You can't get away from His presence." Her voice was soft and gentle, yet strong. "If you go up to heaven, He's there, and if you go down into Hades, He's there, too."

Tears burned his eyes and the back of his throat. He wanted her to stop, to be silent, to leave him alone.

As if reading his thoughts, she continued, "No matter what you believe, you've never been alone, Gabriel Talmadge. Not even in your prison cell. Jesus went there with you."

"You don't know what you're talking about."

She took a step closer. "For I am persuaded, that neither death, nor life, nor angels, nor principalities, nor powers, nor things present, nor things to come, nor height, nor depth, nor any other creature, shall be able to separate us from the love of God, which is in Christ Jesus our Lord." Her voice dropped to a whisper. "Nothing can separate you from the Father's love."

"Go away."

71

"No."

He rose to his feet. "Don't you understand? I turned my back on Him. I made my choice. There's no changing that now. Just like there's no changing that I killed my brother."

"Gabriel—"

"This is my punishment!" he shouted. "Let it be!"

For a long while, silence stretched between them. When she spoke again, still in a whisper, Gabe suspected it was no longer him she addressed.

"A man can endure a sick body, but who can bear a crushed spirit?" There was a hint of tearfulness in her voice. "Oh, Father, help us. Help *him*."

When Gabe heard that, something crumbled inside him. "You don't know what I've done, the things I've seen, the kind of person I am."

"No, I don't. I don't need to know. Christ knows, and He's already paid the price for it all."

"It's too late for me. Maybe once..." His voice trailed into silence.

"Gabe." She reached out, touching his shoulder with her fingertips. "Do you think the Almighty was surprised by what you did? He wasn't. He knew your life from beginning to end. He made provision for whatever you would do in His plans for you. Isn't it arrogance of the highest order to believe your sins are greater than God Himself? His blood covered it all."

How did she know what he was feeling? How could she possibly know him that well?

Once again she responded as if he'd spoken his thoughts aloud. "I know you're far from where you want to be. But you don't have to stay there. Jesus is waiting. He's calling you to come home." She withdrew her hand, then took a step backward. "He's the God of second chances, Gabriel. Take it."

With those words lingering on the calm night air, she turned and walked away.

Akira's sleep that night was fitful, and she was up before the dawn, walking with Cam at her side, talking with the Lord. That was how she happened to see Gabe leading Big Red, the oldest of the three workhorses, out of the barn. The eastern sky was stained the color of peaches at the moment he stepped up in the stirrup and swung his free leg over the saddle. She watched as he gathered the reins in one hand, then nudged the horse with the heels of his well-worn boots. She saw him tug the brim of his hat firmly down on his forehead so it wouldn't blow off.

"Is he running away, Jesus? Has he rejected You again?"

Expecting sorrow to grip her heart, she was surprised instead with a sense of peace flowing through her.

"Yes, Lord, I'll trust You. Thy will be done."

She watched Gabe ride Big Red away from the barnyard. She kept watching until he disappeared over a ridge. Then she headed up the path toward the house.

"Come, Cam," she called to her faithful collie. "There's work to be done."

Reverend Simon Neville's eyesight wasn't what it used to be, but he could still recognize a man carrying the weight of the world on his shoulders. From the window of the parsonage, he watched the tall, slender stranger dismount his horse and walk toward the church. There was something tentative about the way he tried the door, and even from this distance, Simon seemed to feel the man's relief when he found it unlocked.

"Your breakfast is ready, Simon," his wife called from the kitchen.

Should he let the man pray in peace or go to him?

"Dear?" Violet stepped into the parlor. "Did you hear me calling? Your food is growing cold."

Feeling a sudden sense of urgency, he made his decision. "I'm going to the church." He reached for his Bible and his hat.

"But you haven't eaten."

"I'll eat later."

"Simon, whatever—?"

He met her gaze, and her objections immediately ceased. After forty years of marriage, she'd learned to read him well.

"I'll say a prayer," she said after a moment.

He gave her a gentle smile. "Thank you, dear."

Simon whispered his own words of supplication as he covered the distance between parsonage and church, not knowing what awaited him inside.

The door creaked as he pulled it open. Anemic morning light filtered through the stained-glass window above the altar. Simon pushed his glasses up on his nose while his eyes adjusted to the shadowy interior. The man stood at the front of the church, staring up at the large wooden cross on the wall. He didn't turn, gave no indication of hearing Simon's arrival.

After a moment's hesitation, the reverend slid into the back pew and waited.

No matter what you believe, you've never been alone, Gabriel Talmadge. Not even in your prison cell. Jesus went there with you.

Twenty years ago, he'd asked Jesus into his heart, but before the week was out, he'd denied Him. He'd wanted his father's love and approval more than God's. He'd feared his father's anger more than he'd feared God's wrath. There was no forgiveness for that. How could there be?

Nothing can separate you from the Father's love.

Gabe had spent his youth doing whatever he could to get Hudson's approval. When approval didn't come, he'd done whatever it took simply to get his father's attention, even if it meant living for the devil himself. He'd known the things he did were wrong. He hadn't needed anyone to tell him so.

A man can endure a sick body, but who can bear a crushed spirit?

Gabe sank to his knees. He lowered his head to his chest, feeling crushed and broken. "O God."

Do you think the Almighty was surprised by what you did?

God was God. He had to know everything. But it was also true that vengeance belonged to Him. Gabe had to be punished, for he'd chosen all the wrong things. He'd known the Truth, and he'd turned the other way.

Isn't it arrogance of the highest order to believe your sins are somehow greater than God Himself?

Gabe sucked in a breath as he raised his eyes toward the cross once more.

He's the God of second chances, Gabriel Talmadge...

The God of second chances...

Second chances...

"Jesus," he whispered, "I want another chance."

CHAPTER SEVEN

By noon, Akira was in the hayfield, mowing alfalfa that was in full bloom. Sweat trickled along the sides of her face as the sun beat down with brutal fierceness upon the crown of her straw hat. Her back ached and new blisters had formed on her hands, despite her leather gloves, but she kept going. The work wouldn't wait.

At the end of the row, she turned the horses and mowing machine. Then she caught a glimpse of Big Red, with Gabe astride, coming over the rise. Her heart fluttered. Her breath caught in her throat.

He's back!

She slipped the reins over her head and left them trailing on the ground as she hurried across the new-mown field.

Gabe had already dismounted and was standing beside Big Red when Akira came around the corner of the house. Their gazes met, and she halted.

He held out the reins, as if offering them to her. "I brought back the horse. I didn't steal him."

She shook her head. "I knew that."

"I went to see Reverend Neville."

He'd made his peace with God. She could see it in his eyes, hear it in his voice.

"Thanks, Akira."

She didn't ask for what. *Thank You, Jesus.*

He smiled, a look both joyous and tender.

She felt suddenly lightheaded and weak in the knees. *Too much sun,* she rationalized as she fought to regain her equilibrium. *It must be heatstroke.*

Gabe tipped his head toward the hayfield. "Looks like you could use some help down there." He turned. "I'll put up the horse, then give you a hand. It's time I started earning my keep." He led Big Red into the shadowy recesses of the barn.

The instant he disappeared, Akira's sense of balance began to return. She took a few slow, deep breaths. Yes, that was definitely better. A drink of chilled lemonade from the icebox and a few moments seated in the shade and she would feel herself again.

She strode toward the house, sweeping off her straw bonnet as she went. Inside, she hung the hat on a peg near the door. She crossed to the icebox, drew out the pitcher of lemonade, and poured the sweet-tart beverage into a glass. Then she tipped back her head and drained the contents without drawing a breath between gulps.

Much better.

She set the glass on the counter as her gaze shifted to the window. She saw Gabe walk out of the barn, stop, glance toward the house. That confounded weakness in her knees returned.

Maybe she'd better have another glass of lemonade before she returned to the mowing.

The green scent of new-cut alfalfa filled Gabe's nostrils as he walked toward the hayfield. It was a heady odor, but he liked it. For that matter, he liked everything he saw. Today, even the relentless heat couldn't dampen his joy.

Smiling to himself, he sat in the shade of a tree at one end of the field and waited for Akira.

He stared into the distance, where granite mountain peaks met the pale blue of a cloudless sky. The verse Simon Neville had read to him came to mind: *For the mountains shall depart, and the hills be removed; but My kindness shall not depart from thee, neither shall the covenant of My peace be removed, saith the LORD that hath mercy on thee.*

Gabe thought about how the mountains had stood as sentries over this valley for thousands of years. No man could destroy them, not even with all the dynamite in the world. They could cut holes in them, burrow deep mines into their sides. They could blow away portions and cut down trees. Yet ultimately, the mountains would prevail. They would stand against the efforts of man.

But those same mountains would crumble before God's kindness, mercy, and peace would depart from Gabe.

Incredible but true.

"Men have complicated the things of God down through the centuries," Simon had told him. "But God's way is easy. All you need do is ask Christ to rescue you, to forgive you, and He will. The Word says all who call upon the name of Jesus will be saved."

Gabe had started to protest, had tried to explain about all the wrong he'd done, but Simon hadn't let him finish.

"Even the thief on the cross was forgiven in the last moments of his life. He had no time to do good works, no time to make amends. Yet Jesus promised him they would be together in paradise that very day…simply because he asked Christ to remember him."

So simple.

So awesome.

Gabe glanced toward the ranch house and saw Akira's approach, her stride long, fluid, and sure. He remembered how she'd said God had brought him here for a purpose. He hadn't believed it at the time, but now he knew how right she'd been.

Thank God.

He got to his feet.

"Sorry I was so long," she said.

"I didn't mind the wait." He grinned.

Her eyes widened slightly, reminding him of a startled doe caught in a beam of light. She looked…nervous. Not like the Akira he'd come to know. Was it something he'd said or done?

She glanced away. "We'd better get to work. Are you sure you feel up to this?"

"I feel up to everything."

She met his gaze again, and this time she offered a tentative smile of her own.

He couldn't guess what was going on inside her head, but at least her smile told him he hadn't done anything wrong.

"I assume you've never mown hay before," she said as she led the way toward the mowing machine.

"No, I haven't."

"But you can drive a team of horses."

"No. Sorry."

That caused her to look at him again. In the shadow of her broad-brimmed straw hat, he saw her eyebrows lift in an expression of disbelief.

"The Talmadges didn't have carriages or buggies. We always had automobiles."

"Ah."

He was glad he hadn't added, *and chauffeurs.* For some reason, it would have made him feel less in her eyes.

"Well," she said, "you have plenty to learn, then."

He glanced toward the mountains—strong, sure, immovable. "Yes. I've got plenty to learn, but I'm ready."

They worked hard for the remainder of the afternoon, talking little except for Akira's answers to Gabe's infrequent questions. She found him quick to understand and willing to follow directions.

Around and around the field they went, the sharp blades of the mower leaving layers of fragrant cuttings behind them. Sometimes the alfalfa was so thick and tall it bound the sickle. Whenever that happened, Gabe stopped the horses and Akira pulled the pile of matted alfalfa aside. By the time the last row was cut, the first rows had been dehydrating in the sun for several hours. The mowing machine was put away and the team was hitched to the hay rake. They followed the same route around the field a second time, raking the hay into rows and bunches. And when that was done, the cuttings were tossed onto the hay wagon with pitchforks.

Cheat and weeds sifted out of the drying alfalfa, covering Gabe and Akira, sticking to their sweaty necks and arms, working beneath their shirt collars and up their pant legs, chafing and poking and torturing. The irritating dust made their eyes smart and their lungs burn.

Akira was surprised by Gabe's endurance. Eight days before, he'd passed out on the road from hunger, but now he was putting in a full day's labor. True, they rested more frequently than normal, although she didn't tell him that.

Early evening had settled over the valley by the time Gabe drove the wagon, with Akira seated beside him, to the stack yard. Sunlight caressed the trees, gilding the leaves. A slight breeze caused the grasses to undulate, rising and falling like the ocean.

Gabe wore a look of weary satisfaction as he drew the horses to a halt.

"No one would believe you'd never done this before." Akira smiled when he glanced in her direction. "You're a born rancher."

After a moment's hesitation, when he seemed to seriously consider her comment, he replied, "Maybe you're right."

As hungry as he was, Gabe was too hot, too sweaty, too tired to eat much. Even Akira's cooking, which was always excellent, didn't tempt him. She apparently felt the same.

Ten minutes after they'd sat down to supper—just the two of them, Mrs. Wickham having already eaten—Akira pushed her almost untouched plate away, then scooted her chair back from the table.

"Do you swim?" she asked as she stood.

"What?"

"Do you know how to swim?" She did the breaststroke through the air.

He frowned. "Yes. Why?"

"Because I can't stand myself another minute. I need to wash off the dust and get rid of the cheat grass in my hair." She turned toward her bedroom. "I'm going for a swim. You're welcome to join me if you'd like to come along."

She didn't have to ask twice. Nothing sounded better.

He got to his feet. "I don't have any bathing trunks."

"My grandfather kept extra clothes on hand for guests and ranch hands. There's bound to be something in one of the bureaus that will fit you. Wait here." She disappeared into the other room.

Half an hour later, with towels thrown over their shoulders, both of them clad in swimming attire beneath their denim trousers, they rode their horses up a narrow deer track into the forest.

"I usually settle for a creek that runs north of the house," she said over her shoulder, "but it's running low this summer. I wanted a real swim after the work we've done today."

The sky darkened, revealing the evening's first stars. The forest sounds changed as day gave in to night—the harsh cries of the jays silenced, the muted hoot of an owl taking their place. If not for the rising crescent moon, filtered through the branches of towering ponderosa and lodge-pole pines, Gabe would have lost sight of Akira altogether.

"He that dwelleth in the secret place of the most High shall abide under the shadow of the Almighty." Her voice was gentle and low, but it carried back to him on the night breeze, each word clear and true. "I will say of the Lord, He is my refuge and my fortress: my God; in Him will I trust."

"What is that?" he asked when she fell silent.

"The Ninety-first Psalm."

"The Ninety-first Psalm," he repeated softly. Once he could afford to buy a Bible, he wanted to look up that verse for himself.

He had a lot to learn, a great deal of catching up to do. He longed to know more about God. He wanted to know more about farming and sheep ranching and—

"Follow me." Akira reined in and dismounted. "The swimming hole's right over there." She tethered her horse to a bush. "Come on." She vanished between two trees.

Whether out of habit or out of eagerness for the promised swim, he hurried to obey. He came through the trees and underbrush in time to see Akira dive into the moon-silvered waters of the pond.

She resurfaced with a shriek of pleasure. "It's wonderful. Come on in."

He wanted to learn all about Akira, too, he realized, and he wasn't sure that was a good thing.

Not for him.

Or for her.

Chapter Eight

If there was one thing Gabe learned his second week at Dundreggan, it was that a rancher's day began early and lasted long. And with good reason. There was always more to be done than there were hours to do it.

There was the livestock to tend—a half-dozen sheep; two pigs, one due to give birth in a couple of weeks, one meant for butchering come fall; three cows, one for milking, the others raised for beef; a henhouse full of chickens; the saddle- and workhorses. There was a huge garden to tend, rows and rows of corn, tomatoes, several kinds of squash, onions, pumpkins, and more. There was the large patch of berry bushes and also an arbor thickly laced with grapevines. Beyond the arbor was the fruit orchard with apple, peach, and cherry trees.

"This is the easy part," Akira told him the day they weeded the garden. "The canning. Now *that's* the part I hate."

He wondered if she ever rested, but he didn't ask. It would have sounded as if he was complaining, and he wasn't. When he fell into bed at night, bone weary, muscles aching, it was with a sense of accomplishment, a sense of having done an honest day's work. It was a good feeling, and he thanked God for it.

He thanked God for many things every day. At the moment, he was thankful for the litter of newborn puppies Akira had discovered in the barn.

"Aren't they adorable?" she asked, pressing one of the mewling, wheat-colored pups to her cheek.

Gabe thought it resembled a rodent more than a dog.

"I've got to show Mrs. Wickham." Akira stood. "Come with me?"

"I'd better get back to work. Besides, I make the lady nervous. She doesn't care to have an ex-con get too close."

Her smile faded. "She doesn't know you. Give her time."

"Not everyone is as forgiving as you, Akira."

"No matter what you did before, you're different now. Christ has made you so."

"People don't always forgive. Not even Christians." He shrugged his shoulders. "And they rarely forget. It's something I've come to accept."

Her greenish-blue eyes studied him intently. After a lengthy silence, she said, "Tell me about your brother."

The request stopped him cold. No one had asked him about Max in years.

"I'm sorry," she said softly. "I shouldn't have pried." She started toward the barn door.

"No. Wait."

She paused, then turned.

"I'd like to tell you about him."

"Only if you're sure."

He thought about it a moment before answering, "I'm sure." He glanced toward the door. "But do you mind if we walk?"

"Of course not." She returned the puppy to its mother.

They left the barn, side by side, walking with no particular destination in mind, Gabe silently trying to decide how and where to begin.

Funny, the way the mind worked, he thought. Years ago, he'd turned off his memories, closing them away in tight little compartments. He'd learned that captivity hurt less if he didn't remember the way things used to be, if he didn't think about the freedom he'd once taken for granted. If he didn't think about Max and the brotherly love they'd shared.

It took real effort to bring the memories back.

Akira sensed that Gabe needed to gather his thoughts. She said a little prayer, asking God to grant him peace. Then she waited for him to begin in his own way, in his own time.

It felt comfortable to walk beside him this way. In the short time he'd been at Dundreggan, he'd become important to the life of the ranch. Perhaps, to be more honest, he'd become important to her.

She looked forward to seeing him each morning, to discovering the world for the first time through his eyes, to watching him put on weight and grow stronger. Working outdoors had bronzed his skin, and there was new definition in his biceps and shoulders, a new confidence in the way he carried himself.

She'd come to love his smile, too. At first, it had been rare as a blue moon. Now it came more easily, more frequently, and it made her heart skip a beat. Always.

I'll hate it if he goes away.

She cast a surreptitious glance in his direction.

When he leaves. Not if. He won't stay. Why would he?

Gabe caught her watching him. He smiled. "Do you always wear your hair like that?"

Reflexively, her right hand reached for one of her braids where it flapped against her shoulder. "Usually. Why?"

"Just wondering."

"Gets in my way if I leave it down."

"Yeah, I guess it would." His gaze shifted into the distance. He was silent awhile longer, then said, "Max wanted to go to college to become a doctor. Hud wouldn't let him."

"Why on earth would he forbid such a noble calling?"

"He said doctors in these parts get paid in chickens and sides of ham, and that wasn't the life for his son. Max was expected to inherit the Talmadge fortune. He was expected to learn everything about the mill and Hud's other enterprises, not become a do-gooder."

And you? What was expected of you, Gabe?

"My brother would've been a good doctor. He cared about everybody. He was smart and funny. I guess I idolized him. He was Hud's favorite, but he never lorded it over me or Leon. In fact, he took care of us both, giving us the love Hud refused to give." He paused, then added, "Our younger half brother, Leon, died of pneumonia while I was in prison."

Akira acknowledged his words with a nod.

"Everybody liked Max. Everybody. Especially the girls." He released a low chuckle as he shook his head. "All he had to do was grin, and they were swooning at his feet." Gabe glanced at her.

She could understand why the girls swooned if Max's grin had been anything like Gabe's.

"He looked like our mother. Blond hair. Blue eyes. I'm told she was a great beauty." His smile evaporated. "She died when I was born. That's why Hud resented me. He blamed me for her death."

"But that's foolish. It wasn't your fault."

He shrugged and looked away again. "I wish I'd known her. Miss Jane talked about her often, when Hud wasn't around. She wanted me to know who my mother was, especially that she was a woman of faith. But Hud…" He frowned. "Hud hated God—if he believed in Him at all—and he was determined his sons would do the same."

He fell silent, and the expression that crossed his face caused Akira's heart to ache. She wished she could wipe away his painful memories. She couldn't, so she prayed for him instead, asking the Lord to heal the hurts.

They reached the main road, cut across, continued down a narrow trail to the river. The sun rose higher in the morning sky, already warm upon their backs. When they reached the river, they stopped in the shade of a cottonwood. Akira sat on the ground. Gabe picked up a few smooth stones and skimmed them, one at a time, across the water's surface.

When his hands were once again empty, he said, "Max died on my eighteenth birthday." He swallowed hard; his gaze was fastened on some point in the distance. "I overheard him telling Hud he was leaving. He was going back East to medical school. He said I could help run things. He didn't want Hud's money or his businesses. All Max wanted was to be a doctor. But Hud said he hadn't made his fortune to leave it to me. I charged into the office and demanded to know why he hated me. His answer was to hit me. Hard enough to knock me to the floor. I got up and ran out." Gabe flinched, as if reliving the moment. "But first I grabbed a bottle from the liquor cabinet. All I wanted at that point was to get good and drunk."

Akira was blinded by her tears.

"Max found me at the lumberyard. We'd gone there a lot, the two of us, over the years, and he knew where I'd be. We got drunk on Hud's whiskey and plotted how we were going to leave Ransom together." His voice lowered. "Max climbed onto the logs and shouted something about what Hud could do with his money. I grabbed for a rope to pull myself up. I wanted to shout a few things myself. Then the logs started to shift. The rope broke and I fell. When I got up, Max had disappeared." He paused, stooped to pick up more stones, and began tossing them into the river.

Akira rose but didn't move toward him.

Gabe looked at her. "A log had rolled on top of him. When I found him, I tried to move it, but I couldn't. He died before I could go for help. I remember there was blood in the corner of his mouth. He looked at me and tried to say something. Then he was gone."

"Oh, Gabe," she whispered.

He didn't seem to hear her. "Hud had me arrested."

"It was an accident. Didn't you tell him that?"

"He said I'd killed Max on purpose because I was jealous and wanted to inherit everything myself. He said I got him drunk so it would look like an accident. And that was good enough for the jury. If my own father believed it…" His voice trailed into nothingness.

"But it was an accident," she repeated.

He closed his eyes. "Didn't matter. Max was dead, and it was my fault. And maybe Hud was right. Maybe I was jealous. I didn't understand half of what had happened. I just knew it was my fault. If I hadn't been so rebellious, if I hadn't lost my temper so easy, if I hadn't been drinking… There were plenty of what-ifs for me to think about over the next ten years, but none of them brought Max back. Nothing could undo what I'd done."

Before Akira could reply, Cam released a sharp bark, then raced up the trail. A moment later, the sound of a motorcar reached their ears. Both Gabe and Akira turned toward the road.

When she saw the Duesenberg, her heart sank. "It's your father."

But it wasn't Hudson who waited for them at the ranch house. It was Rupert Carruthers. He disembarked from the long black automobile as soon as they walked up the drive a short while later.

"Mr. Talmadge sent me," he said without preamble. "He wants to see you."

Gabe felt an odd tumble of emotions roll through him—anger, helplessness, ragged insecurities, the fear that if he didn't immediately obey an order, punishment would follow.

Rupert motioned toward the car. "I came to drive you into town."

Two weeks earlier, Gabe had returned to Ransom, seeking Hudson's help. More than that. He'd been seeking reconciliation, perhaps even a welcome. He'd been denied both. He no longer needed a job or a place to stay, and God had healed the desperate corners of his soul.

But what about his father? Was there any chance for amends between them? What was the right thing to do?

Jesus, show me Your will! The prayer had scarcely formed before calm settled over him. He didn't know *how* he knew. He simply *did* know what his answer must be.

He met the secretary's impatient gaze and shook his head. "I can't go with you today. I've got work and can't spare the time."

Rupert stiffened. It was obvious that he rarely—if ever—heard someone refuse one of Hudson's commands.

"Tell him," Gabe continued, "that if he still wants to see me, I can come on Sunday. That's the next time I'll be in town. I could drop by after church."

"Church?" Rupert nearly choked on the word.

Gabe couldn't remember a time when Rupert hadn't been his father's yes-man. He supposed, since Hudson was an atheist, that Rupert shared the same viewpoint. He wouldn't dare do otherwise. Not if he wanted to keep his job.

"Mr. Talmadge isn't going to like this," the secretary muttered.

Somewhat amazed by the self-confidence he felt, Gabe couldn't help his wry smile. "No, I don't suppose he will, but it's the way it's going to be." He glanced over his shoulder at Akira, who stood behind him. "I'll see to the repairs on the corral now." He looked one last time at Rupert. "Sorry if this causes you any trouble, Carruthers." Then he strode toward the barn.

CHAPTER NINE

Nora Wickham was feeling a good sight better now than when Charlie had driven the old truck up this drive more than two weeks before. At that time, she'd thought she might be dying, but plenty of rest and no men to tend to had worked wonders.

Shortly after nine o'clock in the evening, Nora settled onto a rocker on the small porch in front of her new home, a bit of mending in her lap, a lantern—already lit, though it was yet daylight—on a stand to her left. The night was warm, but not uncomfortably so. The air was rich with the fragrance of honeysuckle.

It was evident Akira Macauley loved flowers. They bloomed everywhere on Dundreggan, both those she'd carefully planted and cultivated and those that grew wild, like the dark blue forget-me-nots near the steps of this very stoop.

Squinting, Nora slid thread through the eye of a needle, then picked up one of Mark's socks and began to darn the heel where it had worn through, her thoughts remaining on Akira.

Since returning to live with her grandfather back in '25, the young woman had been a sporadic churchgoer, attending when

97

weather allowed, which meant she was seen in town mostly during the summer months. There were some who considered Akira an oddity of sorts, a pretty young woman choosing this difficult, solitary life when everybody knew she could sell to Hudson and come out richer in the end. Nora glanced across the barnyard toward the main house. Akira wasn't odd, she thought, catching sight of her through the kitchen window. Kindhearted. God-fearing. Free-spirited. Perhaps a bit too independent for her own good. But not odd.

A sound drew Nora's gaze toward the barn. Gabe Talmadge leaned against it, to the side of the doorway, one of the newborn pups held against his chest. He was staring off toward the mountains, his expression pensive, his hand idly stroking the pup's coat.

Nora recalled her secret fears about staying on this ranch without Charlie to protect her from a convicted murderer. If she hadn't been so ill at the time, she would have insisted her husband put their belongings back on the truck so they could leave. She'd had no desire to be killed in her bed by the man living in the cabin next door.

She looked down at the sock and took another stitch.

Nora remembered the trial, of course. She, Charlie, and Mark—who was only a youngster at the time—had been new to Ransom. Charlie hadn't worked at the mill more than a few months when Max Talmadge was killed. Folks had said Gabe was a troublemaker, smart-mouthed and rebellious. Max, on the other hand, had been liked by every person in Ransom. Pity, it was said at the time, that it hadn't been Gabe who was killed by that log.

The result of the trial had been a foregone conclusion, and talk of it had filled every conversation for months, both before and after.

Now she wondered about all she'd heard, all she'd thought was true.

He was a hard worker, she'd give him that. Kept to himself. Didn't talk much. At least not around her. And he was always polite.

Of all the things she might think of him, one stood out—he was not at all like his father.

The door to the main house opened with a creak, drawing Nora's gaze from her mending a second time. Akira stepped through the opening. In her hands she carried a tray with a pitcher and glasses on it.

"Care for some lemonade?" she called to Gabe.

He held up the pup. "I'll put him back with his mother."

"Join me at Mrs. Wickham's," she replied, then strode toward Nora. When she reached the porch, she smiled and said, "Beautiful evening, isn't it?"

"Indeed. Not so hot, for a change."

"I brought you something cool to drink."

Nora nodded.

"Gabe's going to join us in a bit, but we won't wait for him." Akira squatted and set the tray down, filled all three tumblers with lemonade, and handed one of them to Nora. Then she took one for herself, stood, and leaned against the rail before taking a sip. "Ooh." She puckered her lips and squinted her eyes. "A wee bit on the tart side. Could have used more sugar."

"I like it tart," Nora said, then took a drink. "Yes, just the way I like it."

Akira looked toward the barn. "We're going into Ransom for church on Sunday. You're welcome to join us if you feel up to it."

Nora considered the long drive to town. Charlie's truck still needed repairs, so they'd have to go in Akira's wagon. The going wouldn't be so hard in the morning, but they'd be returning in the worst heat of the day. Still, it would be nice to see her friends. Simon and Violet Neville, Jane and her brother, Zachary Sebastian, and others...

"Yes," she said, her decision made. "I'd like to go with you."

From within the darker recesses of the barn, Gabe observed the two women on the porch. Their voices—though not their words—carried to him, the sound a pleasant one. He supposed it was an ordinary way to spend an evening, but it still seemed extraordinary to him.

For some reason, he thought of his stepmother Harriet Smith Talmadge. Gabe had been five when Hud married her, but if his father had cared for her, had even said so much as a single kind word to her, Gabe couldn't remember it. He supposed it was nothing short of amazing that Leon had been conceived at all.

Poor kid. Hud had been hard on Gabe, to be sure, but he'd

ignored Leon, which might have been worse than getting hit now and again. Gabe wondered if Leon and his mother had ever longed for an evening on a porch, visiting with friends, talking over the simple events of the day. Had they longed for love and approval as he had?

He would never know. Both of them had died while Gabe was in prison—Leon, at the age of fifteen, from pneumonia, and Harriet the following year from a stroke.

"I wish I'd been nicer to them both," he said, regret washing over him.

Pauline Talmadge, at the age of thirty-four, was still a beautiful woman. Certainly she didn't look her age. She ate little, determined her waistline would never expand beyond its current eighteen inches—a fact of which she was quite proud. After all, how many women who had carried two babies to term could say the same? She used all the latest beauty products to keep her skin soft and free from wrinkles. She tried never to frown, not because she hadn't plenty of reasons to but because doing so formed permanent creases in a woman's forehead.

But she was frowning now.

She met her husband's gaze in the reflection of her dressing-table mirror. "Hudson. How unexpected." She twisted on the vanity stool. "What brings you to my room at this hour?"

"You're going to church on Sunday."

She laughed. "Church? Whatever for?"

"Because I want you to." His eyes narrowed. "Because I'm telling you to."

In the eight years they'd been married, Hudson had never struck her, but instinct warned Pauline that this might be the time if she dared thwart him. She composed her expression and hid the shaking of her hands in the folds of her dressing gown.

"Well, of course. If that's what you wish, Hudson. But please do tell me why. Since the day we were married, we haven't once attended church."

His glare seemed as cold as ice. Perhaps it was because of the piercing blue color of his eyes, but she thought it had more to do with the frozen status of his heart—*if* he had one.

"You've made your feelings about religion quite clear," she added.

"Gabe has returned to Ransom."

"Gabe?" Her eyes widened. "You mean your son? The one who was in prison?"

"Yes."

How long had he been back? Why hadn't someone told her? The reappearance of the only living son couldn't bode well for her, the despised wife.

Hudson took a step toward her. "I've learned Gabe will be at church on Sunday. I want you to meet him there, before he comes to the house."

"He's coming *here?*" She rose from the stool. "I thought you never wanted to see him again."

"I've changed my mind." He reached out, cradling her chin between thumb and fingers, his grip firm but not painful. "And you, my dear wife, are going to become his close friend and ally."

She wanted to shake off his touch but didn't dare.

"You're cunning, Pauline. You've a great talent for deception. I trust it won't fail you in this instance. I want to know everything that's happening on that ranch. I want to know how Gabe lives and what he thinks. I want to know what's going on between him and Akira Macauley. Use whatever skills and wiles you must." He paused before saying, "I believe you know what I mean." He leaned forward to kiss her on the cheek, his grasp tightening on her chin. Then, with his lips still brushing her skin, he whispered, "Do not fail me, my dear. I've paid handsomely for your wifely assistance, and now I mean to collect."

He left as suddenly as he'd arrived, closing the door behind him, his threat lingering in the now silent room.

Akira was sorry when Nora rose from her rocker and announced, "It's time for me to be in bed." Nora yawned, as if to prove the truth of her statement.

Gabe, who'd been seated on the top porch step, his back against the post, stood. "It's been a pleasure, Mrs. Wickham. Thanks for sharing your company."

"I'm sure the pleasure was mine, Mr. Talmadge."

Akira hid her smile. She'd believed Nora would warm to Gabe if she allowed herself to know him. But there'd been a trace of doubt as well, a fear that, if she were wrong, Gabe would be hurt by another rejection. She needn't have been afraid.

"Good night." Nora took up the lantern in one hand and her sewing basket in the other. "Rest well." She went inside.

The moment the door closed behind Nora, Akira and Gabe were plunged into the darkness of a moonless night.

"Suppose I'd best be turning in too," he said. "Morning comes early."

"Yes, it does."

He cleared his throat. "I'll walk you to your door."

She didn't *need* him to. She could find her way blindfolded just about anywhere on the ranch, and she could most certainly walk unescorted between this cabin and the main house. But that she *wanted* Gabe to accompany her was an indisputable truth. The realization caused a peculiar sensation to swirl in her chest.

Neither of them spoke as they covered the short distance, but when they reached Akira's door, Gabe said, "Thanks."

"What for?"

"For what you did tonight with Mrs. Wickham."

She smiled, though she knew he couldn't see her in the dark. "Were my reasons so transparent?"

"Yes." He chuckled. "They were."

"You're a good man, Gabriel. All folks need is a chance to see it for themselves."

There was a lengthy silence before he said, "You're the first person who's believed in me since Miss Jane."

On impulse, she stepped toward him, took hold of his shoulders, and kissed his cheek, surprising them both. Embarrassment was the next thing she felt. She couldn't believe she'd done such a thing.

"Good night," she whispered, then slipped quickly indoors, fighting a ridiculous urge to burst into tears.

If he saw her blubbering, he would think her a complete ninny. Whatever had gotten into her?

Gabe didn't move away. He stood staring at the door, his fingers touching his cheek where, moments before, Akira's lips had brushed against his skin.

He knew next to nothing about women. Although he was the son of the town's wealthy patriarch, he hadn't been the kind of boy mothers wanted for their daughters. *He's trouble,* had been their thoughts, if not their words. He sure hadn't learned anything about women in prison, except that he missed a soft voice, a gentle touch. And since his release? He'd known the kindness of a few women who'd given him a bowl of soup and a slice of warm bread or a place to sleep in a shed or even a suggestion for where he might get a job.

But none of that helped now. None of it explained what he was feeling for Akira.

"Look at me," he whispered, his gaze lifting to the starry heavens. "I've got nothing to offer. Not to her or anybody else." Raising his voice, he added, "I've got nothing. Not even a good name."

I'm falling in love.

That was Akira's first thought when she awakened the following morning.

I'm falling in love with Gabriel.

She sat up in bed, drew her knees to her chest beneath the white folds of her nightgown and hugged them with her arms, watching as the first fingers of dawn reached across her ceiling.

She'd always been certain that love—the romantic kind—wasn't her destiny. She'd been content to work on this sheep ranch with her grandfather and Brodie, to help others in the valley where and when she could, to commune with her Savior and study His word. Never had she felt God calling her to love a man, to be a wife and, perhaps, a mother.

Lord?

But she didn't know what she was asking nor did she hear an answer.

She leaned her forehead against her knees, reliving the impulsive kiss and dreading the next time she would see Gabe. She could only hope he'd thought it a kiss of friendship from a sister in Christ.

She groaned softly.

Even if Gabe thought that, *she* would know the truth. She had thrown herself at him.

She got up and went over to the mirror. The quality of the glass was poor, but it was good enough to see there was nothing particularly pretty or feminine about her that would draw a man's attentions. She was tall and skinny and freckled. She wore denim overalls rather than pretty dresses. She worked in the fields and often smelled of dirt, sweat, and animals. Honest scents but not attractive ones.

"Maybe Mother did have a few things more to teach me," she whispered, then released a lengthy sigh.

She untwined her braids, brushed her hair, then reversed the process.

Do you always wear your hair like that?

Her hands stilled.

"Oh, Lord, what now?"

CHAPTER TEN

If Jane Sebastian lived to be one hundred, she would never forget the moment that Sunday morning when Gabe walked into the Ransom Methodist Episcopal Church with Akira and Nora. The curious hush was thick enough to cut with a knife. But it was nothing compared to the surprise she—and everyone else—felt when Pauline Talmadge entered through those same doors just as the threesome from Dundreggan settled onto a pew near the back of the small sanctuary.

Jane was fairly certain her mouth gaped open a full fifteen seconds before she had the good sense to close it.

Elegant and exquisite, Pauline swept her gaze over the gathering of believers. Finally, she moved to the only unoccupied pew, the one immediately behind Akira.

Jane frowned. She should be glad Pauline had come to church. She couldn't think of anyone who needed to hear the gospel more, with the possible exception of Hudson Talmadge himself. Still, Jane couldn't shake the feeling Pauline hadn't come to hear

Reverend Neville's excellent sermon or to make friends with any of those in attendance.

But when Jane looked at Gabe and found him gazing back at her, she completely forgot Pauline. He obviously wasn't the same man she'd seen nearly three weeks before, and it wasn't simply because he looked healthier. No, this change went much deeper.

The first chords of the opening hymn forced her to straighten in her pew. She rose to her feet and joined the others in song, her heart welling up with joy.

"Amazing grace, how sweet the sound that saved a wretch like me! I once was lost, but now am found, was blind, but now I see."

Reverend Neville couldn't have made a better selection, she thought before beginning the second verse of the hymn.

Gabe had never been to church before. He hadn't known what to expect. The first song nearly broke him. It seemed to be all *about* him, all *for* him. As did the Scripture reading and Simon's sermon about the thief on the cross.

Throughout the service—as he stood singing and as he sat listening—Gabe was overwhelmed by the love and grace God had shed upon him. Praise overflowed in his heart. Praise, wonder, and thanksgiving.

He couldn't help remembering the twelve-year-old boy who had briefly known that love, who had eagerly run to tell his father so he, too, might know it. Only his father hadn't wanted to know, and Gabe, in seeking his earthly father's approval, had turned his back on what he'd found. He'd turned his back on everything good and had become as bad as his father thought him.

But grace had covered it all. It was more than Gabe could comprehend.

When the congregation rose to sing the last song, Akira touched his arm, causing him to look at her. She smiled, then whispered, "You must allow me to introduce you to others when the service is over."

Gabe understood how small towns were. He suspected everybody in this house of worship knew his identity. The news had to have swept through the valley within the first couple of days of his return. He doubted there was anyone left who didn't know he was working at Dundreggan.

Still, he nodded because he knew it would please Akira.

A short while later, they stood outside, on the shady side of the church. Jane Sebastian was the first to approach them.

Without any hesitation, she threw her arms around Gabe and hugged him close, whispering, "You've come home to Jesus."

"Yes."

"Praise the good Lord." As she stepped back, she dabbed her eyes with her handkerchief. "I've been prayin' for you, Gabe. All along."

Tenderly, he smiled. "I know you have."

Another woman's voice intruded. "You must be Gabe."

He looked over Jane's shoulder. An extraordinarily beautiful woman, about his own age, was standing not far behind. He knew he'd never seen her before. He would have remembered if she'd lived in Ransom when he was young.

"I'm Pauline, your stepmother." She smiled, obviously amused by the descriptive word.

Hud's wife? In *church?*

She stepped forward, holding out a gloved hand for him to take. "Your father tells me you're expected at the house today."

"Yes." He shook her hand. "I'm going there from here."

Her smile was spectacular. "Hudson will be glad to see you again." She looked at Akira. "You must be Miss Macauley."

"Yes." There was a wary note in the acknowledgment.

"It was kind of you to help Gabe when he needed it. His father"—her smile faded and her voice lowered, as if she were sharing a confidence with a close friend—"can be a hard man at times."

Akira didn't reply.

Pauline's gaze returned to Gabe. "May I take you in my car?"

"Well, I—" He glanced at Akira.

"I see no reason to put Miss Macauley to the bother," Pauline continued. "I'll make certain you have a ride back." She paused before adding, "*If* that's what you want."

It made sense to accept her offer. He didn't know how long this interview with his father would take. He didn't even know why

Hud wanted to see him. There wasn't much point in making Akira and Nora wait for him.

"Sure," he answered. "I guess that would be okay."

Akira gave a minuscule nod. "I'll be praying for you."

Hudson observed the approach of Pauline's motorcar from his bedroom window. He wondered if Gabe was with her. That had been the plan, but he wouldn't know until he saw them disembark if she'd succeeded.

His wife hadn't been happy about any of this. That had been clear to him by the looks she gave him, by the lift of her chin, by the set of her shoulders. But he couldn't care less about her feelings. He only cared that she did as she was told. She didn't always obey him, but he was certain she would for now. She was afraid. Afraid of him. Afraid of what might become of her—the childless wife—now that Gabe had returned.

He momentarily wondered if Clarice, had she lived beyond her twenty-second year, would have come to despise and fear him as Pauline did. Would she have learned to hate him if she'd survived the birth of Gabriel, the child of her treachery?

He's your son, Hudson. Why won't you believe the truth?

As Clarice's voice from long ago echoed in his memory, he

heard a soft *Crack!* and looked down at his hand. He'd snapped the delicate stem of the wine glass he was holding.

"Welcome to our home." Pauline's voice carried to Hudson through the open window.

He glanced below, saw Gabe standing beside the automobile, looking at his surroundings. Was he thinking that someday this might all be his?

"I hope you are," Hudson muttered. "I hope you want it very badly."

He set the two pieces of the wine glass on a silver serving tray before walking from the room. He descended the staircase only halfway, then waited.

There were two things Hudson noticed when Pauline and Gabe entered the house. First, Gabe no longer looked like a starving tramp. His clothes, though not new, were clean and neat. His hair was well-groomed. He'd gained weight and appeared stronger. He stood tall, moving with more confidence. Not the false swagger of someone pretending to be confident, either. This was genuine self-assurance. The second thing he noticed was more difficult to define, but it was there all the same—a different kind of strength. Something that went deeper. Soul deep.

It momentarily unnerved Hudson.

"Ah," Pauline said, her voice sugary sweet, "there you are, darling."

Gabe glanced up. Their gazes met. Hudson expected the boy to look away first. He didn't.

What's changed about him?

"I wanted to introduce him," Akira said while pacing Zachary Sebastian's front porch. "I wanted folks to get to know him. And she just swooped in and carried him away in that black automobile of hers. Like a vulture."

Jane chuckled. "Would you sit down? Please. You're wearing us out, watching you pace. Isn't that right, Nora?"

"Yes, indeed."

Akira spun toward them. "What did she want with him, anyway? She's never been to church in all these years. Everybody knows that. So what was she doing there today? It can't be for any good reason."

"The Lord knows why," Jane answered softly.

"I wish He'd explain it to me."

"Maybe He would if you'd be still for a moment." Jane's rebuke was mild, but it was a rebuke all the same. "It's hard to hear God when you're doing all the talking."

Akira knew she deserved the gentle chiding—and more besides. "I'm sorry. I shouldn't have said such a thing. I don't know Mrs. Talmadge, and my remarks were unkind."

"Sit down and drink your tea, dear girl, before the ice melts completely. You'll have all the answers you need when Gabe returns to Dundreggan."

When Gabe returns.

That, of course, was the root of her fears, her anger, her

frustration—she was afraid Gabe *wouldn't* return. She was afraid he would never fall in love with her, that he would never know she loved him.

"Good heavens!" Jane exclaimed.

The instant Akira met Jane's gaze, she knew her secret had been discovered. Jane must have read Akira's feelings on her face. She'd never been any good at hiding them. It was too much to have hoped she could do so now.

Jane turned toward Nora. "Would you like more tea?"

"No thank you." Nora waved her hand over the rim of the glass. "This will do me fine."

Akira sat on the empty chair, feeling miserable. She wondered what was happening at the Talmadge mansion. She wondered if Hudson would ask his son to stay. If he did, would Gabe agree? Of course he would. Who wouldn't want to live in such a place? And why else would Hudson have summoned Gabe if it wasn't to extend the olive branch of peace? To welcome his son home.

It's why he came back to Ransom. It's what he wanted, what he hoped for. You should be happy for him.

Yes, she should be happy for him. She should be praying for reconciliation between father and son. She should want it for him.

But what I want is for him to be with me at Dundreggan. I want to love him and have him love me. Is that so very terrible?

The Talmadges had been well-off when Gabe was growing up, but if this house was any indication of his father's wealth, Hudson's fortune had multiplied many times over.

"Would you like something to drink?" his father offered as they sat down in the elegantly spacious drawing room.

"No thanks."

"You're sure? I've got a fine brandy. Or there's whiskey if you prefer."

Gabe shook his head, at the same time wondering when Hudson would get to the point.

Not until I'm suitably impressed, I bet. He had to suppress a smile as the thought crossed his mind. That his father would want to impress *him* seemed ludicrous.

Life often turned on an instant, he reflected, more soberly this time. Such had been proven the night Max died, and it had been proven again the morning he'd surrendered his heart, his sins, himself, to God. Could this be another turning point?

"You're wondering why I asked you here," Hudson said, breaking the lengthy silence.

"As a matter of fact, yes." He looked the older man straight in the eyes and waited for him to continue.

"Things are different now than when you went away."

"Went away?" Gabe cocked an eyebrow, remembering the part his father had played in his arrest and conviction. "I guess that's one way to put it."

Hudson frowned. "You were always belligerent. I see prison didn't change you."

Several different retorts flashed in his head, none of which, Gabe figured, would please God. So he took a deep breath and said, "No, it didn't. I'm sorry."

Judging by Hudson's expression, the apology threw him off balance. He seemed to forget what he wanted to say.

Pauline touched Gabe's knee with the tips of her fingers. "You'll dine with us, of course. Our cook has prepared something special."

"Sorry. I've got chores awaiting me."

"I thought you were supposed to rest on the Sabbath," she said in a slightly amused tone.

"God knows the animals must be fed." He looked at Hudson again. "Why'd you send for me?"

"I want your help with the Macauley woman."

Now Gabe was the one thrown off balance. "My help? With Akira?"

"I have plans. Big plans. They could mean a great deal to the people of Ransom. This economic depression can't last forever. If I succeed in developing this valley, Ransom will thrive in the coming years and so will those who live here. You, too, if you'll help me."

"What sort of help?"

"I want the Macauley property. I *need* it. I've offered good money, more than she could hope for from anyone else, times being what they are. But she refuses to sell. I was hoping she might listen to you."

"Why would she?"

"You're with her every day. And every night, I suspect."

"What do you mean by that?"

His father's laugh was unpleasant and all the explanation Gabe needed.

"Akira is a decent, God-fearing woman."

"And you're a man who was in prison for ten years. If you're not lusting after a woman, even one who stinks of sheep, then you're not normal. Don't think I'm the only person who's guessed what's going on out there."

Gabe stood, his fists clenched at his sides, fighting the anger inside him. "If that's all you've got to say, then I'll be off."

"That isn't all." Hudson stood too. "You came back to Ransom because you wanted something from me. You wanted me to give you work and a place to stay. You came begging for it. You looked around at everything I have, and you wanted a piece of it. Well, you may even get some of it, but I'm asking something in return. Prove yourself worthy of being called a Talmadge. If you succeed, you'll be handsomely rewarded."

"Prove it how?"

"Use your imagination," his father answered.

Gabe wasn't the hungry, hopeless tramp who'd arrived at the mill a few weeks back. He wasn't the man who'd been broken beneath the weight of his own sins, his own guilt and shame. He was different. Forever different. Hudson didn't know that yet. But Gabe did.

"I never wanted anything from you except a father's love." He lowered his voice. "And you don't have anything I want now." He turned toward Pauline. "It was nice to meet you, Mrs. Talmadge."

Without another glance at Hudson, Gabe strode out of the drawing room. The butler was waiting near the front door, Gabe's hat in hand, his expression studiously neutral. Gabe took the hat, nodded, then left the house.

As the ornate door swung closed behind him, he heard Hudson bellow in rage.

Gabe actually felt sorry for him.

After their visit with Jane at the Sebastian farm, where they shared the noon meal, Akira and Nora returned to Dundreggan. Akira had half hoped she would find Gabe already there. After all, an automobile could cover the distance in much shorter time than the team and wagon. But he wasn't home yet.

The hours of afternoon lengthened, along with the shadows, while Akira went about her chores, her thoughts confused and disjointed. She tried to pray but couldn't. No, that wasn't true. It wasn't that she couldn't pray. She was *afraid* to pray. Afraid God's answer might be different from what her heart wanted.

Countless times she looked down the drive toward the main road, watching for a telltale cloud of dust to signal an automobile's approach. It was never there. She thought about going after him, driving right up to the Talmadge mansion and demanding he return home with her.

"Love hurts," she told Cam as dusk settled upon the valley.

Lying at her feet, the collie whimpered.

Akira grabbed another ear of corn from the feed sack and continued shucking. "I never knew that before," she added. "That love hurts."

This time, Cam raised her head from her paws and stared at her mistress with wide brown eyes.

"You're no help." She smiled sadly as she stroked the dog's head.

Cam rose on all fours and looked toward the road, her ears cocked forward. Akira set aside the corn and stood too, looking to see what had drawn the dog's attention. Her heart pattered erratically in her chest. But there was no sign of an approaching vehicle, no unusual sound of any kind.

Disappointment flooded through Akira as she sank onto the chair.

Suddenly the collie jumped off the porch and raced up the drive. A few moments later, Gabe strode into view. He'd removed his suit coat and carried it slung over one shoulder, held there with an index finger crooked beneath the collar. His sleeves had been rolled up to his elbows, and even from this distance, she could see rings of perspiration dampening the white shirt beneath his arms.

He stopped when the dog reached him, leaned down and stroked her head, spoke, ruffled her ears. Then he straightened, looked toward the front porch, and lifted a hand to wave at Akira. She saw him smile.

She couldn't find words to describe what she felt. She didn't think there were any.

Gabe walked toward her, Cam leading the way.

I was worried, she thought. *What kept you so long?*

"Warm evening," he said.

"I made iced tea. Would you like some?"

"Please." He draped the suit jacket over the porch railing before settling onto the top step.

She went inside, filled a large glass with the cool drink, then carried it to him. She found him shucking corn.

What happened at your father's?

"Here you go," she said softly.

"Thanks." He took it from her. "It's a long walk from town."

"I thought Mrs. Tal—"

"I preferred to walk." He put the glass to his lips, tipped back his head, and drank, his Adam's apple sliding up and down with each swallow. When he'd drained the glass, he set it beside him on the porch and reached for another ear of corn.

"Folks are talking, Akira. About me. About us."

"Us?"

He didn't look at her. "Hud suggested some think we're…" He let the words drift into silence.

Understanding dawned. "Oh." Heat rushed to her cheeks.

"I ought to leave. It isn't good for you to have an ex-con on your place." His expression darkened. "There's those who would use me and what I am to hurt you."

"You can't leave, Gabe." She leaned toward him, tamping the panic in her heart. "There will always be talk, no matter where you go, because you did time in prison. You know that's true. People are the same the world over. There are mean, small-minded folks everywhere. But there are good ones, too. Ransom's got its share. Stay and give them a chance to come around. Like Mrs. Wickham did."

"It won't stop the talk. About you and me."

"Short of the two of us getting married, I don't see how we can stop it."

His eyes widened.

She was stunned into silence by her own words.

Gabe stood, reached for his jacket, stepped off the porch. "I'd best turn in."

"Wait!" She was afraid. So afraid. "I have something for you. I'll get it." She rushed into the house.

Married?

Married to Akira.

It was a crazy, wild, outlandish notion.

She was everything good and true and pure.

He'd seen the evil men did. He'd lived it. God might have pardoned him, but that didn't wipe away what he'd done, what he'd been.

Married to Akira.

It was worse than crazy. He would never be good enough for her. She deserved the best.

Akira reappeared in the doorway, carrying a black book in her hand. "It's a Bible." She held it toward him. "Miss Sebastian sent it to you. It belonged to a young man she was to marry, but he died. That was when she came to Ransom to live with her brother. She wants you to have it now."

Gabe took the book, then rubbed his fingers over the worn leather cover. "I never knew Miss Jane was engaged." More to himself than to Akira, he added, "This must have meant a lot to her to keep it all these years."

"Yes, but you mean more." She dropped her gaze to a spot on the porch. "Please don't hold what I said against me. About stopping folks from talking. I never meant—"

"You don't have to say anything, Akira. I know you didn't mean it like it sounded." He lifted the Bible in front of his chest. "I'll thank Miss Jane for this."

She watched as he walked away in the gathering dusk.

"But I *did* mean it, Gabriel," she whispered when she was sure he was out of hearing. "I meant it with all my heart."

CHAPTER ELEVEN

Gabe closed the Bible, then lay back in the tall grass near the river's edge and stared up at the evening sky.

What a wondrous thing the word of God was! No matter what he read—Old Testament or New, single verses or entire chapters—it spoke to his heart. He'd known he wanted a Bible. He'd known he needed one in order to learn more about Jesus, more about how he should live his life.

But he'd never imagined it would be like this.

"'For the word of God,'" he quoted, "'is quick, and powerful, and sharper than any two-edged sword.' Hebrews, chapter four, verse twelve."

He grinned, pleased with himself for remembering the verse.

Yesterday, Akira had called him a sponge. He liked the idea. He wanted to soak it all in. He wanted to immerse himself in it, to understand it and live it.

He recalled another passage. "But He that is spiritual judgeth all things, yet He Himself is judged of no man. For who hath known the mind of the Lord, that he may instruct Him? But we have the mind of Christ."

Another voice chimed in. "First Corinthians, chapter two."

He sat up and glanced behind him, watching Akira's approach.

"I thought I'd find you here," she said as she drew near.

"It's cooler by the water."

She settled onto the ground beside him. Hugging her knees to her chest, she closed her eyes, then took a deep breath. "Mmm. I love the smell of August."

"What does August smell like?"

"I don't know." She let her head drop back, her face turned toward the sky. "Dusky?"

He might have said her answer didn't make sense, only he was distracted by the length of her exposed throat—pale, soft, and elegantly arched.

Things had been different—awkward and tentative—between them this week, and he knew why. Her offhanded remark about getting married to stop the gossip had put images in his head that shouldn't have been there. It had started him thinking what it might be like to have a wife, a home, maybe children. And more than once he'd found himself wanting to take her in his arms and kiss her, taste her mouth, feel the warmth of her body against his.

Which, he figured, made him as bad as his father had suggested.

Akira straightened and looked at him. "Next week I'll be taking supplies up to Brodie and the others. Would you mind going to town tomorrow to get a few things we're short on?"

"No." He glanced away so she wouldn't see the yearning in his eyes. "I don't mind."

"Gabe?" Her voice was soft, gentle. "What's wrong?"

He shook his head. "Nothing."

After a lengthy silence, she said, "'Therefore, if any man be in Christ, he is a new creature: old things are passed away; behold, all things are become new.' Second Corinthians, chapter five, verse seventeen." She stood. "Look it up. It's talking about you." Then she walked away.

Gabe stayed beside the river long after night had blanketed the valley.

Hudson leaned back in his chair as he read the last paragraph of the senator's letter.

...and despite my best efforts, I have been unable to per-
suade any of my colleagues in the Senate to support your
proposal. While it may be that a dam and reservoir south of
Ransom are possible in the future, we have no legal grounds
to force Miss Macauley from her land. Unless you are able to
convince her to sell her property to you, I'm afraid there is
nothing further I can do.

Hudson crinkled the paper in his hand and tossed it across his office. Senator Quincey Fortier was a sniveling, worthless, spineless excuse for a man. He was even less of a senator. Nothing further he could do for Hudson, indeed! Just wait until the next election.

He stood and strode to the window. The mill was silent, the workers long since gone to their homes for the evening. Looking toward town, he saw the lights of his mansion on the hillside. Pauline wasn't waiting up for him, of course. She never did. They'd barely spoken to each other since the day Gabe had come to the house.

Hudson shook his head and frowned.

That interview certainly hadn't gone as he'd expected. Gabe had stood up to him. Not in the rebellious, angry manner of his youth, but with a quiet confidence. He'd reminded Hudson of Clarice.

His mood darkened.

If only Gabe hadn't gone to work for Akira. This was her fault. All of it. But she wouldn't win. He didn't care what he had to do, she wasn't going to win. Nobody got in his way.

Nobody.

Akira should own a truck, Gabe decided as he drove the team toward Ransom the following day. With any luck, the parts for the Wickham's Ford would have arrived at the hardware store by now.

Charlie had said Akira was free to use it once it was repaired. Until then, their only means of transportation was by wagon or horseback.

Akira didn't seem to mind not having an automobile or a gasoline-powered tractor or any number of other modern conveniences. She didn't have a telephone. She didn't have an electrical stove—but then, she didn't have electricity, either. She didn't even have a bathroom with running water.

Yet she was content with what she had. He wondered if she ever worried about anything.

With Hudson resolved to get his greedy hands on her land, she *should* be worried.

Gabe frowned. Why *did* his father want Akira's land? Was he determined to take it from her because she'd helped Gabe? No, that couldn't have been the reason. He knew Hudson had offered to buy the land and she'd refused to sell. That was before Gabe had returned to Ransom. So it didn't have anything to do with him. Or rather, it hadn't until Gabe refused to help his father. Now, knowing Hudson as he did, the reasons would have become personal.

He should leave. It would end the gossip, and maybe it would keep his father from doing anything to hurt Akira.

Maybe.

His arrival in Ransom put a stop to his ruminations. He drove the wagon to the feed store. From there he would go to the hardware store and then the dry-goods store. If he could afford it, he planned to buy himself a new hat and a pair of overalls that fit him better than the ones Akira had given him.

Inside the feed store, he received a less than warm welcome from the proprietor who watched him with a suspicious gaze.

Making sure the ex-con doesn't steal anything.

He shouldn't have been surprised. He'd grown used to those looks after his release from prison, but being with Akira at Dundreggan had caused him to forget, however momentarily, what many folks thought of him.

He made his purchases as quickly as possible and left the store.

Things were a little better at the hardware store. Zachary Sebastian was inside, and he greeted Gabe in a boisterous manner, slapping him on the back while shaking his hand. The farmer looked a great deal like his sister, except his face was deeply etched with wrinkles from a lifetime spent in the sun and wind. His hair, sparse as it was, was the color of granite, and liver spots dotted his scalp.

"Am I glad to see you," Zachary said. "I could use your opinion about something. Come over here and take a gander at this. I've been thinking of ordering me a new tractor. Sure does help a body make a decision when he can talk it out with another fella."

"I don't know much about tractors."

"Don't matter none. It's the talkin' that helps, not the advice." Zachary grinned, displaying a gap where he'd lost a tooth.

They spent the better share of the next half-hour turning the pages of the catalog, comparing models and prices. They also discussed the weather, especially the drought in what had come to be known as the Dust Bowl.

"Goes to show we could be worse off than we are." Zachary looked toward Richard Martin, the hardware store's manager, who was standing on top of a ladder at the back of the store. Raising his voice, he said, "Ain't that right, Martin? Things could be worse than they are."

"I reckon so," the man answered, "though I sure hope it don't get worse." He turned around and sat on the top step of the ladder. "Don't know what I'd do if Mr. Talmadge ever decides to close the store." He glanced nervously at Gabe, then back at Zachary.

Understanding hit Gabe like a sledgehammer—Richard Martin feared for his job, simply because Gabe was in the store. A store owned by Hudson.

"I'd better get on with my errands. It's a long drive back to the Macauley ranch. Good luck deciding which tractor to buy, Mr. Sebastian."

"You call me Zach. We're old friends."

It wasn't the truth, but it made Gabe feel a bit better.

"Say hello to Miss Macauley and Mrs. Wickham for me."

"I will. You do the same to Miss Jane. Oh, and thank her for the Bible. Tell her I'm reading it every day."

Zach nodded and smiled. "She'll be mighty pleased."

Turning around, Gabe asked Richard Martin about the parts for the Wickham truck and was told they were in. The store manager fetched the order from the back room. Gabe paid for the parts and, after a final farewell to Zachary, left the hardware store.

Beneath the branches of a tall silver maple growing near one end of the barn, Akira gripped the saddle horse's hoof between her thighs and spread salve over a cut on the animal's leg.

She wondered if Gabe was on his way back from Ransom yet. She wondered if he might learn to feel something more for her than gratitude. She wondered what she would do if he decided to leave Dundreggan.

"It'd break my heart to see him go. Don't let him go, Lord. I don't want to lose him. He's become mighty important to me. Mighty important."

Eyes closed now, she set down the horse's leg, then straightened, placing her fingers in the small of her back and bending slightly backward, stretching out the kinks. When she opened her eyes again, she saw Nora walking toward her, carrying something wrapped in a towel.

"I baked a rhubarb pie," Nora said. "Care to have a bite with me?"

Akira smiled as the delicious odor reached her nose. Rhubarb pie was her favorite. "I'd love some. Thanks. Give me a second to put Wally up."

She untied the halter rope, then led the horse into the corral where she turned him loose. A short while later, she joined Nora on the front porch of the main house.

She savored the first bite of the pie. "This is delicious, Mrs. Wickham."

"What it needs is some ice cream."

"Mmm. Sounds heavenly."

Nora closed her eyes. "We have a freezer packed in one of our trunks." She smiled softly. "Can't tell you how many summer evenings we've spent, all taking turns on the crank, Charlie, Mark, and me. Nothing quite so good as just made ice cream on a warm summer night."

"No, indeed."

"Maybe I could find it. Charlie would know right where it is, but I'm afraid I don't. I was so ill when he lost his job and we were forced from our home."

There was an uncomfortable silence and Akira sought to change the subject. "If I'd known you had a freezer, I'd've had Gabe buy some rock salt while he was in town."

Another period of silence followed.

"I like that young man," Nora said after a spell.

Akira felt a fluttering sensation in her stomach. "Me, too." She kept her gaze turned away lest the other woman see more than she should.

"I didn't expect to, you know."

"Yes, I know. No one did."

"It isn't going to be easy for him, Akira. And it isn't only 'cause he went to prison. There are folks who remember him from before."

"Was he really so bad?" she asked, looking at Nora again.

"Some would say so. Young, handsome, rich, and full of anger."

"Poor Gabe."

Nora touched her shoulder. "Be careful. I'd hate to see you get your heart broke."

It might very well be too late already, she thought.

Gabe stood near the wagon, the new beige-colored trilby in his hand. He ran his index finger and thumb along the deep crease in the hat's crown, enjoying the feel of the soft felt. He supposed he shouldn't have bought it. He could've made do with the one he had. Then again, he was glad he'd bought it. Made him feel good. A man ought to have something of his own that made him feel good.

Looking up, he saw Pauline strolling along the sidewalk, looking at the window displays, a parasol shading her from the harsh August sun. He didn't want to talk to her, but if he didn't move quickly, she would see him. Then he wouldn't have any choice.

He ducked into the nearest building, which turned out to be the Ransom River Bar. The dimly lit room was empty of customers.

"What kin I git fer ya?" the bartender asked.

Gabe had heard enough preachers railing against the evils of drink to figure he shouldn't order anything, but through the small window in the door, he could see Pauline had stopped to visit with another woman on the sidewalk.

"I'll have a root beer."

"Root beer." The bartender nearly snorted over the words. "This ain't no drugstore lunch counter, mister. They done lifted Prohibition. You want a drink or not? If not, you kin git on out of here."

He looked out the window again. Pauline was still there.

"All right." He tossed a coin on the counter, hoping it was enough. "I'll have a beer."

A few moments later, glass in hand, Gabe slid into a booth in the corner, wondering how long he would have to sit there. If he got up to check the window, it would be obvious what he was doing, and for some reason, he didn't want the bartender to know. Pride, he supposed. A grown man shouldn't be hiding from a woman.

The door opened and two men entered the bar. They ordered a couple of drinks, then ambled to the booth next to where Gabe was seated. Their voices carried over the divider, but Gabe was too lost in his own thoughts to pay attention to their conversation.

Until he heard a familiar name.

"You're right about Akira. Folks think she's sweet enough sugar won't melt in her mouth, but it's an act. I would've warmed her bed myself instead of her lettin' the jailbird do it. All she had to do was ask."

A low chuckle. "As if she'd give you a second look. She already turned you away twice."

"She'll be fair game after his old man runs him outta town. No decent folks are gonna have anything to do with her after that."

"Maybe you're wrong about her, Danny. Him, too. I heard he got religion."

"Not a chance."

"I swear that's what I heard. Gabe Talmadge was at the Methodist church last Sunday."

"Well if'n he was, I'm tellin' you it's all part of an act to keep the sheriff from givin' him grief. The time'll come he'll have to move on. He sure ain't never gonna get nothin' from that old man of his if'n he stays. And when he moves on, I'm gonna pay Akira a personal visit." More suggestive laughter, low and guttural. "A *very* personal visit."

The other man laughed too.

Murder flared to life in Gabe's heart. He wanted to snuff out the laughter, to silence it for good. If he stood up, if he grabbed that Danny whatever-his-name-was by the shirt collar and punched him in the face, shoving those ugly words down his throat, helped him choke on them—

His hands closed around the beer glass, as if holding on to it would keep him from doing something stupid. And it would be stupid to get into a bar fight. Even in his rage he knew that. It would prove he was exactly what they said he was. It would send him back to jail, and it would leave Akira unprotected, a victim of their filthy minds.

Above everything else, he had to protect Akira.

But how do I protect her? Gabe wondered as he drove the wagon toward Dundreggan. It wasn't easy to stop folks from talking. It wasn't easy to keep men like those two in the bar from thinking the worst and then acting on it.

"Short of the two of us getting married..."

Those had been Akira's own words. But she hadn't meant them, had she?

No. And even if she had, he wouldn't be willing. Would he?

If it would keep her safe, maybe I would.

Gabe owed Akira Macauley a great deal. She'd taken him in, given him food and work, treated him with respect. That was more than anybody else had done for him. He wouldn't be much of a man if he didn't repay her in some way. If his presence on the ranch brought scorn upon her or danger to her doorstep, then he owed her more than his appreciation.

It might not be so bad to be married. If they did marry, theirs wouldn't be the first union formed without love at its roots. There were lots of reasons for two people to wed. Lots of good, respectable reasons.

He looked heavenward. "How else do I protect her?"

The only other choice was for him to leave Dundreggan, to leave Ransom and this valley for good. He could warn Brodie before he left, of course. He could make sure the old Scotsman kept an eye on Akira.

But would that be good enough? Not if Brodie was out with his sheep.

No, Gabe couldn't leave Akira's safety to anyone else. Besides, it was his fault that folks were gossiping about her, right?

So he was back where he started. There was no other answer. He would have to marry her. It was the only way.

The tiny thrill in her heart when she saw Gabe was familiar to Akira by this time. She felt it whenever he'd been away for a few hours and then returned.

Drying her hands on a small towel, she composed herself before stepping out of the kitchen into the shade of the porch awning. The sun was already low in the western sky, and she had to squint against its glare as she watched Gabe drive the team up to the barn.

Thanks, Lord, for bringing him back safely.

She dropped the towel onto the nearby chair, then went down the porch steps and walked across the barnyard toward the wagon. Gabe was already unhitching the team.

"You must be hungry," she said when he looked up and saw her.

"Plenty hungry." He returned his attention to the rigging.

She laid a hand on the broad back of one of the horses. "I didn't think you'd be this late."

"Neither did I."

He seemed agitated. She wondered what had gone wrong in town.

As if hearing her thoughts, he straightened and met her gaze a second time. His expression was grim, his eyes clouded. "You were right. There's only one way to stop the gossip. I want you to marry me, Akira."

"Marry you?" she whispered, disbelieving her ears.

"Yes." He took a step toward her. "I thought maybe my going away would make things okay, but it won't. You wouldn't be safe."

"Safe?" She didn't know if she spoke the word or only thought it.

"I don't know what sort of husband I'd be, but I'd do my level best. I'd treat you kind, and I'd go on working hard around the place." The words rushed out of him, as if he'd been practicing them for hours and needed to get them said as fast as he could. "I know there's no love between us. Leastwise not the romantic kind. But I think we like each other well enough, and maybe one day it could grow to be more. You wouldn't have to let me move into the main house if you didn't feel comfortable having me there. I'd understand."

Unlike most other young women, Akira hadn't dreamed of her future husband or planned for her wedding day from the time she was a little girl. Instead, she'd dreamed of returning to this ranch, of living out her days here, working the land, raising sheep and keeping livestock. She'd enjoyed her independence, the freedom to make her own choices, and had never felt she was missing out by not having a husband or a family.

But something had changed within her when she fell in love with Gabe—she wanted more. In those secret moments when she'd allowed herself to imagine a proposal of marriage from him, this hadn't been it. She would have liked a declaration of his undying love. She would have liked to declare the love she felt for him too. But here he stood, telling her he wanted to marry her to keep her *safe*.

"I think we ought to do it, Akira. But if you think I'm wrong, if you'd just as soon not be married to me, then I'd best leave Dundreggan. Staying will only make things worse."

She tried to hide the panic those words caused in her heart, words that made her decision for her. She couldn't bear it if he went away. Selfish or not, crazy or not, she wanted to keep him with her.

"All right, Gabe. I'll marry you."

CHAPTER TWELVE

"Excuse me, sir," Rupert said as he stepped into Hudson's office early on Wednesday morning. "I'm sorry to trouble you, but I've learned something I believe you should know."

"What is it?"

"It's about your son, sir."

Hudson glowered at his secretary. Ten days since Gabe's visit and he felt the same anger as he had the moment Gabe refused to help him. It galled, the way the boy had walked out on him. There weren't many men who were either that stupid or that courageous—Hudson hadn't yet decided which of those adjectives described Gabe.

"It's about him and...and Miss Macauley." Rupert swallowed nervously.

"What about them?"

"Well..." Rupert's gaze darted toward the window behind Hudson's desk. "They're at the church, sir. They picked up a license yesterday at the county seat, and now they're getting married."

Hudson felt something twist in his belly, a sudden apprehension, as if he'd fallen off a cliff and was plummeting into a bottomless pit. But he'd never been a man given to premonitions, nor did he give credence to those who had them.

He swiveled his chair toward the window. "Married," he repeated thoughtfully.

There was a part of him that resented the notion of Gabe marrying without his permission. Then again, perhaps the marriage would serve Hudson better than any plan he might have concocted. The law wasn't quite as helpful as in days of old, when a wife's properties transferred ownership to her husband on their wedding day, but it could be nearly as good. *If* Gabe played his cards right.

"Maybe I underestimated him."

"Sir?"

Hudson flicked his hand at his secretary, dismissing him. "Nothing, Carruthers. That'll be all. I'll let you know when I need you."

"Yes sir." Rupert let himself out.

Married. Akira Macauley and Gabe. Hmm.

Gabe knew Hudson wanted that land. It could be he was marrying the fool girl so he could get control of Dundreggan, then sell it to Hudson. It could be he wanted Hudson's money, but on his own terms.

"Maybe there's Talmadge blood in him after all."

There were seven people present in the Ransom Methodist Episcopal Church that morning: the minister and his wife, the bride and groom, and three others—Jane Sebastian, Brodie Lachlan, and Nora Wickham. Akira probably could have asked half the town to be her guests; she hadn't. Gabe was fairly certain it was for his sake. After all, whom did he have to invite? His father and step-mother?

"Dearly beloved," Simon began, "we are gathered together here in the sight of God, and in the presence of these witnesses, to join together this man and this woman in holy matrimony, which is an honorable estate, instituted of God, and signifying unto us the mystical union which exists between Christ and His Church..."

She'd left her hair down. It fell over her shoulders and down her back in thick red waves. Gabe had wondered what it would look like, freed from those braids she always wore, but he hadn't expected it to be so beautiful, so inviting. He was tempted to reach out and touch it, see if it felt as soft as it looked.

"I require and charge you both, as you stand in the presence of God, before whom the secrets of all hearts are disclosed, that, having duly considered the holy covenant you are about to make, you do now declare before this company, your pledge of faith, each to the other..."

God, don't let me bring any heartache upon her. She's pure and innocent. The very things I'm not. I'm beginning to understand how You've cloaked me in Your righteousness, and I'm thankful for it. But I also know the evil that lurks in the hearts of men. I don't want Akira to pay for my mistakes.

"Gabriel Talmadge, will you have this woman to be your wedded wife, to live together in the holy estate of matrimony? Will you love her, comfort her, honor and keep her in sickness and in health, and forsaking all others, keep you only unto her, so long as you both shall live?"

Akira lifted her eyes, looking at him as if uncertain what his answer would be.

"I will," he said.

"Akira Macauley, will you have this man…"

He wished things were different. He wished he'd come to her without all the complications of his past. He wished he weren't the son of Hudson Talmadge, that he'd been raised in a home with a father and mother who loved each other. He wished he could have seen what a good marriage was like. He wished he'd been able to court her properly, to maybe make her want and respect him as a man, to love him as more than a fellow believer in Christ.

"I will," she answered, a soft quaver in her voice.

Simon looked over Akira's shoulder. "Who gives this woman to be married to this man?"

Gabe didn't need to see the scowl upon Brodie's face to know it was there. He could hear it in the Scotsman's voice as he answered with obvious reluctance, "On behalf of her mother, I do."

"Repeat after me," the reverend continued. "I, Gabriel, take thee, Akira, to be my wedded wife…"

144

He listened carefully to the words, and when he repeated them, he looked directly into Akira's eyes, wanting her to understand that he meant his pledge. He would be with her from this day forward, for better or for worse, richer or poorer, in sickness and in health. He would cherish her until death parted them one from another. This marriage may not have come about under the best of circumstances, but he swore to himself he wouldn't make her regret this day. Not if it was in his power to prevent it.

When it was her turn to say the same vows, he felt something stir in his heart. Perhaps it was only hope. Or perhaps it was something much, much more.

How was it possible, Akira wondered, for a person to feel both overwhelming joy and overwhelming sorrow at the precise same moment? Possible or not, that was how it was for her. She loved Gabe and wanted to be his wife, and that brought her joy. Her sorrow came because he didn't feel the same thing for her.

She thought of the two witnesses standing behind them. In their own ways, they represented Akira's contradictory emotions. Jane was probably smiling while tears streamed down her cheeks. She believed the couple would be blessed with happiness. Brodie, on the other hand, had left no doubt about his displeasure or his concerns for Akira's future. He'd come down from the sheep camp under protest, telling her countless times in the past two days that she was making a grave mistake.

The feel of the ring sliding onto her finger drew her attention back to the ceremony.

"Forasmuch as Gabriel and Akira have consented together in holy wedlock, and have witnessed the same before God and this company, and thereto have pledged their faith each to the other, and have declared the same by joining hands and by giving and receiving of a ring, I pronounce that they are husband and wife together, in the name of the Father, and of the Son, and of the Holy Spirit. Those whom God hath joined together, let no one put asunder. Amen."

"Amen," Akira whispered, closing her eyes lest tears escape.

"Let us pray. O eternal God, creator and preserver of all, giver of all spiritual grace, the author of everlasting life. Send Thy blessing upon this man and this woman, whom we bless in Thy name, that they may surely perform and keep the vow and covenant between them made, and may ever remain in perfect love and peace together, and live according to Thy laws."

It was useless to fight the tears. They came anyway, slipping from beneath her eyelids as she listened to the prayer.

"Look graciously upon them, that they may love, honor, and cherish each other, and so live together in faithfulness and patience, in wisdom and true godliness, that their home may be a haven of blessing and a place of peace. Through Jesus Christ our Lord. Amen."

Akira heard Gabe say, "Amen." Then his left arm slipped

around her shoulders, drawing her closer to his side. She opened her eyes and looked up at him. He offered a tender smile, one that made her heart miss a beat.

"Congratulations," Simon said as he took Gabe's right hand and shook it. Then he looked at Akira. "Every happiness, Mrs. Talmadge."

Mrs. Talmadge. Akira almost glanced behind her in search of Pauline, then realized he meant her.

Violet Neville stepped to her husband's side. "God bless you both."

"Thank you."

Gabe's arm tightened as he gently turned her around. She found both witnesses looking exactly as she'd imagined them, Jane crying and smiling, Brodie frowning.

"Ye make the lass happy," the Scotsman said in a gruff voice.

"You have my word on it, Lachlan."

Brodie grunted, a clear sign he didn't believe Gabe.

"Oh, stop it," Jane all but sputtered as she elbowed Brodie in the ribs. "Can't you be glad for them, you old goat? Two young people with so much love to give each other. Mark my words. God will see them through whatever lies ahead."

Akira had to smile. The look of surprise on Brodie's face was too priceless for words.

"There." Jane leaned forward and kissed Akira's cheek. "That's better. You keep on smilin'. You hear me? Don't you care one bit what anybody else thinks or says. You just care about yourself and Gabe here. You make sure to think of each other first."

Gabe spoke before Akira could. "We will."

"Love the Lord God above everything," Jane continued. "As you draw closer to Him, it'll bring you closer to each other, like the two sides of a triangle comin' together at the top." She kissed Gabe's cheek. "Go on with you. Spend the day together. You're man and wife now. I'll see that Mrs. Wickham gets home all right."

Man and wife.

Those words repeated in Gabe's mind throughout their return to Dundreggan.

You're man and wife now.

He glanced to his right. Akira was staring into the distance, lost in her own thoughts. Gabe took advantage of her daydreaming to study her. He'd always thought her pretty, but never had he seen her looking lovelier than she did today. Her red hair blazed in the sunlight, wisps dancing around her face, ruffled by the warm afternoon breeze. She wore a simple cotton dress, the floral print the same color as her eyes.

She turned her head, caught him watching her, smiled almost shyly.

"I didn't tell you how nice you look," he said.

"No, you didn't."

"Sorry. I meant to."

She blushed and dropped her gaze away.

"I like your hair down."

Her blush intensified. "I thought you might." She pushed it back with one hand. "But it's a bother. It gets so tangled this way."

The team's pace quickened as they turned off the road and followed the drive to the ranch house.

"I don't guess there was ever a prettier bride."

"Oh, Gabe."

She laughed, and for the first time that day, he thought she looked genuinely happy and relaxed.

He grinned too. "Did I say something I shouldn't?"

"No, though I'd say you were stretching the truth some."

"A man's supposed to think his bride's pretty."

Her smile faded slowly.

He wanted to kiss her. He should have kissed her back at the church. He should have kissed her in front of everybody. Why hadn't he?

She looked away. "I cleared space for your things in the bureau and wardrobe. You might as well take care of that while I fix us a bite to eat."

"Are you sure that's what—?" he began.

"Yes," she interrupted. "I'm sure." She met his gaze, looking almost angry with him. "I wouldn't've married you if I wasn't sure. I'm your wife. A man and his wife are supposed to live together."

He'd been fooling himself, he realized. He'd wanted to believe he asked her to marry him in order to protect her from gossip and

evil men like those two he'd overheard in the bar. He'd pretended
he was being altruistic. But the truth was, he'd done it for himself,
for selfish reasons. He'd wanted to stay on Dundreggan Ranch.
He'd wanted to stay with Akira. He hadn't been able to bear the
idea of ever leaving, of not seeing her smile or hearing her laughter.

Moreover, he'd wanted the right to hold her and kiss her and
know her as only a husband could.

He let the horses have their heads, knowing they would take
the wagon straight to the barn without any help from him. Then
he placed his palm on the side of her face. "You never do anything
halfway, do you, Akira Macauley?"

"Talmadge," she said, her eyes swimming with tears but her voice
filled with determination and pride. "My name is Akira Talmadge."

He didn't try to resist this time. He simply kissed her.

Marriage, Gabe soon decided, suited him.

He especially liked the first few moments in the morning, before
he was quite awake, when he became aware of his wife lying close
beside him. Invariably, he drew her into his embrace, her head on his
shoulder. She always released a sleepy groan, then sighed—a sound
of contentment that made him smile—and nestled closer still.

On this particular morning, more than a week after their wedding, with predawn painting the bedroom ceiling with soft shades

of gold and peach, Gabe braced his head against the heel of his hand and raised up on his elbow in order to watch her sleep. The corners of her mouth were slightly curved, as if her dreams were pleasant. She lay on her back, one arm above her head, the other draped over her abdomen. Her breathing was slow and steady. Her hair flowed over the white sheets and pillowcase like a dark red stain. He knew she left it loose to please him.

She did much to please him.

How did this happen, Lord? Why have You blessed me so?

He hadn't expected theirs to be a real marriage. He'd had no right to expect it. And yet, that was what had happened. Akira had welcomed him into her home, into her bed, into her arms, and into her heart.

As he'd said to her on their wedding day, she did nothing halfway.

Sometimes it frightened him, the love she gave so willingly, so completely. She'd never said the actual words, but she didn't have to. She showed her love for him in hundreds of ways every single day.

She had come to mean the world to him…and that frightened him even more.

An unwelcome memory surfaced in his thoughts. He saw again the three-by-eight-foot cell in "Siberia," the cellhouse used for solitary confinement, punishment for convicts who broke prison rules. He heard again the steel door slamming behind him, felt the terror of not knowing when he might be let out of that torture hole, a place of limbo where there was nothing to sort one day from the next, one week from the next. In Siberia, he'd slept on the concrete floor with a couple of cotton blankets for his bed. No metal frame. No mattress. Just cold hard concrete. A three-inch-wide opening overhead had provided ventilation and sunlight, and a small hole in the floor had served as the toilet. Bread and water, served twice a day, had been his only sustenance.

Even an animal deserved better treatment than what men in Siberia had received. But then, they'd been considered lower than animals by the prison guards.

How had he come from that place of dark despair to this state of bliss? What had he done to deserve it?

Nothing.

He didn't deserve it. He never would.

Akira opened her eyes and revealed a languorous smile. "Why aren't you asleep?" Her voice was husky. She snuggled closer.

He buried his face in her hair, breathing deeply.

You deserve so much more than me, my sweet Akira. So much better than what you got. I'm sorry for that. I'll always be sorry for that.

Marriage, Akira was learning, was about hearing one's husband, even when he wasn't speaking. At the moment, she heard Gabe's secret hurt.

"What's wrong?" she asked, her cheek against his bare chest.

"Nothing."

She knew that was a lie, of course. He held so many things inside himself. She wanted to be his helpmeet, if only he would allow it. If only she knew how to break through that invisible wall.

He shifted slightly. "I'd better take care of the milking."

"Not yet." She tightened her arms around him. "It can wait awhile longer."

"Nothing I'd like better than to stay in bed with you all day." He kissed the top of her head.

The pleasures of physical love had taken Akira by surprise, pleasures heightened by the knowledge that Gabe desired her. She hadn't known he would. After all, he'd been willing for this to be a marriage in name only.

"But," he continued, "the chores won't wait."

She released a heavy sigh as she let him slip from her embrace. "All right. You win."

She watched as he rose from the bed, already familiar with his morning routine. He would put on his trousers, leaving the suspenders dangling against his thighs, then he would shave the dark stubble from his jaw. He usually hummed to himself as he shaved, a tune of his own creation, made up as he went along. Sometimes he would catch her watching him in the mirror's reflection. Then he would wink at her.

It made her feel special. It made her feel as if he loved her. Really loved her. The way she loved him. With all her heart.

I want him to love me that way, Lord. Is it possible he ever will?

CHAPTER THIRTEEN

Pauline stood at the front door of the Talmadge mansion and watched Hudson drive away in his Duesenberg. The moment the automobile disappeared from view she felt an immense sense of relief.

Four weeks with the house completely to herself. Four weeks to do whatever she pleased. Of course, she knew Hudson's little spy, Rupert Carruthers, would keep an eye on her and report back to his boss. That was part of his job. Still, it was far better than having her husband around. His mood had been foul for weeks.

Shivering—either from the nip in the morning air or from her thoughts about Hudson—she stepped back inside and closed the door.

"Would you like your breakfast served now, ma'am?" Opal Young, the housekeeper, asked.

"No thank you, Mrs. Young. I'm going back to bed for a while. See that my coffee and breakfast tray are brought up to me in an hour."

"Yes ma'am."

Pauline started up the stairs.

"Excuse me, Mrs. Talmadge."

She stopped.

"Eugene asked if you'll want the car in the morning."

"In the morning?"

"For church, ma'am."

"Oh yes. Tomorrow's Sunday. Yes, I'll want the car."

"Thank you, ma'am. I'll tell Eugene."

With a nod, Pauline continued up the stairs, pondering her response.

For six Sundays in a row, she had attended services at the Methodist church in Ransom. She'd gone because Hudson commanded it. He'd wanted her there to check on his son. But Hudson was on his way to Washington, D.C., and would be away for at least four weeks. She wouldn't be able to tell him if Gabe was in church or who Gabe talked to after services or how well he seemed to get along with others in the community. She wouldn't be able to report any gossip she overheard.

So why was she bothering to go?

In her room, she removed her dressing gown, dropping it on the floor. Then she got into bed and drew the covers over her shoulders. She stared at the canopy overhead, her desire for more sleep forgotten.

Why *was* she going to church now that Hudson was away? She'd never cared a fig about religion. She'd given scant thought to matters of eternity. She was a woman who cared about the here and now and the pleasures to be found in it. She wasn't an avowed atheist like her husband, but neither was she particularly concerned about the condition of her soul...if she had one.

Yet Pauline knew she would go to church in the morning. She would go, and she would listen to the reverend's gentle voice and earnest words. She would stand with others in the small congregation and hold the hymnal in her hands and join in the singing.

And when she returned to this huge house on the hill—a beautiful but lonely and loveless many-roomed mansion—she would feel better for some unknown reason.

"You look tired, Mrs. Wickham," Akira said. "Why don't you sit a spell? I can finish this last batch myself."

Nora nodded. "Maybe it would be good for me to rest a bit. And you ought to do the same. You've been at it since sunup. You may be near half my age, but even the young get wore out after a day like this."

It was true. Akira was tired. But it was a good kind of tired. When she looked at the rows of mason jars—filled with fruits and vegetables—lining the shelves in the cellar after two weeks of harvesting and canning, she felt a sense of accomplishment, along with a gratefulness for the bounty God had provided.

"Why don't you go see how your husband and the other men are coming along with the butchering?" Nora settled onto a straight-backed chair near the open front door where the September breeze could reach her.

My husband. Akira smiled, taking pleasure in the simple words.

"Go on. There isn't anything here that a delay will harm."

"Maybe I will." She dried her hands on a towel, then removed her apron and laid it over the back of a chair. "I won't be long."

"Take all the time you want. I'm gonna rest my eyes until you get back."

Storm clouds had moved in while the two women were busy with the preserving, and the air smelled like rain. Rain would be welcome on any other day, but Akira hoped it would hold off until the butchering was done.

Zachary Sebastian and George Edwards had arrived that morning with their own hogs in the back of Zachary's truck. They'd slaughtered all three animals, then scalded the carcasses in a vat of hot water over an outdoor fire. The scalding loosened the bristles so they could be scraped off with knives. By tonight, big sides of pork would be hanging in the smokehouse.

And next week would find Akira frying and stirring the ground fat and storing the resulting lard in buckets in the cellar. Then would come more grinding of sausage, mixing in the seasoning spices and salt, frying it and packing the patties in quart jars. Hams and shoulders and bacon would be packed in a wooden barrel and covered with a briny solution. Pigs feet would be pickled in vinegar. The head would be boiled and used to make a big pan of head cheese.

By Friday Akira would swear off eating pork for as long as she lived. She knew she would swear it because she did it every time they slaughtered a hog.

She heard Gabe's laughter, mingled with that of the other men, before she could see them. It was a sound of masculine camaraderie. She didn't have to be told to know it was something he'd known little of during his adult life.

Reaching the barn, she paused, unnoticed, and observed her husband.

My husband, she thought again.

She and Gabe had been married a month. She wondered if he was aware of the special significance of this day. Or did such things matter to men?

He worked with his shirt sleeves rolled up to his elbows. His head was bare, his hair damp. Sweat made his forehead glisten. He looked tired, but more importantly, he looked strong and healthy. No sign remained of the hungry hobo she'd found on the road last July.

I told You, Lord, I'd rather have a man who knew sheep. But You know what I really need, and I'm grateful You answer for my best. She leaned her shoulder against the barn. *Sometimes I think I'm too happy with Gabe, that I love him too much, that I think on him when I ought to be thinking on You. Is that a horrible thing, Lord? Loving him that much?*

Gabe straightened. He placed his fingers in the small of his back and arched. Then he saw her. He smiled and waved. Heart fluttering in response, she pushed off from the barn and walked toward him.

"How's it coming?"

"Zach thinks we'll be done before the rain comes." He wiped his brow with his forearm. "You finished in the kitchen?"

"Not quite. Mrs. Wickham's taking a rest, then we'll do the last batch." She looked at Zachary and George. "Will you eat with us before you leave?"

"That's kind of you, Mrs. Talmadge," George answered, "but I promised the missus I'd be home for supper."

"And I've got chores awaitin' me," Zachary added.

The wind whipped up, causing a dirt devil to whirl across the yard. All three men glanced upward.

"We'd best hurry," Zachary advised.

Akira took that as her cue to leave them to their work.

Walking back to the house, she hummed softly to herself. She was nearly to the porch before she realized it was the same sort of melody Gabe hummed each morning.

"And they shall be one flesh," she quoted softly. She stopped and looked at the stormy sky. "It means so much more than the intimacy of the marriage bed, doesn't it? It means we think alike and act alike, that our lives are tied irrevocably together. What an amazing thing it is, Lord."

She smiled, tipping her head back farther while holding out her arms. The first raindrops struck her face. She closed her eyes.

"I never knew I could be this happy. How kind You are to me, Your unworthy servant."

The rain fell in relentless sheets, driven by a mournful-sounding wind.

By the time Gabe bid Zachary and George a good evening and saw them headed back to their own farms, he was soaked clear through to the skin. He stood on the front porch and watched the dusty barnyard turn to a muddy mush.

"You'd better peel out of those wet things," Akira said from the doorway, "before you catch your death."

He turned toward her. *I wonder if I'll ever get used to somebody caring whether I'm warm and dry.*

"Come on. Your supper's waiting."

"Is Mrs. Wickham joining us?"

"No. She went back to her cabin. Said she was going straight to bed. I hope she isn't getting sick again."

Gabe sat on the chair inside the doorway. He removed his boots and set them on an old newspaper. "She's probably wore out. The two of you put in a mighty long day." He stood again.

"No more than you." Akira lifted a kettle off the stove. "You'll want to wash up." She walked into the bedroom.

Gabe followed her there, watching as she filled the wash basin with hot water, steam rising like smoke from a campfire.

"You'd better hurry out of those wet clothes," she said in a raised voice, apparently not knowing he was in the room with her. "You must be starved."

"Ravenous."

She turned, a flush warming her cheeks, her eyes bright with surprise.

"You spoil me," he said, his voice low.

"It's my pleasure to spoil you, Gabriel."

He liked it when she called him that.

"Gabriel," she whispered, her gaze unwavering and filled with trust. "A strong man of God."

Her belief in him was daunting. He wasn't sure he could live up to her expectations. After all, who was he to deserve her trust?

"God looks on the heart," she said, as if reading his thoughts. "He'll provide what you need. He's changing you from glory to glory, into the very image of Christ our Lord."

"Is your faith ever shaken, Akira?"

The look she gave him was a tender one. "Of course it is. I've questioned the Almighty. Sometimes I'm like a petulant child. But He's patient with me, and if I wait on Him, He always shows me the way, even if He doesn't show me the why."

"I can't imagine you being petulant. I think you're wonderful in every way."

The blush returned to her cheeks. Her gaze dropped to the floor. "Thanks."

He paid her too few compliments, he realized as he watched

her hurry from the room. She meant so much to him, yet he'd never told her how he felt.

Why not? he wondered. Why couldn't he put into words the feelings in his heart?

In the kitchen, Akira placed the kettle back on the stove, then pressed her cool hands to her overheated cheeks.

I think you're wonderful in every way.

Her heart trilled as Gabe's words replayed in her mind.

"I love him, Lord," she whispered. "And I desperately want him to love me too. Is it possible he might? Please let it happen. Please."

She heard Cam's toenails clicking on the floor as the collie crossed the room to stand near the front door. A moment later, the dog growled a warning. Then a knock sounded. Akira went to answer it.

Sheriff Andrew Newton, a stocky man in his midthirties, stood on the other side of the screen. Although he'd lived in Ransom only a few years, Andy—as he was better known—had become a trusted and well-liked member of the community.

"Evenin', Miss Macauley," he said, almost apologetically, removing his hat as he spoke.

Something tightened in her belly. "It's Mrs. Talmadge." She

pushed the screen door open with her left hand. "Come in, Sheriff. It's a bit chilly out this evening."

"Thanks." He stepped inside. "Is your...husband at home?"

"Yes. He's washing up for supper."

Andy glanced toward the kitchen table, then back at Akira. "I need to speak to him for a minute or two."

"I'll get him for you."

"No need," Gabe said from the bedroom doorway. "I'm here." He strode forward, his face an expressionless mask. "What can I do for you, Sheriff?" He didn't offer his hand.

Andy ran his fingers along his hat brim. "Maybe we should step outside onto the porch."

"That won't be necessary," Akira said before Gabe had a chance. She quickly moved to stand beside him.

The sheriff cleared his throat. "It's about your parole."

"My parole?"

"I understand it was discharged by the commission."

"Yes." Gabe paused, then softly added, "More than two years ago."

Andy glanced toward Akira, then back at Gabe. He moistened his lips with his tongue. "I'm afraid there's some question about whether the timing was...appropriate."

"Appropriate?" Gabe's tone was flat and emotionless.

Akira took hold of his arm. "What does this mean?" she asked, addressing her question to the sheriff.

"Not much really. I need Mr. Talmadge to check in once a month. There's a bit of paperwork to complete. It's all pretty routine."

"But it's not routine two years after a parole's been discharged," Gabe said. "Is it, Sheriff?"

An uncomfortable silence preceded the man's reply. "No. No, it isn't routine."

"Is my father behind this?"

Andy's mouth thinned into a straight line. His silence was answer enough.

"Can he do that?" Akira demanded of Gabe. When her husband didn't answer, she turned toward the sheriff. "Can he do that to Gabe?"

Andy shook his head. "I can't say if Mr. Talmadge had anything to do with it or not, ma'am."

He *couldn't* say. He hadn't said he didn't know. Only that he couldn't say.

"It's not right." Her voice rose in anger. "It isn't fair."

It was Gabe's turn to take hold of her arm. "Don't, Akira. What's done is done. Sheriff, I'll be in your office on Monday to take care of the paperwork."

"Thanks, Mr. Talmadge. I'm sorry for the mix-up."

It was no mix-up, and everyone in the room knew it.

Gabe followed the sheriff outside.

Why, Lord? Akira wondered silently. *This isn't fair. It isn't right.*

Shouldn't right prevail? Isn't there something we can do to stop this injustice? Gabe doesn't deserve this to happen. Not now. Not when he's come so far.

As if in answer to her prayer, she recalled her own words from a short while before: *He always shows me the way, even if He doesn't show me the why.*

A door slammed. An engine roared to life, then slipped into gear. Above the sounds of the rain, she heard the sheriff's car drive away.

"Show us the way, Lord," she said aloud, "even if You don't show us the why." She released a deep sigh. "Except right now, I really would like to know why."

Chapter Fourteen

Why, Lord?

The question echoed in Akira's mind again and again, but she received no answer. Not the night the sheriff came. Not the next day. Not now.

She glanced at Gabe, seated beside her in the wagon. He rode with his arms resting on his thighs, the reins looped loosely through his fingers. By all appearances, this was an ordinary trip into Ransom, but both of them knew it was not.

Why, Lord? Why now? He's made his peace with You. Why are You allowing this to happen to the man I love?

She was angry at the injustice of it all. She was furious that a man like Hudson could manipulate the legal system in order to harm others, in order to harm his own son. It wasn't fair. Gabe's stoic acceptance of the situation only made it seem worse.

I'm angry, God. You shouldn't have let this happen to him. You shouldn't have let it happen to us.

She gasped softly, shocked to discover it was God Himself with whom she was angry.

Gabe frowned at her. "What's wrong?"

"Nothing." She shook her head.

He looked back at the road. "You should've stayed home."

She didn't reply, and they fell into silence once again.

I've never been angry at God. I've always believed He knew best. What's wrong with me? Where's my faith?

She shivered, suddenly chilled.

Father?

She couldn't feel His presence.

Lord?

There was only silence in her heart.

Gabe stopped the team in front of the jail. He stared at the sign that read "Sheriff's Office" and fought against the painful memories lurking around the edges of his mind. He fought and failed.

He felt again the handcuffs clamped tightly around his wrists. He remembered the despair and anguish of knowing, even in his state of drunkenness, that he was at fault for his brother's death. He heard his father's furious accusations of murder and understood now, as he had then, how much his father hated him.

"Shall I go with you?" Akira asked.

"No." His answer was abrupt and firm.

"Gabe—"

"Do your errands, Akira. I'll find you when I'm done."

He hopped down from the wagon seat and strode toward the door. Something heavy pressed against his chest as he stepped inside the office. He wanted to turn and run. Instead, he closed the door.

Andy Newton appeared a few moments later from the doorway leading to the two jail cells at the rear of the building. His eyes widened slightly, as if he was surprised Gabe had kept his word. Then he said, "Talmadge."

"Sheriff."

"Didn't expect you this early in the day."

"Just as soon get it over with."

The sheriff nodded, then motioned toward his desk. "I've got the paperwork over here. Have a seat."

Without a word, Gabe moved to a chair and sat down.

"You've been back in Ransom how long now?" Andy asked. "'Bout two months? That right?"

"Yes."

"By the way, congratulations on your marriage. You're a lucky man."

Gabe wondered if there was a hidden meaning behind the sheriff's words.

"Folks around here think a lot of your wife. They liked her grandfather, too, from all I've heard." As he spoke, Andy slid a sheet of paper across the desk toward Gabe. "Gotta respect a woman who can run a sheep ranch near single-handed. 'Course, there's Brodie, too. Guess he's been at Dundreggan almost from the beginning."

"That's what I've been told." Gabe started filling in the spaces on the form.

The sheriff leaned back in his chair, his action accompanied by a mournful squeak. "Small towns are interesting. Everybody knows everybody else's business. I grew up in the big city myself. But my wife, she's from a wide spot in the road over in Colorado. She didn't take to city life much, and that's how we ended up here."

Gabe stared at the next question on the page, wishing the sheriff would shut up so he could get finished and get out of there.

"Sheriff Plunkett, from what I've heard, was a tough old bird."

"Yeah," Gabe muttered, "he was tough."

"Loyal to your father from all reports. Blind loyal, if what I've heard is true."

Gabe's jaw hurt. Maybe from clenching his teeth. Maybe from remembering the night Plunkett had arrested him. When Gabe had tried to speak, the crusty old lawman had punched him, knocking him clean off his feet. Of course, it hadn't helped that Gabe was in a drunken stupor.

"I'm a different kind of sheriff from my predecessor."

Gabe signed his name, then pushed the paper toward Andy. He met the other man's watchful gaze. "Anything else you need from me, Sheriff?"

"As a matter of fact, yes." Andy sat forward, leaning his arms on the desk. "I need to tell you to keep your nose clean, no matter what else happens."

Gabe didn't reply. What was there to say?

The sheriff's gaze narrowed. "I'm not sure you understand me. This"—he pointed at the form on the desk between them—"isn't normal. You know it and I know it. Somebody wants you to make a mistake. Don't make one. Don't make my job more difficult than it has to be."

It took a moment for Andy's words to sink in. He'd thought the sheriff wanted a chance to throw him back in the slammer. Instead, he seemed to be acknowledging that an injustice had been done to Gabe.

"The town's different now than it was fourteen years ago," the sheriff commented.

Gabe stood. "Lots of things are different. Me included."

"Talmadge?" Andy stood too. "I'm here to help if ever I can." He held out his hand. "Remember that."

Somewhat reluctantly, Gabe shook the man's hand, then turned and left.

It had been an odd encounter, he thought as he strode along the sidewalk toward the general store. Not at all what he'd expected.

His footsteps slowed.

I didn't trust You, did I, Lord? I should've trusted You, and I didn't. I expected everything to be like it's always been. Even now, when You've given me so much, I'm still expecting things to be like always. I'm expecting the worst. Wish You'd let me know what's happening, what it is I'm supposed to do. I know You speak to me in Your Word, but I don't know it well enough, and I don't always understand what I do know.

He turned the corner, stopping when he saw Akira loading supplies in the back of the wagon.

She hears Your voice. Really hears it. I know she does because I've seen that certain look on her face when she knows You've spoken. Wish I could hear You as clearly. I'm probably wanting more than's rightfully mine. But I guess nothing's rightfully mine, is it, Jesus? You've already done more for me than I deserve.

Akira tossed another feed sack onto the wagon bed. She was strong for such a slight thing. And there sure wasn't another woman he'd ever seen that could look as pretty in a baggy pair of overalls, her head covered with a floppy straw hat.

She deserves better than me for a husband.

He leaned his shoulder against the wall of the bank.

I'm not good enough for her. Not as a Christian. Not as a man. Don't make her pay for my mistakes, God. I'm asking that much. Don't let anything I've done or ever do hurt her in any way. She's a good woman, and she loves You with all her heart.

If ever he found himself wondering if God loved him, Gabe figured all he had to do was look at Akira.

My wife.

He pushed away from the building, standing straight, staring at her.

Was it possible what he felt was more than affection? Was it love? And more importantly, was it possible she loved him? Not the love Christians were supposed to feel for the hurting and the lost, but the kind a woman felt for a man.

An odd mixture of emotions filled his chest. Fear and hope. Dread and joy. God had promised to open the windows of heaven and pour out an overflowing blessing until he couldn't take it in.

And so He had.

Akira slung the last burlap bag onto the wagon bed, then paused to wipe the perspiration from her brow. When she turned, she saw Gabe standing at the street corner, watching her. She waved but didn't smile, uncertain what had transpired since she left him at the sheriff's office. Had it been worse or better than he'd expected? She'd been praying unceasingly for it to be better.

He started toward her.

Oh, Father. Please...

"You should have waited for me," he said when he stopped beside the wagon. "I would have loaded the heavy sacks."

"They weren't too heavy." *What happened? Tell me what happened.*

The hint of a smile curved one corner of his mouth.

Her heart skipped a beat in response to it.

After a long, breathless moment, his gaze shifted from her to some point beyond her left shoulder.

She turned to see what had stolen his attention. It was Pauline, disembarking from her chauffeur-driven automobile, looking like a motion picture star in her high-fashion dress, shoes and silk stockings, her hair perfectly coiffured.

Akira felt suddenly dowdy, dusty, and sweaty.

"I won't be long," Pauline said to her driver. It was only then she seemed to notice Gabe and Akira. She smiled broadly and started toward them. "Well, hello. Is everything all right at your ranch? I didn't see you at church yesterday, and I was wondering."

"Things are fine," Gabe answered, stepping up to stand next to Akira. "We've been busy with harvesting. It's a lot of work this time of year, you know."

"No, I can't even imagine." Pauline's laughter was melodic, a sound as beautiful as the woman herself. "Good heavens! I don't grow my own flowers. I swear, I merely look at a plant and it withers. Without our gardener, our yard would be a sorry sight."

"You should talk to Akira." Gabe placed his arm around her shoulders. "Dundreggan has flowers everywhere. She can grow anything."

Pleasure flowed over her, like warm honey over a biscuit, a balm on her insecurities.

Pauline's gaze shifted from Gabe to Akira. "I would love to see your flowers. Would you mind if I came for a visit next week?"

Hudson's wife as a guest in her home? It was unthinkable.

"Of course, I wouldn't want to put you out," Pauline continued, sounding slightly less sure of herself.

Akira shoved aside her uncharitable thoughts, ashamed of her reaction. "You wouldn't be putting me out. Please do come. Come whenever it's convenient, Mrs. Talmadge."

"Pauline." She held out her white-gloved hand. "Please call me Pauline. After all, we're *both* Mrs. Talmadge now."

Akira paused. Her hands were filthy after tossing around the feed sacks. And even if they were clean, the calluses on her palms would snag the delicate lace fabric of Pauline's glove.

Pauline obviously misunderstood the hesitation. She pulled back her hand, placing it against her abdomen, as if holding in something painful. Her expression revealed nothing, and yet, Akira sensed she was disappointed, perhaps hurt.

Instinctively, she extended both arms, hands open, palms up. "I didn't want to soil your gloves."

Pauline stared at Akira's hands for a moment. Then, ever so slowly, the shadow of a smile returned. As it did so, Akira became aware of something else—Pauline's smiles never quite reached her eyes. They were sometimes dazzling, sometimes amused. But they seemed never to come from a place of real joy.

With sudden discernment, she knew Gabe's stepmother was lonely and not at all what Akira had expected her to be.

They were halfway back to Dundreggan before Gabe asked, "Do you think Hud put her up to it?" The question had been plaguing him for the past hour.

Akira didn't ask for him to clarify, so he was certain Pauline had been on her mind, too.

"I don't know," she answered.

He glanced at his wife. "You didn't have to invite her to the ranch."

"I know." She met his gaze. "But I wanted to. She seems so…so unhappy."

Gabe couldn't argue with the truth. Still, Pauline hadn't been to church in Ransom until he started going—or so he'd been told. That in and of itself made her motives suspect. He was familiar with his father's ability to manipulate the actions of others. Was he manipulating Pauline?

"It must be terrible to have no one," Akira said softly.

"She's got a husband and a house full of servants."

Akira spoke no words, but her eyes said plenty.

He looked back at the road. "Yeah, I guess you're right."

It wasn't easy, being surrounded by people but having no one to trust, no one in whom one could confide. If anybody should understand, it was Gabe. It was only because of Akira that folks in Ransom, other than Miss Jane, had anything to do with him. Even with her at his side, there were plenty who preferred to steer clear of the convicted murderer.

"I guess she deserves the benefit of the doubt," he said, unable to disguise the reluctance in his voice.

After a few moments, Akira's left hand covered his right one where it rested on his thigh. He glanced down.

Did Akira own a pair of pretty lace gloves, he wondered, like the ones Pauline had worn? She should. She should have lots of pretty things. If he could give them to her, he would.

She deserved so much…

And he had so little to give.

Chapter Fifteen

The sheep returned to Dundreggan on one of those beautiful Indian summer days when the whole earth seemed wrapped in a golden haze. Almost overnight, the greens of summer had been replaced by the colors of autumn. The air smelled of just-turned earth and burning leaves.

When Akira heard the tinkle of the lead sheep's bell, she ran to meet them. After waving to the Wickhams, she gave Brodie a hug, then kissed his bearded cheek.

"I've been watching for you all week," she told him as she stepped back.

"*Ach!* 'Tis the same every year, lass. Glad ye are t'see us gone, and glad ye are t'see our return."

She laughed.

"Now let me have a good look at ye." He scowled as he stared at her face. "Ye look right enough. 'Tis well with ye, then?"

"Aye," she answered, mimicking his brogue. "'Tis very well with me."

He looked past her toward the ranch house. "Is he about?"

"Yes, *he* is about. Gabe's in the barn, trying to fix the old wireless."

"Radio." He made the word sound foul.

Akira didn't think his disgust was about the radio. "Brodie?" She placed her hand on the big man's chest. "I love Gabe. We're happy together. Can't you be at least a little glad for me? Won't you give him a chance? He's not who you think he is."

"He's a Talmadge."

"And so am I."

He made a guttural noise in his throat.

She took a step backward, lifted her chin, placed her fists on her hips. "I'll hear no more against my husband, Brodie Lachlan. I've run out of patience. You've been like a member of my family for near as long as I can remember. As close as my grandfather. But I'm Gabe's wife, and it's time you got used to it. If you can't, then...then maybe there's no place for you at Dundreggan any longer."

She didn't know which of them was the most surprised by her outburst. She couldn't remember a time when she'd spoken to him in such anger.

Brodie rubbed his beard as he stared down at her, his eyes narrowing as the moments passed. Finally, he nodded. "So be it, lass."

His words were like a knife in her heart. Would he really choose to leave rather than make peace with Gabe?

"I'll say no more against yer husband. If ye see good in him, then good there must be."

Tears sprang to her eyes. Her throat burned. "Oh, Brodie," she whispered. "Thank you."

"*Ach!* Why stand ye there cryin' when there's work t'be done, lass?"

He strode away, all bluster and bravado, but he didn't fool her. If he'd stayed, she suspected he might have shed a few tears himself.

"Forgive me for speaking in anger, Lord," she said softly, "and thank You for keeping Brodie here. Soften his heart toward Gabe. I'd be grateful if they could become friends, but I'd settle for cordial if that's the best he can do." She shook her head, smiling as she added, "Stubborn old Scot."

The reception on the battery-powered Philco was less than ideal, but Akira's expression when the *Amos 'n' Andy* broadcast began that night made it seem perfect to Gabe. She sat in a straight-backed chair, leaning forward, her elbows on her thighs, her chin resting on the heels of her hands. Her eyes were round and bright.

"I can't believe you were able to fix it," she said, glancing over at him.

Pride welled in his chest. She made him feel as if he'd accomplished the impossible.

"Mr. Martin at the hardware store told me I'd have to buy a new one," she continued, "but you fixed it."

He shrugged, then shook his head. He wasn't used to compliments; they made him uneasy. Seeming to understand, Akira turned her rapt attention back to the program, leaving Gabe to his thoughts.

He loved her. He understood that now. His feelings went beyond gratitude and appreciation, beyond affection and devotion. It went beyond the marriage bed. So why didn't he tell her? What kept him from saying it? He understood that women liked to hear the words. Was it because she hadn't declared her love for him? Or was there some other reason?

She laughed at something one of the program's characters said, and the pleasant sound drew his gaze.

God, I love her. With my whole heart. I don't know why You put us together the way You did. She deserves much more, much better, in a husband. I want to be the man she thinks I am. How do I do that? How do I become him? 'Cause I'm not him yet. Maybe I never will be.

But I want to know You the way she does. Really know You. I want to be closer. I want to hear You speaking to me. You've blessed me, and I don't know why. Help me understand what You've got planned for me, Lord. Help me walk in Your ways.

Akira rose from her chair and turned the knob on the Philco, plunging the house into sudden silence.

"I'd forgotten how much I enjoy that program," she said, facing him again. "We should invite the Wickhams to join us next time."

"Sure." He stood, hoping she wouldn't ask what he'd thought of the show since he hadn't been listening.

She reached out, touched the side of his face with her fingertips. The caress didn't last long. It was merely a whisper, and then it was gone.

"I'd better get those dishes washed," she said, her voice as whispery light as her touch.

"I'll help you."

Wordlessly, she nodded, then turned and walked to the kitchen.

Akira took the kettle from the stove and poured hot water into the dishpan, then added soap and cold water until the temperature was right. Throughout the ritual, she was aware of Gabe standing nearby, dishtowel in hand.

"I spoke with Lachlan this afternoon," he said as she placed the first of the dishes into the pan. "He says you'll be shipping lambs to market next week."

A lump formed in her throat. She didn't know why, but she felt a little like crying. In fact, she'd felt weepy all week long. Happy or sad, it didn't matter. She seemed always on the verge of tears.

"You must be glad to have him back at Dundreggan."

She scrubbed the plate, unable to see through a blur of tears.

"Something bothering you, Akira?"

"No," she managed to say, adding, "Tired, I guess."

He didn't press.

She was thankful for that.

Gabe took the just-rinsed plate from her and dried it before setting it on the shelf in the cupboard. "George Edwards told me there's a barn dance up at the Candleberry farm tomorrow night. I'd like us to go."

"You would?" She glanced over her shoulder, surprised.

His smile was tender, causing her heart to skip a beat. "Yes. When was the last time you did something for fun?"

"I'm not much of a dancer."

"Neither am I."

Although he didn't say it aloud, she knew he mentally added, *Not many dances in prison.* It made her heart ache.

He continued, "But as long as we're dancing together, what does it matter?"

Tears blinded her completely now.

Next thing she knew, he was holding her close against him, the wet dishrag in her hand soaking their clothes.

"What's wrong?" he demanded gently, his lips brushing the top of her head.

"Nothing."

He withdrew slightly, cupped her chin with his fingers, tipped her head back. He dried her eyes with a corner of the dishtowel. "Akira, what is it? Tell me."

"Nothing's wrong."

"You've never been less than honest with me. Not until now."

She shook her head.

"Is it something I said? Something I did?"

She kept shaking her head.

"I know I'm not good with words." He pulled her close again, pressing her cheek against his chest. "I didn't mean to hurt you, whatever I did or said."

"Oh, Gabe," she whispered. "You haven't hurt me. Honest, you haven't. I don't know why I'm crying. I'm not sad."

"You sure?" He sounded skeptical.

"I'm sure." She sniffed as she drew back from him again. She forced a smile as she met his gaze. "See?"

He didn't look convinced.

I love you, Gabriel Talmadge. I love you so much. You've come to mean the world to me. And I think you love me too. Why don't either of us say it?

The question lingered in her mind, keeping her awake into the wee hours of the night.

CHAPTER SIXTEEN

Somewhere near sunrise Akira found the answer to her question. She hadn't told Gabe she loved him because she was trying to protect her heart. As if not speaking the words would shield her from pain should he never love her in return.

But it wouldn't shield her. Nothing could.

It came to her, as she lay there, listening to the sound of Gabe's steady breathing and watching as the first pale streaks of dawn inched across the ceiling. The Bible told wives to submit to their husbands and husbands to love their wives. God hadn't told wives to love their husbands. Was it because women found it easier to love?

And harder to submit.

She turned her head on the pillow. She couldn't see him clearly, caught in shadows as he was, yet she knew his features so well by now it seemed she could. She knew the sharp angles of his face. She knew the morning stubble that darkened his jaw. She knew the way his hair stuck out in odd directions when he first got up.

She didn't have to be afraid, she realized. God knew what she needed. God knew she needed her husband to love her. He'd begun a work in Gabe, and He would complete it. Nothing could keep Him from it.

Father, I'm sorry. Forgive me. I've harbored anger and resentment all week long. Not just because of Gabe's parole. Because of what I want and when I want it. But You know what I need. You know what we both need, Gabe and me. Why have I acted as if You don't know or care?

She sat up, still staring at Gabe. He'd been rejected by his father time and again. The approval he'd sought hadn't been there. He'd tried to be what Hudson wanted, but he had failed. Gabe hadn't yet grasped the Father's unconditional love. No wonder he didn't understand her love for him.

I'm going to tell him. He needs to know.

A huge weight lifted off her chest, and joy rushed in to take the place of the anger she'd released into God's keeping.

Smiling, she slipped from beneath the blankets.

Gabe opened his eyes and watched Akira's quiet departure from the room. He hated it when she was the first to rise. The bed felt too large without her beside him.

He frowned, remembering her strange mood last evening. She could deny it all she wanted, but he knew he was responsible for her tears. She wasn't a woman who cried at the drop of a hat. If she was sad, it had to be because of him.

He draped an arm over his eyes as he stifled a groan. Everything she'd done for him was kind and caring. She'd taken him in when he was nothing more than a starving bum. She'd given him work when his own father wouldn't do it. She'd rejected the opinions of the townsfolk of Ransom—not to mention Brodie Lachlan—and treated him with respect. And finally she'd agreed to marry him. He owed her a great deal. The least he could do was find a way to make her happy.

How do I do it? How do I make her happy? God, don't let me fail her. Not Akira.

He heard the front door close and knew she'd gone to do the milking. Time he was up and about too. He had a full day ahead of him, and he needed his chores done early if they were going to the barn dance.

And they *were* going.

He liked the idea of dancing with Akira. He liked the idea of showing her a good time. Maybe the Wickhams and Lachlan would join them. Maybe they could take the Wickhams' truck, if Charlie thought it would make it all the way north to the Candleberry farm.

Pauline glanced out the window at the passing countryside. She'd traversed this road countless times in the years she'd been married to Hudson, going to Boise to shop or to see her parents and visit friends. Any excuse that would take her away from her husband.

If only I could get away from him for good.

She'd never loved Hudson, not even in the beginning, and eventually, she'd learned to despise him.

Now she feared him.

He'd called last night from Washington, D.C. Although she didn't know the nature of his business in the nation's capital—and Hudson wouldn't dream of telling her—it had been clear he wasn't happy with what had transpired thus far. She didn't know why he'd called her, other than that he'd needed someone to intimidate. He'd chosen her.

"It worked too," she muttered softly to herself.

Eugene, her chauffeur, slowed the automobile, then turned off the road. Sheep—hundreds of them, she supposed, maybe thousands—grazed in the rolling pastureland on both sides of the long and winding driveway. In the distance, she saw a man with a shepherd's staff standing near a tall pine. He motioned with his free hand, and a dog took off at a run, its body in a slightly crouched position as it approached some sheep. She couldn't see what happened next as her car went over a rise and the shepherd, sheep, and dog disappeared from view.

She looked ahead, toward the collection of buildings that made up the Macauley ranch. Or was it the Talmadge ranch now? That was what Hudson wanted it to be.

She frowned. Why did he want this piece of land so badly? He owned much of the land hereabouts, not to mention nearly every business in Ransom. Didn't he have enough?

You know what you have to do, Pauline. Now do it. Do you understand, my dear? She shivered, remembering the threat that had been so clear in his false endearment.

Eugene braked, bringing the car to a stop. He got out and came to open her door. He offered his gloved hand, which she accepted, allowing him to assist her as she stepped from the automobile.

She looked around. There were several log houses, the larger of them set apart from the others. Different kinds of outbuildings of various sizes surrounded a spacious barnyard. The place had a rustic appearance, but everything seemed solid, too. Built to last for generations. Of course, she had little knowledge of farms and ranches. She was a city girl. She didn't know how she'd ended up in this backwater logging town.

No, that wasn't true. She was here because she'd wanted to be rich. Obscenely rich. She'd wanted it for herself, and her parents had wanted it for her. And so she'd sold herself to the devil to get it.

Something twisted in her chest.

At that moment, Gabe appeared around the corner of one of the outbuildings. He hesitated when he saw her there, then continued forward.

"Morning."

"Good morning, Gabe." She smiled. "I hope I haven't come at an inopportune time. To see the flowers? Remember? I would have called, but..." She shrugged, tipping her head slightly to one side.

Get close to him, Pauline. Real close. You understand me?

Oh yes. She understood Hudson's meaning. But could she do what he wanted? A year ago, even a few months ago, she'd have had no qualms using her charms to seduce Gabe. He was tall, handsome, and near her own age. It would be a pleasure to spend time with him.

But things were different now. *She* was different now, although she couldn't explain why or how. She only knew she didn't want to deceive him. She didn't want to use him for her own gain. She didn't want to hurt his wife, either. Akira had been kind to her. Kinder than anyone in Ransom had been in the years she'd lived here.

Not that she'd given others much of a chance to be kind or otherwise. She'd always thought herself above them.

"Come on in the house," Gabe said, interrupting her thoughts. "Akira's fixing us something to eat."

"Oh, I'm sorry. I didn't realize it was so close to dinnertime. Why don't I wait out here until you're—".

"Akira will insist you join us, so there's no point in arguing."

Akira did seem glad to see Pauline. She smiled and greeted her warmly, insisting she sit at the table and eat with them, as Gabe had said she would.

Hudson would be pleased, Pauline thought, but she took no satisfaction in it.

The food was both simple and delicious, and although Akira and Gabe discussed ranch matters, things of which Pauline had no knowledge or experience—separating grown lambs from ewes, preparations for shipping to market and the expected price they might bring, plowing fields under for winter—Akira somehow made her feel like a participant.

When the meal was over, Gabe rose from his chair and began gathering the dishes. "You show our guest around. I'll see to these."

"All right," Akira agreed. She looked at Pauline. "It's too late in the year for most of the flowers, of course. You'll have to make sure you come in the summer when they're at their best."

Pauline wasn't listening. She was trying to imagine Hudson clearing the table of dirty dishes. Then she tried to imagine her husband watching her with an adoring gaze, the way Gabe had watched Akira throughout the meal. She tried and failed.

There was no point, she realized, in throwing herself at Gabe. Hudson could threaten all he liked. She would be wasting her time. Gabe couldn't even see Pauline. Not as a woman. He had eyes only for his wife.

Lucky Akira.

Gabe saw more than Pauline guessed. A man didn't spend a third of his life among the devious and dishonest without learning to read people. Pauline wasn't the sort of woman who came calling for no reason. Akira thought it was because she was lonely. Maybe. But there was more to it than that.

Through the window, he watched Akira and Pauline stroll side by side down the drive.

His father's wife was a beautiful woman…and aware of it too. He suspected she could turn the charm off and on at will. From what he understood, Pauline had stayed aloof from the townsfolk since marrying Hudson in '25. So why was she making a point of becoming Akira's friend now? It wasn't as if the two of them had a whole lot in common, the society dame and the shepherdess.

"Judge not," the Scriptures said. He'd read the verse that morning.

Maybe he *was* judging her, but he couldn't help it. Maybe? Well, okay. He *definitely* was judging her. But somebody had to protect Akira from her own sweet innocence. If he didn't do it, who would?

Brodie Lachlan would, for one.

The lass might convince him to accept her husband, but there was no way on God's green earth Brodie would ever trust the wife of Hudson Talmadge.

From the hillside upon which he stood, he observed the two women as they returned to the large black automobile. He watched them clasp hands, then Pauline got into the rear seat, aided by her chauffeur.

"'Tis an ill wind what brought ye here," he muttered.

He rubbed his thigh, his leg aching, a reminder of one more reason not to trust a Talmadge. His so-called accident had been the work of Hudson's lackeys, trying to be rid of him so Hudson could take Dundreggan from Akira. Brodie didn't have proof of his suspicions, of course, but he didn't need any. He knew. Deep in his gut, he knew.

He turned and walked slowly toward the flock grazing on the upper hillside.

The lass had changed in the weeks he'd been away from Dundreggan. Marriage had changed her. She'd always been a strong one, physically and spiritually. She'd always been wise beyond her years. But now there was a deeper maturity about her. Brodie couldn't say he understood it, but it was there all the same.

"Akira Talmadge." He glanced up. "Old Fergus must be rolling in his grave."

Frowning, he admitted Gabe didn't *seem* to be like the man who'd sired him. Nor did he resemble the reckless, spoiled youth of Brodie's memory, the one whose temper and anger had brought about his brother's death. For that matter, Gabe didn't much resemble the man who'd first arrived at Dundreggan, hungry and hopeless.

He makes Akira happy.

Brodie grunted.

Aye, she's happy.

He'd even admit the lad had accomplished a lot around the place. Gabe was a tireless worker, now that he had his strength back. It had been years since the fences were in such good repair. The main house had new screens over the windows. Gates and doors swung open without the squeal of rusty hinges. The hen-house sported a new roof to keep out the rain and snow, as well as tightly strung wire to keep out predators. The stack of firewood had multiplied many times, promising warmth throughout the coming winter.

And he makes Akira happy.

Brodie grunted again.

It was possible, he supposed, the lass hadn't made a mistake in marrying Gabe.

But only possible.

Akira prayed for Pauline as the automobile disappeared from view, leaving a cloud of dust lingering in its wake.

She's so lonely, Father. Let her know she's not alone, no matter the circumstances. And forgive me for all the unkind thoughts I had toward her when we first met.

"Pauline wants something," Gabe said, coming up behind her.

She looked at him, then followed his gaze toward the road. "Everyone wants something."

"She's seeking you out for some reason. I'd like to know why."

"God must have His reasons for sending her here."

Disapproving silence was his answer.

Strengthen Gabe's faith, Lord. He looks through a glass darkly. Help him see things with Your eyes and not the eyes of the world.

"Well," he said, "I'd better get to my chores. It'll be time to leave for the Candleberry farm in a few more hours."

"My word!" She looked at her wrist, but she wasn't wearing her watch. She glanced up again, meeting his gaze. "It can't be that late."

"It's past two-thirty."

"I've a dozen things to do before I can go. Maybe—"

He grabbed her by the shoulders, drawing her to him. "Don't," he said, his voice deep and low. "Don't even suggest we forget going. I mean to dance with my wife." His kiss was brief but oh-so-sweet.

Dizziness swept through her, and she was thankful for Gabe's strong hands, still holding her by the shoulders.

The lightheaded sensation almost made her giggle. Who'd have thought she would become the sort of woman who swooned when kissed by her husband? Not her. Not even in a million years.

Chapter Seventeen

The Candleberrys were a large, boisterous, close-knit family of ten—Weston, Ursula, and their eight grown sons, ranging in age from twenty-nine down to twenty: Wadsworth, Dickens, Byron, Tennyson, Keats, Clemens, Butler, and Kipling. Saddled with such names, the Candleberry boys had been involved in plenty of schoolyard fights when they were youngsters. Much to their mother's dismay, none were inclined toward literary endeavors as had been her hope.

Since the start of the Great Depression, the Candleberry boys had scattered across the western states, leaving the valley each February, riding the rails, working wherever they could find jobs, sending home what money they had to spare. They returned again every fall at about this time. To help their dad with the harvest was the official reason, but everyone in the valley knew it was because that was how Ursula wanted it. And none of the boys intentionally disappointed their mother.

Until this year.

The Wickhams and Talmadges had scarcely disembarked from

the old truck before the juicy gossip was passed along to them in hushed, excited voices.

"You'll never believe it," Irene Hirsch said to Nora. "Woody"— as Wadsworth was called—"brought home a wife, and she's big as a barn with child. Nary a phone call or a letter saying he was getting married, let alone about to become a father." She turned her gaze toward Akira. "*Claims* they've been wed since last February."

"Ursula's beside herself," Lilybet Teague chimed in. "Just beside herself."

Akira smiled, pretending not to understand their implications. "Well, of course she is. This will be her first grandchild. We must go give her our best wishes." She slipped her arm through Gabe's. "If you'll excuse us."

They walked toward the barn, leaving the Wickhams to Irene and Lilybet. *Poor Charlie and Nora.* Akira felt a twinge of guilt for deserting her friends. But only a twinge. She was certain she would have said something she oughtn't if she'd remained.

Music spilled through the large open doorway of the barn, along with light, laughter, and an overflow of people. The crisp evening air was cloaked in the fragrance of new-mown hay and home cooking.

Gabe's footsteps slowed. "Ever wonder what those two battle-axes must've said when they heard we were married?"

"You shouldn't call them names." Actually, she'd thought worse than that about them, but she didn't want to admit it.

"Do you?" he persisted, ignoring her admonishment.

"No." She tilted her chin. "Women like that only find the worst to say, no matter what."

In the dusky evening light, she saw him frown.

"Akira? Are you happy?"

"Happy?"

"With me?"

"Oh, Gabe," she whispered. "Don't you know?" She touched the side of his face with the palm of her hand. The time had come to tell him she loved him.

"Gabe. Akira," Jane Sebastian said as she walked into view. "I thought maybe you weren't coming."

"We just arrived," Gabe answered, turning toward her.

"Have you heard the news about Woody?"

Akira replied, "We heard. Mrs. Teague and Mrs. Hirsch met us when we arrived."

Jane's expression soured. "Those two. I'm sure they had nothing good to say." She motioned for them to follow her. "Well, come inside and meet the bride. She's a lovely girl. Shy as a church mouse and overwhelmed by all the hullabaloo, but lovely all the same."

Akira took hold of Gabe's hand, squeezing it briefly. Her declaration of love would have to wait a little longer.

201

Gabe felt more than a little sympathy for Celia Candleberry, Woody's unexpected—and very expectant—bride. Her complexion was chalky white, making her eyes seem overly large in her face. She sat on a chair, her husband standing beside her on the right, her mother-in-law seated beside her on the left. Gabe recognized a person who felt trapped when he saw one.

But then Akira took Celia's hand as they were introduced and spoke softly to her, smiling all the while. It was like watching a miracle take place right before his eyes, the way Celia's tension visibly eased.

How does Akira do it? What did she say to her? It's like she brings sunshine into any room she enters.

Just as she'd brought it into his life.

Akira turned toward him. "This is my husband, Gabriel Talmadge. He was raised in Ransom, but he's been away for many years. He understands how overwhelming it is to feel like a stranger. Don't you, Gabe?"

"That I do," he said, nodding at Celia. "Pleased to meet you, Mrs. Candleberry." He lifted his gaze. "Good to see you again, Woody. Congratulations on your marriage."

Gabe and Woody hadn't run with the same crowd when they were teens. For one thing, Gabe was three years older. For another, the Candleberry boys, while a fun-loving bunch, hadn't participated in the sort of shenanigans Gabe had been known for as a youth. If they'd gone home pie-eyed on hooch or been caught smoking cigarettes, their father would've hauled them to the woodshed for a licking, and their mother would've had them scrubbing the big farmhouse from floor to ceiling for a month of Sundays. Gabe couldn't recall for certain, but he suspected he'd ridiculed them, thinking them "duds" because they'd obeyed their parents.

He wondered what Woody had thought of him back then.

He wondered what he would think of him now.

"I'd heard you were back." Woody held out his hand. "And I guess congratulations are in order for you, as well." He glanced at Akira, then back again.

Gabe took his hand and pressed it firmly. "Yes. Thanks."

He recognized Woody's expression. A bit of skepticism, a healthy dose of doubt. But Gabe didn't turn away from the look as he would have at the start of the summer. He was grateful for that—and a bit surprised, too. He'd been anxious about tonight. No doubt about it.

He felt as if he'd passed the first test.

Akira slipped her hand around his arm. "I think you promised a dance to me, Mr. Talmadge."

"I think I promised you all of them."

She smiled, and he felt something soften inside him.

He'd told her he wasn't a good dancer, which was the truth. And yet, as he took her in his arms and they moved in time to the music, he felt like Fred Astaire in *A Gay Divorcée*. Last winter, cold and wet from an endless drizzling rain, he'd used a precious dime to get into a movie theater. What he'd been after was a brief period of warmth, not entertainment. But now he remembered watching the actor as he'd twirled around on the screen, and he could almost believe himself capable of the same.

"What?" Akira asked.

He raised an eyebrow.

She grinned. "You're wearing a strange smile. What are you thinking?"

"You wouldn't believe me if I told you." He drew her a bit closer, tightening his grip on her right hand.

What he'd like to do was kiss her. Soundly kiss her. Right there for every Tom, Dick, and Harry to see. Why shouldn't he want to? She was his wife...and he loved her.

I love her so much it scares me, Lord. What if I fail her? What if I can't measure up? She trusts me. I see that in her eyes. She has no reason to. Not really. There's plenty in this room who only see an ex-con when they look at me. But not her. Not Akira.

He was sorry when the music changed from the more romantic melody of "I Only Have Eyes for You" into a rousing rendition of "Happy Days Are Here Again." He didn't let on, however, as he gamely twirled her around the dance floor, pretending he knew what he was doing. She released a peal of laughter, a joy-filled sound, her gaze locked with his, and he figured Fred Astaire's days were numbered should he, Gabe Talmadge, ever decide to head for Hollywood.

They were both winded when the song ended.

Still laughing softly, Akira fanned herself with her hand. "Oh, my. I thought it was cool when we got here, but I was wrong."

"Want to sit one out?"

She nodded.

"I'll get us some punch."

Her eyes sparkled in the lantern light.

"You look for a place to sit. I'll find you," Gabe said.

She nodded again, squeezing his hand once before letting it slip from her grasp.

Grinning, feeling pleased with the world, Gabe made his way through the crowd toward the refreshments. He didn't mind the looks of disdain from a trio of men standing beside the ladder to the loft. He didn't mind the two women whispering behind their hands while casting suspicious glances toward him as he walked by. Tonight he was a better dancer than Fred Astaire; he was richer than Daddy Warbucks; he was flying higher than Charles Lindbergh Who cared what others thought as long as Akira was happy?

And she is happy.

He stopped, turned, looked through the crowd for a glimpse of her shiny red hair.

She's happy with me.

"Good evening, Gabe."

He swallowed the lump in his throat before turning toward Simon Neville. "Good evening, Reverend."

"Fine party, isn't it?"

"It sure is."

"I'm glad you came. I assume your lovely wife is with you?"

He couldn't help grinning. "Yes sir, she is. I came to get her a glass of punch. She was feeling a bit overheated."

"Took a few turns around the dance floor, did you?" Simon frowned. "No, wait." He waved with his hand to keep Gabe from interrupting him. "Kipling says my language is woefully outdated. He's given me some pointers. What I should have said is, 'Did you tote your frame onto the scud track'?"

"Come again?"

The reverend grinned. "It does sound a bit preposterous, coming from a man my age."

"I haven't a clue what it means."

With a chuckle, Simon translated, "Did you escort your dance partner onto the dance floor?"

"Hmm. Take my advice, Reverend. Don't listen to Kipling anymore." Gabe picked up two glasses of punch, then faced the reverend again. "I'd better take Akira her punch. She'll be wondering what happened to me."

"Hope to see you both at church in the morning."

Gabe walked away, muttering to himself, "Tote my frame onto the scud track." Then he chuckled deep in his chest. Wait until he told Akira.

He craned to see over the heads of the milling partygoers. His wife's distinctive red hair should have made her easy to find, but he couldn't see her. She wasn't seated with the older women or with the young mothers with babies and toddlers. She wasn't near the raised musicians' platform, and she wasn't in any of the straw-strewn stalls.

He was growing anxious when he came upon Jane.

"She went outside for a breath of fresh night air," she said in answer to his query. "I left her a moment ago, outside the doorway there." She touched his arm. "Don't let her stay out too long. The night's turned colder than she thinks. She could take a chill. You don't want her getting sick now."

"No. Of course not. I'll bring her back in."

But he didn't find her beyond the barn doors. He didn't see anyone. Miss Jane was right. The night *had* turned cold. He could see a cloud of mist in front of his mouth when he breathed out.

He turned to go back inside.

Keep looking.

He didn't know why he thought those words. He only knew they stopped him in his tracks.

And then he heard a sound. Nothing loud. Yet he knew it signaled something wrong. Something very wrong. Something with Akira.

He tossed the glasses of punch aside. Long strides carried him deeper into the moonlit night.

"No!"

Her voice was no more than a hoarse whisper, but in Gabe's ears, in his heart, it was a ringing cry of desperation. He rounded several vehicles parked near the house.

"You're not too good for that jailbird, but you're too good for me. Is that it? Never givin' me the time of day." As the man spoke, his voice slurred, he yanked Akira toward him. Then he tried to kiss her.

Something feral exploded inside Gabe. He didn't think. He

couldn't. He just reacted. He slammed his body into the man, and the two of them rolled across the ground, exchanging punches in a mad flurry.

Gabe thought he heard his name shouted from a distance. He wasn't sure. He was sure of only one thing. He had to make certain this rotting piece of garbage—whoever he was—never touched his wife again.

Never.

His hands closed around the man's throat.

"Gabe, don't! Gabriel, *don't!*"

An instant after Akira's words registered through the red fury that possessed him, Gabe felt ironlike hands grasp his arms and haul him to his feet.

"He tried to kill me," the man on the ground said between gasps. "He tried to kill me."

"That wasn't smart, Talmadge."

Gabe glanced in the direction of the low voice, then realized it was Andy Newton who'd spoken. It was the sheriff who still held his upper left arm.

Slowly, the world righted itself. Gabe became aware of the buzz of voices behind him, and he looked over his shoulder. The barn seemed to have emptied. They were all standing there, all those who'd come to this farm to dance and enjoy the evening, staring at him. Staring at Gabe Talmadge, the ex-con, the convicted murderer.

"He was protecting me, Sheriff," Akira said, coming to stand before them.

The sleeve of her dress was torn at the shoulder. Her hair had tumbled down, the pins lost. She looked ghostly pale in the moonlight.

Bravely, she continued, "Mr. Peck is drunk, and he…he…" Her voice faltered as she fingered the collar of her dress.

Peck. Danny Peck. Gabe should have recognized him, but he'd been too blinded by rage. He hadn't cared who the man was. He'd only wanted to hurt him.

Andy released Gabe. "Take your wife into the house, Talmadge. I'll be in to talk to you both in a few minutes." He turned toward the onlookers. "Go back inside, folks. There's nothing more to see. Excitement's over."

"You're not gonna let him go," Danny rasped as someone helped him to his feet. "He like to killed me. You seen him."

Jane grabbed her brother's arm as she watched Akira and Gabe walk away. "Zach?"

"It'll be all right. Andy Newton's no fool."

She blinked away hot tears. "Oh, Lord," she whispered, "don't let this hurt that boy."

Danny Peck made a vile comment about Akira, slurring his words but not so much he wasn't understood. Jane heard several women gasp behind her, then heard the grumbling of some men.

"I think it's time you got on home, Peck," the sheriff said, his voice like steel.

"I wanna know if you're gonna arrest that—"

"I said, it's time for you to go. If I need to, I'll come see you tomorrow."

Through his fog of intoxication, Danny seemed to realize he'd stepped over some invisible line. He retrieved his hat from the ground and slapped it onto his head, then beat a wordless and hasty—if unsteady—retreat.

"You suppose I should go be with them?" Jane asked Zachary. "With Gabe and Akira?"

"No. Let them work it out 'twixt themselves. They're man and wife. They gotta deal with these things as a couple."

She nodded, fighting another wave of tears.

Zachary put his arm around her shoulders and gave her a squeeze. "You worry too much."

"But Gabe—"

"There isn't a man here who wouldn't have fought to protect his loved one from that drunken sot."

"I hope you're right, Zach."

Akira wasn't often afraid, but she had been frightened during her brief struggle with Danny. Mostly because he'd caught her off guard. She'd been staring up at the clear night sky, enjoying the wash of white moonlight and the twinkle of stars against an ebony heaven, when he'd grabbed her, tearing her dress in the process. He'd been drunk and angry and beyond reasoning. That's what had frightened her. The absence of reason.

But the look on Gabe's face as they sat opposite each other at the Candleberrys' kitchen table frightened her more than anything Danny had said or done.

"Gabe."

He stared at his hands, palms up. "I could've killed him."

"But you didn't."

He looked at her. "I reacted in violence."

"You came to my aid."

"I haven't changed." He got up and walked to the window. "I'm supposed to act like Christ would act. I'm supposed to act in love. Jesus didn't strike out. He didn't lose Himself in rage or try to hurt His fellowman. He wasn't a constant failure at everything He did."

"Neither are you."

"It would have been better for everyone if I'd never come back."

His words cut like a sword through her heart.

"All I'll ever do is disappoint you." He hesitated, then added, "And disappoint God."

"You're wrong. You aren't a disappointment to Him. He loves you more than you'll ever know."

He turned toward her.

She stood. "You'll never be a disappointment to me, either. I love you too."

The door opened, drawing both their gazes. The sheriff stepped inside. He looked briefly at Akira, then toward Gabe. He removed his hat. "You okay, Talmadge?"

Gabe nodded.

"This incident could hurt your parole."

"Yeah."

"But I don't think it will. Peck was drunk as a skunk, and enough folks saw your wife's torn dress—" He nodded apologetically at Akira. "Sorry." He looked back at Gabe. "I figure most folks understood why you did what you did, even if they didn't approve of the way you did it."

"Then we can go home?" Akira asked.

"Yes." He put his hat on his head again. "Keep away from Peck. He's a fool and a drunk, and a drunken fool is dangerous." He bent his hat brim toward Akira. "Evening."

The door closed behind the sheriff, leaving Gabe and Akira in silence. She didn't know what to do. She didn't know if she should go to Gabe or stay where she was. She didn't know if she should speak or keep quiet.

Why did this have to happen, God? Why?

Chapter Eighteen

Hudson set aside the letter from Rupert, then tapped his chin with an index finger as he contemplated its information.

That Gabe had lost his temper and attacked a man—in front of nearly the entire town, no less—could prove useful. According to Rupert, Gabe hadn't been seen in town in the three weeks since the incident.

"Put your tail between your legs and ran away, didn't you, boy?" he muttered with disgust. "I said you'd never amount to anything."

He rose from his chair and strode to the window of his New York hotel room. He'd start home tomorrow, a week later than originally planned. He'd done everything he could here and in Washington. It was clear he would get no help from either the politicians or the men of business. It looked as though he'd have to do this himself.

And do it he would. Hudson Talmadge didn't like to lose. Ever.

He *would* obtain rights to the land north of the river's fork, and he *would* build a dam and create a reservoir. He *would* control water rights for hundreds of miles around. He *would* control the lumber industry in the region. See if he didn't. When the economy improved and people were once again building homes and farming the land, they—private citizens and government alike—would have to come to him for their lumber and water. And they would pay a premium for it too.

He stared at the busy street below. Men in suits and felt hats, briefcases in hand, walked swiftly along the sidewalks, their heads bent into a brisk October wind. Few women could be seen among them; he supposed it was too cold and windy for most shoppers.

If Pauline were here with him, she wouldn't let a little bad weather stop her from shopping.

Pauline...

He frowned.

Each time he'd called home, the maid had informed him Mrs. Talmadge was out of the house. He suspected that was a lie. But why would she risk lying to him? Rupert reported Pauline had paid a few visits to the Macauley ranch since Hudson left Ransom and that she'd attended church every Sunday. Since she was following his instructions to the letter, he saw no reason for her to avoid his calls. Yet there had to be a reason.

He muttered a few unsavory words in reference to his wife, then quickly forgot her. Right now, he needed to formulate a plan regarding land and water rights. Everything else had to take a backseat to that.

"Gabe. Please." Akira touched her husband's shoulder. "We need to talk."

He shrugged off her hand. "What is there to say?"

"We can't go on like this."

He didn't look at her. He hadn't met her gaze for more than an instant since the night of the barn dance. "Leave it be."

Father, how did this happen? Why has he retreated to that dark place again? Why can't he hear You? Why can't he hear me? And what can I do to reach him with my love?

She stood, then picked up her lunch plate. "Don't shut me out. I'm your wife." She left the table, crossing the kitchen to the sink.

She heard his chair scrape against the floor. Her heart fluttered. She waited, hoping…

Footsteps carried him away from her. The door opened and closed, and he was gone.

Tears blurred her vision. Were they caused by heartbreak or anger? She didn't know for certain. Perhaps both.

Day after day, they sat down to meals together and spoke hardly a word. Night after night, they lay beside each other in bed, not touching. They'd never spoken again of the night of the barn dance, of what Danny Peck had done to Akira, of the fight that followed, or of her declaration of love. Gabe had erected a wall so high and so thick she couldn't storm it.

The door opened again. She held her breath, hope flaring to life. She dashed away her tears, not wanting him to know she cried, then turned.

Jane Sebastian stood in the opening. "I saw Gabe. He told me to come on in."

Akira was nearly crushed by her disappointment that it wasn't her husband.

"You don't have to tell me," Jane said. "I already know what's going on. I can see it in both your faces."

A sob tore from her chest, a sound of anguish. She covered her mouth with the back of her hand.

Jane hurried forward, opening her arms wide, and Akira fell into them.

"There now. There now. Go on and cry it out." Jane stroked Akira's hair. "That's it. No shame in cryin'. No shame at all. The good Lord Himself cried. There. That's it. Let it out, dear child. Let it out."

And she did. She wept as she'd never wept before. She wept until she was spent and too weak to stand.

Gabe strode swiftly down the drive, not stopping until he came to the road. He looked south, away from Ransom.

How hard could it be to walk away from everything? To head

down that ribbon of highway? Away from everyone who knew anything about him? To disappear once again into the ranks of homeless men looking for work?

He'd arrived in Ransom with nothing. But now he had good boots on his feet and a coat to keep him warm, and his belly was full. He'd been a whole sight worse off before. If he left today, this moment...

FIGHT THE GOOD FIGHT OF THE FAITH.

He clenched his jaw. *I don't know how to fight a good fight. I only know how to fight with my fists, to fight to hurt. There isn't anybody who doesn't know that now. Not after what I did.*

He'd had murder in his heart the night Danny kissed Akira, and he understood that made him a murderer in spirit, if not in deed. Hud had been right about him all along. He wasn't any good. He wasn't ever going to be any good.

THERE IS NONE RIGHTEOUS, NO, NOT ONE.

He wished those scriptures would quit popping into his head. He didn't want to think about them. He didn't want to think about God. All it did was serve to remind him how he'd failed. He couldn't even control his own temper. He was never going to be good like Akira or Reverend Neville or Miss Jane.

HAVING DONE ALL, TO STAND.

He looked over his shoulder toward the ranch house. He'd hurt Akira, refusing to talk, walking out on her that way. He didn't want to hurt her, but he seemed helpless to do anything else.

You aren't a disappointment to Him. He loves you more than you'll ever know... Her voice was as clear in his head now as it had been the night she spoke those words. *You'll never be a disappointment to me, either. I love you too.*

He'd wanted to believe her, but he couldn't. He never would be worthy enough. Couldn't be. Not worthy of her love nor of God's. He was like the apostle Peter when he'd said to Jesus, "Depart from me, for I am a sinful man." Peter had known he was too evil to be near the Lord. And so was Gabe. Too evil for a holy God. Too evil for Akira.

BUT I DIDN'T LEAVE PETER AS I FOUND HIM.

Gabe felt something tighten inside him.

NEITHER WILL I LEAVE YOU, GABRIEL, MY SON.

"He blames himself." Akira wiped her eyes with the handkerchief Jane had given her. "He blames himself for everything that goes wrong."

"It takes awhile to shed the thinking of the world. Sometimes a long while. Most never manage to do it altogether. I sure haven't."

"He won't go to church. He's ashamed of what others think of him now." She stared at the cooling cup of coffee on the table before her. "He's accepted Jesus with one hand, but he clings to the past with the other. He still sees himself as a convicted murderer. How do I help him see the truth of who he is in Christ?"

Jane touched her shoulder, drawing her gaze. "You don't, child. That's the work of the Holy Spirit."

"But—"

"Don't attempt to do God's job. You won't succeed. Maybe the Lord's got another path for Gabe to follow than the one you've got in mind."

Akira's vision blurred again. "He doesn't want my love," she whispered hoarsely.

"Now that's got to be the most foolish thing I've heard in all my born days."

"No. It's true." She swallowed.

"Akira Talmadge, you quit talking nonsense this minute. Just 'cause a man has a hard time sayin' the words doesn't mean he doesn't feel it." Jane leaned forward, staring at Akira. "You hear me?"

"I hear."

"Now, you go wash your face so when he comes inside he won't know you've been crying. You show him your smile, and you love him right where he is, and you pray like you've never prayed before in your life, and then you trust God to work it out. He's got it all in control."

"I know." *But why does everything feel out of control, Father?*

"Go on." Jane stood. "Go wash your face. I'll take care of these dishes."

"You don't have to do that. I'll—"

"I'm a stubborn woman. Don't bother to argue with me when I'm in one of my moods."

Akira managed a flimsy smile in response, then did as she'd been told.

Once in her room, with the bedroom door closed, she knelt beside her bed, folded her hands, and prayed.

"Lord, I can't do Your work for You. Jane's right about that. I fail every time I try. I told Gabe You love him, but I confess it was me I wanted him to love in return. Only he's got to love You more, doesn't he? Because only then can he love me completely. So I'm letting him go. Right now. I'm giving him to You. Whatever You choose to do is all right with me. Not my will but Thine."

Gabe sat beside the river. The water was no more than two inches deep in this section. It gurgled and splashed over the smooth stones lining the river bottom. Sunlight danced across the water's surface, the flashes nearly blinding him with their brilliance.

THAT I MAY KNOW HIM…

The passages of Scripture wouldn't stop coming, no matter how much he wanted them to.

…AND THE POWER OF HIS RESURRECTION…

If only he understood what it all meant. If only he could piece together the wretched fragments of his life. On that morning he'd returned to Christ and accepted God's forgiveness, he'd thought it would all fall neatly into place. But it hadn't.

...AND THE FELLOWSHIP OF HIS SUFFERINGS, BECOMING CONFORMED UNTO HIS DEATH.

"Jesus," he whispered, overwhelmed by the feelings roiling inside him.

THAT I MAY KNOW HIM.

He covered his face with his hands. "Jesus, help me."

KNOW ME, GABRIEL.

Jesus?

I WILL LIFT UP MINE EYES UNTO THE MOUNTAINS.

He lowered his hands and looked up.

KNOW ME.

"I don't understand what I'm to do."

KNOW ME, BELOVED.

Dusk settled early over Dundreggan, a pewter cloak dropped upon a valley turned gold, red, and orange in the final days of October.

As the darkness of evening entered the house, Akira lit the kerosene lamps while continuing to pray. Her prayers consisted of the same words, repeated time and again: "Not my will but Thine, Lord. Not my will but Thine."

Cam alerted Akira to Gabe's return. The dog lifted her head and whimpered softly, looking toward the door. A moment later, it opened, and her husband stepped inside.

Their gazes met across the living room.

Akira felt lightheaded; her knees were weak. With joy? With relief? She didn't know, didn't care. All that mattered was that he'd returned.

Gabe closed the door, pushing it with the heel of his boot, shutting out the crisp night air.

She wanted to run to him, to hold him, to tell him she loved him. She didn't move.

"Akira," he said at last, "I'm sorry."

"No, Gabe, it's I who—"

"Please." He raised a hand, palm out. "Let me have my say."

She swallowed the rest of her protest.

"I'm sorry I've refused to talk, and I'm sorry I've refused to listen."

Not my will but Thine.

"I've been walking all this time. Walking and sitting, thinking and praying." He looked down at the floor, then up at her again. "I think God's been talking to me."

Tears burned her eyes.

He raked the fingers of one hand through his hair. "I don't know if this is going to make sense, but I feel like He's telling me to go up into the hills for a while. Just Him and me." His voice lowered. "So I can *know* Him." He took a step toward her. "But I'm not running away. Not from you. Not from the folks in Ransom. Not from Danny Peck and not from my father. Do you under-stand?"

She nodded, although she didn't understand. Not completely.

"You see, I think I've stayed in a prison of my own making. Even after Jesus set me free, that's where I've stayed. Because it was familiar. Because I was used to it. Because I didn't think I deserved anything better than that. But I don't want to stay in that prison any longer." He shrugged and shook his head slowly. "Sounds a bit crazy, I guess."

"No, it doesn't."

"You'll be all right while I'm gone?"

She couldn't speak for the lump in her throat, so she nodded a second time.

Several long strides reduced the remaining distance between them. He took hold of her upper arms, his grasp gentle. "When I get back…" He didn't finish the sentence, instead letting it drift into silence.

But there was a wondrous love shining in his eyes. He didn't have to say the words for her to hear them with her heart.

She threw her arms around his neck and pressed herself into his embrace. "I know, Gabriel. I know. Go with God. Go into the mountains, and come back to me at the proper time. I'll be right here waiting for you."

CHAPTER NINETEEN

Gabe had only been gone a few days, and already it seemed months. Akira almost wished she was still busy with canning or that it was lambing season or any season when there was enough work to keep her going from dawn to dusk. But early winter was upon them now, and while there was plenty to do on Dundreggan at any time of year, this November had far too many idle hours. Or maybe it was Akira's frame of mind that made it seem that way.

"'Tis a fine thing, yer husband leavin' ye alone," Brodie grumbled as Akira ladled hot cider from the kettle on the stove into a large ceramic mug. "Ye shouldn't have let him go, lass."

"Oh, my dear friend, I wouldn't have stopped him, even if I could. God called him away."

"*Ach!* I'll never understand ye and the way ye think."

Arriving at the table with the cider, she kissed his bewhiskered cheek. "You will one day. I'm praying for you, Brodie."

He grunted. "Ye'll not be makin' a saint out o' me."

"Nothing is impossible with God." She smiled at him.

"Mmm."

Cam rose from the rug near the stove and padded across the kitchen to stand near the front door. Her ears were cocked forward, her head tilted to one side as she listened intently.

Maybe he's back! Akira thought as she hurried to the window, looking out just as the chauffeur-driven automobile came into view.

"Who's come?" Brodie asked.

"Pauline Talmadge."

He made a sound of displeasure as his chair scraped back from the table. "I'll be going about my business, then."

"Brodie—"

"I was wrong about Gabe, but I'm not wrong about her. She's trouble."

Akira sighed. There wasn't any point in arguing with him. He'd made up his mind.

Brodie made a beeline for the door and was halfway to the barn before Pauline got out of her car.

Akira grabbed her sweater from the back of a chair and slipped it on, then stepped outside. She crossed her arms over her chest, shivering slightly. It smelled like snow, and the gray, overcast sky confirmed it was a strong possibility. Gabe could get snowed in at that old miner's shack if they got an early blizzard. Would he have enough food until the storm cleared? Did he have enough warm clothes? What if—

"As usual, Mr. Lachlan is less than pleased to see me," Pauline said, breaking into Akira's worrisome thoughts.

O ye of little faith, she scolded herself before moving her gaze from the cloudy heavens and turning it toward the bottom of the steps where Pauline now stood. "I was thinking it might snow."

"Eugene says it will."

Akira looked toward the automobile. "Would your driver like some hot cider? It's on the stove."

"He has a thermos of coffee with him. He'll be fine." Pauline came up the steps. "I hope you don't mind me dropping by this way. It would be nice if you had a telephone."

"You're always welcome." Akira motioned toward the door. "Come inside. It's getting colder as we stand here."

A short while later, they sat at the kitchen table, steaming mugs of cider before them.

"I wanted you and Gabe to know Hudson's coming home." Pauline pursed her lips, then added, "He should arrive by tomorrow night."

Akira didn't know what to say to that news. Her feelings about Gabe's father were confusing, to say the least.

"Things will be...different...once he's back."

Akira wondered how Gabe would react. Would it matter to him? He'd been angry about his father's involvement with the parole matter. Would his anger return, perhaps even worsen?

"Akira?"

She looked at Pauline.

"How does a person... No. How do *I* know I won't go to hell for the things I've done? For my...sins."

A shiver ran up Akira's spine, and her breath quickened. She might be witnessing a life about to change. It wasn't a moment to take lightly.

She reached out and laid her hand over Pauline's. "It's simple," she answered. "You've already taken the first step by acknowledging you've sinned. Now all you need do is accept what Christ accomplished for you on the cross. He died for your sins, covering them with His shed blood. Ask His forgiveness and then live for Him." She tightened her grasp. "If you'd like, I'll pray with you."

"I don't know." Pauline's gaze drifted toward the window, her expression taut, her eyes misty. "I don't know."

She's afraid, Lord. Open her eyes and heart.

"Maybe I shouldn't have come." She tried to withdraw her hand.

Akira wouldn't let go. "God's grace is sufficient. Whatever's troubling you, God knows what to do about it."

Pauline looked at her again. "Must I tell you what it is?"

"No." She smiled gently. "Just tell Him."

"Then I'd like you to pray, Akira. Before it's too late, I need you to pray."

The wind whipped around the corners of the one-room log cabin, causing tall trees to sway and bend before it. The sky was the color of slate and growing darker by the hour. The temperature had dropped a good ten degrees since noon.

Gabe pulled up the collar of his coat to protect his neck and ears before walking to the lean-to where his gelding was stabled. The horse stood with its back to the wind, head slung low and eyes closed. But it perked up when Gabe tossed several flakes of hay over the gate.

"Not much longer," he promised the animal. "A few more days is all."

The gelding snorted.

"Yeah. Guess I'd feel the same if I were living outside in this weather."

He returned to the cabin, thankful for the fire in the stove and the large stack of wood beside it. He poured himself a cup of coffee, then took a sip. It was bitter after sitting on the stove for hours, but he was glad for it, nonetheless. He sat down at the table, ignoring the wobble caused by the uneven legs.

His thoughts drifted to Akira. He'd missed her more than he'd expected to. He'd lost track of the number of times he'd discovered something new in the Word of God and wanted to share it with her only to remember she wasn't there.

He leaned back in the chair. "Thank You for the gift of Akira." As he spoke, he rested his Bible on its spine and let it fall open. "What have You for me this afternoon, Lord?"

He didn't begin reading. Not yet. Instead, he waited, trusting that God would speak to him at the proper time. He was no longer surprised by the Shepherd's voice whispering in his heart, conversing through the Scriptures, instructing him, guiding him, revealing Himself.

Last summer, after he'd sought God's forgiveness, he'd come to love the Bible. But now his love for this book had become something deeper still, something richer, wider, higher. Something…more.

"To *know* You," he said with a smile.

That's why he loved the Scriptures. Because they helped him know God.

Like a caress, a sense of warmth flowed over him. "Jehovah God, my Provider. The just and exalted One. The God who sustains me."

He sat silently, meditating on God's attributes.

And then, he thought of his own father.

THERE SHALL BE TRIBULATION…

The quiet words in his heart shook him, and he knew, without a shadow of a doubt, that there would be obstacles to overcome when he returned from the mountaintop, his father chief among them.

"Jesus," he whispered, not knowing how to pray, making the name a prayer in itself.

He turned his gaze upon his Bible. It was open to the book of Ephesians, chapter six. He began to read: *Put on the whole armor of God, that ye may be able to stand against the wiles of the devil. For our wrestling is not against flesh and blood, but against the principalities, against the powers, against the world-rulers of this darkness, against the spiritual hosts of wickedness in the heavenly places. Wherefore take up the whole armor of God, that ye may be able to withstand in the evil day, and, having done all, to stand...*

STAND, MY SON. STAND.

"I'm not afraid," Pauline whispered, her voice full of wonder. She looked up, meeting Akira's gaze, her eyes sparkling with tears of joy. "I'm not afraid."

Akira smiled and nodded.

"Thank you, Akira."

"Thank God."

"Yes. Thank God." She laughed softly.

Akira took hold of Pauline's hand again. "When you go back to town, you should stop to see Reverend Neville. It's important you tell him what's happened."

"I will. I promise." She looked toward the window. "I suppose I should go now. It's getting darker."

Akira rose from her chair at the same time Pauline rose from hers. Before she could take her first step, a wave of dizziness washed over her. She sank backward, missed the chair, and fell to the floor.

"Akira!"

Akira ran one hand over her face, feeling utterly foolish. "I'm all right."

Pauline knelt on the floor beside her and slipped a hand beneath Akira's head. "Are you sure?"

No, she wasn't sure, but she said, "Yes," in a weak voice, keeping her eyes closed and hoping the dizziness would soon pass.

"You're as white as a sheet. You'd better lie still. Should I send Eugene for Mrs. Wickham?"

"No. Give me a second or two, and I'll be fine."

"Has this ever happened before?"

"No."

"Look at me," Pauline ordered.

Akira did.

"Have you been feeling faint whenever you straighten suddenly? Has your stomach been queasy? Especially when you smell fried foods?"

"I guess so."

"I thought there was something different about you." Pauline grinned. "Mrs. Gabriel Talmadge, I suspect you may be with child."

"*What?*" Akira tried to sit up, but she began to black out a second time. She lay back, forcing herself to take long, deep breaths.

"Pregnant," Pauline said with finality.

"Pregnant," Akira whispered.

"Won't Gabe be surprised?" She paused, then said, "Come on. Let's get you to bed."

With thoughts whirling madly in her head, Akira was scarcely aware of Pauline helping her up from the floor and walking her to the bedroom.

Won't Gabe be surprised? That was an understatement. Surprised and...and what?

O Lord, is it possible I'm really with child? If I am, will Gabe be happy about it? What if—?

No, she decided, stopping herself abruptly. She wouldn't question the Almighty about this. If He'd given them a baby, then that meant now was exactly the right time.

CHAPTER TWENTY

Hudson's return to Ransom was delayed two days by the early season snowstorm. He'd hoped to make use of his unexpected stay in Boise by wining and dining Quincey Fortier, but the senator, he'd been told, was unavailable.

"Unavailable," Hudson muttered as he drove the Duesenberg up the drive to the Talmadge mansion. "Fortier's a coward *and* a liar."

Even as he spoke those words, he had the oddest feeling he'd lost his grip on something vitally important. Which only served to make him angry. He was a self-made man. He determined his own destiny. He decided what was important, and then he did whatever was necessary to bring it to pass. And nobody was going to stand in his way.

The car fishtailed as it rounded an icy curve in the drive.

Hudson swore beneath his breath, his anger building with each passing second. There hadn't been a blasted thing that had gone right for months now.

He stopped the car in front of the house. The main door opened and Eugene Holcomb, Pauline's chauffeur, appeared. He came down the steps two at a time.

"Welcome home, Mr. Talmadge," Eugene said as he opened the door of the Duesenberg.

"Bring in my bags." He got out of the car. "I'll need my brief-case in my study right away."

"Yes sir."

Hudson's foot landed in a puddle of melting snow. He cursed again, loudly this time, then strode toward the front door. He found Pauline standing in the entry, as if waiting to greet him. She smiled hesitantly. He glowered back at her.

"Did you have problems on the road?" she asked, her smile gone.

"What do you think?"

She took a step backward. "Can I have something prepared for you to eat? You must be hungry."

"Yes. Have it brought to my study. I have work to do." He swept past her.

"Hudson?"

Something in her voice caused him to pause. He glanced over his shoulder.

"I…I'm glad you're home."

He arched an eyebrow. "Out of spending money?"

She shook her head.

He stared at her a moment longer. There seemed to be some-thing different about her, though he couldn't put his finger on what that something was. It reminded him of someone else. Who?

With a shake of his head, he proceeded down the hallway.

As the door closed behind her husband, Pauline leaned against the wall. Hudson loathed her. That much was clear in his voice and in his eyes. What point was there in trying to be a good wife? He didn't care. He never had.

"But then, neither did I," she whispered. "All I wanted was his money."

The truth hurt. She didn't like seeing herself as selfish or greedy, but she supposed God couldn't change her until she confessed her faults.

She straightened and walked toward the kitchen. She would have the cook prepare Hudson a dinner tray. Maybe after he'd eaten, he would be in a better mood. Then perhaps she could find the courage to tell him what had happened to her while he was away.

A shiver coursed up her spine.

Tell Hudson she'd embraced Christianity? He would be furious, outraged. He had no patience with, as he put it, "weakminded sops who need a God to see them through life." She'd heard him say that often enough. He'd sent her to church to be his spy, not to find a savior.

Yet it seemed important she tell him. Perhaps it was something she'd heard the minister say from the pulpit several weeks before, something about Christ denying those who denied Him. She didn't want to be denied by the Lord.

And maybe Hudson would see the truth for himself. Maybe he would want the same joy she'd found, the same freedom, the same love.

Love.

How she had yearned for love in the years she'd been married to Hudson. She'd been starving and hadn't even known it.

Akira stared out the window, her gaze set upon the tall mountain peaks in the distance. Cold air seeped through the glass, and she instinctively crossed her arms against the chill.

A baby. Gabriel's child, growing inside her.

The wonder of it hadn't worn off. In fact, it seemed to increase with each passing day. A year ago, even less, she had thought her life complete. She'd wanted nothing more than this ranch, good friends, and the fellowship of her Lord. She hadn't sought a husband or children.

And now…

She placed the flat of one hand over her abdomen, marveling at the miracle of life.

"Mary pondered these things in her heart," she whispered, feeling an unexpected kinship with a woman who'd lived nearly two thousand years before.

Joy washed over her, all-encompassing, warming her. She closed her eyes and gave herself to the sensation.

"Thank You."

She imagined her grandfather, seated on the front porch, holding her baby in his arms. How he would have rejoiced in her happiness. How he would have celebrated.

In her mind's eye, she watched her baby—a son, she believed—growing into manhood, along with several brothers and sisters. She pictured them working the land beside their father, raising Dundreggan sheep, growing crops and harvesting them. Most importantly, she envisioned them knowing and serving God.

"Thank You, Jesus."

"Amen."

She gasped in surprise, her eyes flying open. She hadn't heard the door open or felt the rush of air announcing it. Yet there Gabe stood, a dark, short beard covering his jaw, his cheeks and nose bright red with cold.

She wanted to run to him, but she didn't. "You're back," she said, knowing it sounded inane but not caring.

He smiled, the expression gentle, even serene. "I'm back."

"I didn't know how long it would take."

"Neither did I."

"I was afraid it would take all winter."

"It didn't."

She took a step toward him. "You found what you went after." It wasn't a question.

"Yes, I found it." He paused, then said, "No. God revealed it, and I listened. Really listened." He removed his coat and hung it on the peg in the wall near the door. "I have much to tell you, Akira."

And I have much to tell you, she thought, her pulse quickening.

He came to her then, gathering her into his arms, holding her close against him. With his lips near her ear, he said, "God is faithful, even when we're faithless. I spent hours and hours up on the mountain, looking back over the years of my life, and I saw so many ways He kept calling out to me, drawing me to Himself. Even when I answered His call and returned to Him and knew He'd forgiven me, I didn't forgive myself. I think I wanted to be punished. I *needed* to be punished." His hand gently stroked her hair. "I didn't deserve all the good things He was pouring out on me. I didn't deserve you, so I purposefully built a wall between us. A wall made of my own guilt."

She swallowed the lump in her throat.

"If I got what I deserved, I'd be in hell," he said softly.

She suspected he was talking to himself rather than to her.

Gabe drew back. He cupped the sides of her face with his hands, tilting her head slightly until her gaze met his.

"Husbands, love your wives, even as Christ also loved the church, and gave Himself for it."

He spoke in a low voice, quoting the verses slowly and deliberately.

"That He might sanctify and cleanse it with the washing of water by the word, that He might present it to Himself a glorious church, not having spot, or wrinkle, or any such thing; but that it should be holy and without blemish."

He leaned down and brushed his lips against her forehead. She closed her eyes.

"So ought men to love their wives as their own bodies. He that loveth his wife loveth himself. For no man ever yet hated his own flesh; but nourisheth and cherisheth it, even as the Lord the church."

His breath, as he continued, was warm upon her skin.

"For we are members of His body, of His flesh, and of His bones. For this cause shall a man leave his father and mother, and shall be joined unto his wife, and they two shall be one flesh."

As his words faded into silence, he kissed her on the mouth, not with passion but with gentle adoration.

"I love you, Akira, and I'm grateful for the love you showed toward me when I was far from deserving." He drew back again, caressing her face with his gaze. "You've been an example of Christ's love toward me from the first moment we met."

"Oh, Gabe." She touched his bearded jaw, thinking she rather liked the way it made him look. "Gabriel, a strong man of God."

"Akira," he echoed softly. "My anchor."

For a short while, they stood in silence, looking into the other's eyes.

Then Gabe smiled, and so did she.

241

"I've lots more to tell you," he said, a hint of laughter in his voice, "but I can't remember what it is. It went clear out of my head when I kissed you."

"I have things to tell you too."

He drew her close again. "Let's let the talking wait until later. All I want to do now is hold you." He rubbed his cheek against the top of her head. "I'm going to be a different man from this day forward. A better man. I promise you that."

She nodded, deciding it could wait until later to tell him about the baby. She was content for now simply to love and be loved by this man, her husband, her heart.

Rupert had a great deal to report after Hudson's lengthy absence. Seated in a leather-upholstered chair before the large cherry wood desk in Hudson's study, he rifled through a stack of papers, reeling off figures and names associated with his many business ventures.

Hudson wasn't pleased with what he'd heard thus far. It seemed his life had been spiraling downward ever since summer.

He rubbed one hand across his face. "Yes, yes," he said, interrupting Rupert. "I've heard enough. You can leave all that with me to look over later."

"Yes sir."

"What about Gabe and that Peck fellow? Any further altercations?"

"No sir."

"Too bad. What do you know about Danny Peck?"

"He does odd jobs for whoever will hire him. Drinks whatever he earns, which doesn't seem to be much. He's not well thought of around town."

"How old a man is he?"

"Younger than Gabe, I'd guess."

There had to be some way he could take advantage of the bad blood between the two men, Hudson thought.

"Gabe hasn't been seen in town since the barn dance," Rupert continued. "He seems to have quit coming to church. At least Mrs. Talmadge hasn't reported him being there."

"Pauline's still going?"

"Yes sir. Regular as clockwork."

"Hmm." He glanced toward the closed door to his study.

"Sheriff Newton went out to the ranch for Gabe's last parole report."

Hudson muttered an oath. That blasted sheriff! What gave him the right to interfere?

Rupert cleared his throat. "I believe the sheriff is recommending the parole be discharged once again. He...ah...he seems to believe there was an error made. Because of the reversal, I mean."

"An error." That ever-present anger began to heat his chest.

"An error? By heaven, is a murder so easily forgotten these days? Does he get off scot-free for killing my eldest son?"

"Gabe did serve ten years, sir," Rupert answered quietly.

The comment was met with stunned silence. Then, with a sudden sweep of his arm, Hudson knocked everything within reach off the top of his desk.

"Ten *years!*" He rose to his feet, shouting, "Ten years is nothing! Max is dead, and Gabe is responsible for it. Those idiots on the parole board had better not go back on our agreement or I'll—"

The study door opened. "Hudson?" Pauline took two steps into the room, then stopped, looking from him to Rupert and back again. "What happened?"

"None of your business," Hudson snapped. "Get out!"

She paled but didn't move.

"Did you hear me, woman?" He moved toward her, his fist raised. "Get out!"

She fled as if pursued by demons.

Breathing hard, Hudson continued to stare down the hallway, fighting for control over his fury.

"Sir?"

"What is it?" He turned.

"Mrs. Talmadge was out at the ranch…at Dundreggan…again. Earlier this week. She…she seems to have formed a friendship with Gabe's wife. At least, that's what Eugene called it. A friendship."

Had Pauline betrayed him too, like the sheriff? Would she dare? Surely not.

"Go on home, Carruthers. We'll talk more tomorrow. Be in the office by seven. I'll want an early start."

"Yes sir," Rupert replied, a quaver in his voice.

Cowardly little weasel of a man.

At the moment, Hudson couldn't think of one good reason why he'd kept Rupert Carruthers as his secretary all these years.

With the coming of night and the burning down of the fire in the stove, the house had cooled. But Gabe barely noticed it as he lay in bed, holding his wife in his arms, her head resting on his shoulder. He loved the way she fit so perfectly against him. He loved the softness of her skin and the sweet fragrance of her hair.

If he died tonight, he would die a contented man.

How amazing! How his life had changed in a matter of months. It wasn't so long ago he'd slept beneath railroad bridges, clothed in little better than rags, eating whatever he could beg or scrounge. Before that, he'd known only the loneliness of a prison cell and the scorn of his guards.

Thank You. He kissed the crown of Akira's head. *Thank You, God.*

"Last Monday," she said.

"Last Monday what?" He kissed her forehead.

"Gabriel Talmadge, have you listened to a single thing I've been telling you?"

"Of course."

"Liar."

"Guilty as charged." He chuckled as he hugged her closer. "I'll repent tomorrow."

"It isn't funny, Gabe. I was telling you about Pauline."

He released a groan.

"That's unkind."

"I know, but I don't want to talk about—"

"She accepted Christ. You should be rejoicing. The angels in heaven are."

"Mmm."

Akira drew back and raised herself on one elbow. "It was real, Gabe. I prayed with her."

"I believe you," he said, stubbornly drawing her head to his shoulder once again.

She acquiesced, and for a long while after that, they lay in silence.

Gabe slowly stroked his fingers over her cascading hair, enjoying the silky feel of it against his work-roughened hands. Sleep and pleasant dreams tugged at him.

"I'll be glad when winter is behind us," Akira whispered, adding, "Spring is my favorite time of year."

"Mmm."

"It's a time of new things. Puppies and kittens. Lambs and colts and calves. Life renewed throughout the land. Trees dressed in green leaves and wildflowers blooming." She sighed. "But next spring will be the best spring of all."

"Uh-huh."

"I'm glad our baby will be born then."

"Mmm…me, too." His eyes flew open. "Wait. What did you say?"

"I said, I'm glad our baby will be born then. In the spring."

He sat up, slipping his arm from beneath her head. He turned toward the lamp on the nightstand, found the matches beside it, struck one and lit the wick. With the room bathed in light, he turned again to his wife. She was smiling the most beautiful smile he'd ever seen.

She nodded. "In the spring. Around the first of June, I think."

"You're sure?"

She laughed softly. "I'm sure." She sat up too. "You're pleased, then?"

"Pleased?" He whispered the word, knowing it didn't begin to describe it, knowing he lacked the vocabulary to properly say what he felt.

She touched the side of his face. "How good the Lord has been to me. How great are His blessings to His daughter."

And to me, God. He pulled her close. *More than I could ever have hoped or dreamed.*

"We ought to have an automobile," Gabe announced the next morning at breakfast.

Akira set before him a plate of scrambled eggs, fried bacon, and toast slathered with melting butter. "Horses have served us well up to now."

"You've never been pregnant before."

"True." She smiled as she settled onto her chair, the proposed car forgotten as thoughts of the baby intruded.

Gabe wasn't giving up that easily. "We're too far away from town or another ranch. We don't have a telephone. What if there was an emergency? We need a car at Dundreggan."

"There's the Wickhams' truck. They've said we can use it whenever we wish."

"We can't depend on that truck. It only runs about half the time. Besides, what if they decide to move on, maybe look for work in another sawmill?"

"Has Mr. Wickham or Mark said they want to leave? Nora hasn't mentioned a word to me about it."

"No. Nobody's said anything. I was just supposing."

She released a sigh. "Thank God. Charlie and Mark have proven to be good shepherds, and they get along so well with Brodie."

"I still say we need an automobile of our own," Gabe persisted, not allowing her to change the subject. "I know you don't have a lot of cash set aside—"

"We. *We* don't have a lot of cash set aside."

"We," he agreed, giving her a quick smile. "But I was thinking, there's got to be some broken-down vehicles around this valley somewhere. I could probably buy one cheap, then get it running again. I know a few things about engines. I used to work with my brother on his Coupelet."

She loved the note of confidence in his voice. Not for the world would she do anything to change it. "If you think we should, then we should."

"I'll ask a few folks at church on Sunday." He speared some eggs with his fork. "Winter's coming fast. I'll need to find a car and get to work on it as soon as I can. The roads won't be easy to travel before long."

"I'm glad we'll be going to church again."

He set down the fork without taking a bite. "Long as the weather holds and the roads are safe, it's where I plan for us to be on any given Sunday." He met her gaze. "Worshiping God with the rest of His people."

She smiled.

"Besides"—he grinned back at her—"we need to share the good news about the baby with our friends."

That ever-present joy welled up in her chest. "Yes," she whispered, blinking away a blur of tears.

Gabe was silent awhile, his smile fading. "I should probably tell Hud, too."

"Yes, you should. This is his grandchild. He should know." She felt a flutter in her heart as she spoke the words. Not fear, precisely, but something akin to it.

"Akira?"

"Yes."

"When I was up on the mountain…I believe the Lord warned me of trouble ahead. And it has to do with Hud." He raked his fingers through his hair. "I wish I understood more about my father."

"God will give you understanding as you need it."

"I hope you're right."

Pauline stared at her reflection in the mirror. The discoloration on her left cheek was an ugly purple, much worse than it had been last night, a few hours after Hudson struck her.

Her stomach rolled at the memory, and bile burned her throat.

It had happened so quickly. He'd asked her if she'd made friends with Akira, and she'd said she had. She had smiled as she'd recalled Akira praying for her. And then all she remembered was the pain that shot through her as she was catapulted from her chair and thrown against the dining room wall. She'd never known such terror as she'd felt at that moment. No one had ever hit her before.

She gingerly touched the bruise on her cheekbone where he'd backhanded her. There was a thin red scab forming near the corner of her eye where the edge of his ring had cut her.

"God, I'm supposed to tell the truth. But if I do, I'm afraid he'll lose control and kill me."

Tears flooded her eyes and spilled down her cheeks.

"I'm afraid," she whispered. "I'm so afraid."

She wished she could talk to someone, to Akira. But she couldn't. Hudson had forbidden her to leave the house. He'd forbidden her to use the telephone. She didn't dare defy him. Not with the mood he was in.

She rose from the stool at her dressing table and walked to the large window overlooking the valley. She could see Ransom from here, smoke curling above chimneys.

"Ransom," she whispered.

She pressed her forehead against the cool pane of glass.

Christ gave His life as a ransom for many.

She knew so little about Jesus, but she did know He loved her, had always loved her. He'd ransomed her. No one could take that away. Not even Hudson.

The fear began to ease a little.

"Whatever else comes," she said aloud, once again fingering her bruised cheek, "I *will* remember Your love for me."

CHAPTER TWENTY-ONE

Akira sat in the kitchen, the lamp in the center of the table casting a warm circle of light onto the blank stationery. In the living room, music—and a fair share of static—played on the wireless. Gabe reclined in an overstuffed chair, his long legs stretched out before him, crossed at the ankles. His eyes were closed, and every so often, she heard a soft whiffling snore. She found the sound oddly comforting.

She released a sigh as she glanced down at the blank sheet of paper. Then she picked up her fountain pen and began to write.

Dear Mother,

It has been far too long since I wrote to you last. There is no excuse for it, and I can only say I'm sorry. I hope this letter finds both you and Sidney in good health and fine spirits.

There is much to tell you. I scarcely know where to begin. Dundreggan sheep have done well despite the harsh drought. We lost less than 10 percent this season to disease and predators. Because of water from our spring, which

thankfully has not gone dry, the hay crop should be sufficient to see us through the winter and lambing. God willing,
the drought will break next year, and new grass will be available early.

Brodie Lachlan suffered an accident in midsummer. He
took a nasty tumble, injuring his leg, and was on crutches for
quite a spell. We hired two former millworkers, Charlie and
Mark Wickham, and they helped take the band to summer
range. They have proven to be excellent shepherds, and I hope
they will decide to stay on with us permanently. Mr.
Wickham's wife, Nora, is living in the large cottage. You would
like her. She is a very nice woman, though not in the best of
health. You should see the wonderful needlework she does.

She stopped writing, sighed while tapping the butt of her pen
against her chin, then pressed on.

Mother, I have wonderful news to share, and I'm certain no
one will be more surprised than you when you hear what it is.
I am now a married woman. I was wed in August to
Gabriel Talmadge.

She knew what Miriam Wisdom would want to know next.
Was Gabe the son of the town's wealthy founder, Hudson
Talmadge? And once Akira confirmed it, her mother would be
mentally counting Akira's potential fortune.

"Forgive me, Lord," Akira whispered. "I don't mean to think unkindly of my mother, but You know it's true. She cares about wealth and social standing more than anything. She was even embarrassed for anyone to know she was the daughter-in-law of Fergus Macauley, and Grandfather was the finest man I ever knew."

Another involuntary sigh escaped her.

No doubt you remember Hudson Talmadge. Gabe is his second son.

She saw no reason to say anything more. If her mother had heard any of the scandal surrounding Max and Gabe, she would be sure to bring it up herself.

Jane Sebastian and Brodie Lachlan stood with us at our wedding. We were married at the Ransom Methodist Episcopal Church by Reverend Neville. We chose to have a simple, quiet ceremony without other guests. However, our church family has been kind to us with their congrat- ulations and good wishes.

Akira could imagine her mother's facial expression when she read that paragraph. A simple wedding without guests? Then what was the point of getting married at all? One was supposed to make a statement by one's wedding.

"Oh, Mother. You and I aren't much different than Gabe and his father, are we? Why must it be this way? Why can't we love others the way they are instead of trying to change them into something else?"

She cringed, immediately condemned by her own question. Did she withhold love from her mother because of who Miriam was? She feared she did. At least a little. Or else she would have written this letter weeks ago.

I have saved the best news for last. God has chosen to bless Gabe and me with our first child. Our baby is due in June.

I hope you and Sidney will plan to come to Idaho for a visit around the time the baby is born. I'd like Gabe to know my mother and stepfather, and of course, we want you both to know your grandchild. I realize it isn't easy for Sidney to get away from the city for an extended time, but please try to come for a few weeks at least.

Her pen stilled, held a hairsbreadth above the stationery. She prayed silently, then wrote:

I love you, Mother. I know we've had our differences, and I know I didn't turn out the way you hoped I would. You wanted a debutante, and you got me. But where and how I choose to live doesn't change the fact that I love you. I appreciate all you did for me. I thank you for seeing that I received a good education and for caring about my future.

Give Sidney my love too. Please write soon. And think about coming to Idaho to be with me when the baby is born.

Sincerely,

your daughter, Akira

With his eyes half-closed, Gabe observed his wife as she addressed an envelope. The tip of her pink tongue parted her lips, and her brows were drawn together in a small frown of concentration. Her hair lay in a thick braid over her left shoulder.

"How did I get so lucky?"

She looked up, her gaze meeting his.

He grinned sheepishly. He hadn't meant to ask the question aloud.

"What did you say?" she asked.

He suspected she knew exactly what he'd said and only wanted him to repeat it. He obliged her. "How did I get so lucky?"

"There's no such thing as luck." She smiled. "Only God's blessings."

"Okay." He rose from the chair. "How did I get so blessed?"

"Just lucky, I guess." She laughed.

He cocked his head to one side. "You can be a contrary woman."

"Aye." She added a touch of brogue. "'Tis the Scot in me."

He stepped over to the Philco and turned it off. The house was plunged into silence. Then he walked toward the kitchen table, stopping behind her chair. He placed a hand on each shoulder and began to massage her muscles.

"Mmm." She closed her eyes. "You're welcome to do that as long as you like."

"Okay." He leaned over, kissed the crown of her head, continuing to knead her neck and shoulders.

After a lengthy silence, punctuated at intervals by more of her pleasurable moans, Akira said, "I wrote to my mother. I told her about the baby."

"Will she be glad?"

"I don't know." She sighed. "Probably."

"I want to be a good father."

She reached up with her right hand, covering his left one on her shoulder. Then she tilted her head to the side, holding their hands there. "You will be, Gabriel."

He thought of Hudson. "It's not as if I've got a great example to go by." He tasted bitterness on his tongue, not liking himself for giving in to it but helpless to stop its coming. "There'll always be somebody who'll want to remind any child of mine that his father's an ex-con."

"'There is therefore now no condemnation to them that are in Christ Jesus,'" she quoted before twisting on her chair to face him. "We can do all things because He strengthens us. That includes raising our child to be unafraid of the darts others might fling his way."

He caressed her cheek. "There's a lot of shame that'll go with being the son of a convicted murderer. People can be cruel. Especially kids. When he's old enough to go to school—"

"Then we'll teach him to forgive the unforgivable."

"You make it sound easy."

She shook her head. "I don't mean to. I'm sure we'll make plenty of mistakes." She circled her arms around his neck and drew his face toward hers. "But we don't have to repeat the ones our parents made." She kissed him lightly.

"I love you," he whispered against her parted lips.

She smiled. Her eyes glittered in the lamplight as she leaned back and looked up at him. "See? You've got nothing to worry about. Loving your child's mother is the first step toward being a great father."

Chapter Twenty-Two

"Praise be to God!" Jane proclaimed when she heard the news about the baby.

The older woman hugged Akira, nearly crushing the breath from her lungs. Then Jane repeated the action with Gabe. In moments, word ran through the members of the congregation, and more folks came to congratulate the happy couple. Men shook Gabe's hand and slapped him on the back. Women hugged Akira and kissed her cheek.

Watching the men congratulate Gabe caused Akira's heart to well with indescribable joy. Their acceptance of Gabe—despite what had happened the night of the Candleberry barn dance—revealed their hearts. Truly, a tree was known by its fruit, and the tree called Ransom Methodist Episcopal Church was bearing good fruit this morning.

"Akira," said Wallis Greer, known far and wide as the best seamstress in the valley. "You must come to my home before the baby arrives. When my sister moved away, she left a trunk full of infant clothes. She would be pleased as punch if you'd make use of them. I know she would."

Thomasina Attebury leaned forward. "I have a lovely perambulator my father brought from England when I was a mere baby myself. It's gathering dust in my attic. Goodness knows, those children of mine seem to have no intention of making me a grandmother."

Akira imagined strolling around Dundreggan in her overalls and floppy-brimmed straw hat, pushing a black baby carriage. It made an amusing picture in her mind, but she swallowed her laughter lest she offend Thomasina.

"God willing," Violet Neville said, "we'll have a new doctor in Ransom before your child is born."

"Amen to that," Jane responded.

"Goodness." Thomasina shook her head. "In my day, women didn't have doctors fussing over them when they gave birth. Why, when my oldest boy was born…"

Akira knew she would be listening to several stories of other women's childbirthing travails before she left for home.

Standing at the back of the church with several other men, Gabe waited for one of them to answer his question regarding old automobiles.

Richard Martin scrunched up his face in thought and tapped

his chin with his index finger. Then his eyes widened and he grinned. "I know. Looney Lindy. That's who you need to see."

"Looney Lindy?" Gabe echoed, glancing from Richard Martin to Simon Neville to Zachary Sebastian. "Who's that?"

"Lindy Jones." The reverend frowned at Richard. "She's a widow woman who lives up on Bobcat Mountain with her children. Never comes to town, not even when her husband, Ned, was still living."

"She's a strange one," Zachary offered. "There's no getting around that."

"I hear Looney Lindy's got a bunch of old cars 'round her place." Richard studiously ignored the reverend. "Don't any of 'em run, more'n likely. Her husband was a worthless cuss who never had two cents to rub together, but he did like to collect things. He was forever draggin' junk back to that place of theirs. Don't know if she'd be willin' to sell any of them. Zach's right—she's a strange one."

"Where exactly is Bobcat Mountain?"

Zachary pointed out the window. "South of your place, maybe another ten, fifteen miles by road, I suspect."

"The word 'road' is a generous term." Richard released a derogatory laugh.

The others nodded in agreement.

Zachary explained, "It's more of a trail than a road. The Joneses didn't ever much care for visitors. Liked to keep to themselves."

"Well," Gabe said, "I haven't got anything to lose by going to see her."

"Unless Looney Lindy tries to shoot you," Richard commented dryly. "She's a crack shot with that rifle of hers. Or so I've heard tell."

"I'll keep that in mind."

Zachary patted Gabe on the shoulder again. "I'd better haul my sister away from Akira and get us back to the farm. The sky's starting to cloud over. Could be in for more snow."

Simon rubbed his elbow. "My joints say you're right about that."

A short while later, the church had emptied of all but Gabe and Akira.

He looked across the sanctuary to where she was standing near the window. She met his gaze. He smiled. She smiled back.

"They're good folks," he said.

"That they are."

He moved toward the center aisle between the two columns of pews.

She did the same.

He embraced her.

She hugged him close.

"It's time for me to go see Hud," he whispered into her hair.

"I'm going with you." She pressed her cheek against his chest.

"I think you should wait here."

"Think what you like. I'm going."

He sighed. They'd had this discussion before coming into town. He hadn't won the first round. He didn't suppose he'd win this one, either.

"Besides," she added, "I want to see Pauline. Mrs. Neville says this is the first Sunday she's missed in weeks."

"Okay," he said, resigned. "Let's go."

He took her by the arm and escorted her outside.

"Sir?" came the butler's voice from the hallway.

"What is it?"

The study door opened a fraction. "You've got callers."

"Callers?"

"It's your son, sir. Gabe. And his wife, too. I showed them to the drawing room."

Gabe and Akira? Here?

Hudson rose from his leather desk chair, wondering about this unexpected visit. It could be they'd come to their senses and were ready to sell Dundreggan, but he suspected not. Akira Macauley was as stubborn as her grandfather before her.

"Tell Mrs. Talmadge to come down from her room," he told the butler. "Then get our guests something to drink. I'll be out shortly."

"Right away, sir." The door eased closed.

Hudson flicked at an imaginary piece of lint on his jacket, his eyes narrowing as he mulled the various possibilities that might have brought Gabe to his door. Maybe he'd come to ask his help in discharging his parole. After the Peck incident, he would need all the help he could get.

"Well, he won't get it from me," he muttered, adding a few coarse words for good measure. Then he frowned. His influence with people of power had waned over the summer. Much as he hated to admit it, he doubted he could help Gabe even if he wanted to, which he didn't.

He opened the door and listened for Pauline's footsteps. He hadn't long to wait. She knew better than to defy him again.

He left his study and crossed to the base of the stairs. She hesitated briefly when she saw him. A flicker of fear flashed in her eyes, and her complexion paled. He liked the reaction.

"Come along, Pauline," he said softly. "We have guests awaiting us."

She continued her descent.

He took hold of her arm above the elbow, tightening his grasp a little more than necessary. "Remember your loyalties, my dear."

She didn't look at him, didn't acknowledge his comment.

"Remember your loyalties," he repeated as he propelled her forward.

Gabe's last visit to his father's house hadn't ended well. For an instant he wondered if he'd done the right thing, coming here today.

As if reading his thoughts, Akira squeezed his hand, offering silent comfort and encouragement.

He might have spoken to her if his father and Pauline hadn't entered the room right then. They stopped just inside the entrance.

Gabe stood, his gaze locked with Hudson's. It seemed vitally important that he not be the first to look away. His father thrived on finding a person's weakest point and then attacking. Gabe was determined to show no weakness. Otherwise, there was no hope Hudson would listen to what he'd come to say. If it was a battle of wills his father wanted, he would get it.

"We missed you at services this morning, Pauline," Akira said.

Her voice broke the silent battle between the two men. Both of them looked at her.

She smiled at her father-in-law. "Good afternoon, Mr. Talmadge. You're looking well."

There was true moral courage, Gabe thought, feeling ashamed of himself. Unlike him, Akira wasn't out to prove anything. He wondered if Hudson recognized grace when he was looking at it.

"What brings you here?" Hudson asked gruffly. "Money trouble? Or is it that business with Peck I heard about?"

"Neither one."

Hudson escorted Pauline to the sofa. She sank onto it, never raising her eyes from the floor. There was something about the way she moved, about the way she looked...

What was it that bothered Gabe about Pauline? When Akira squeezed his hand again, he knew she'd noticed it too.

"Well?" Hudson sat on the end of the sofa.

Gabe glanced over his shoulder, locating a pair of brocade chairs. He motioned for Akira to take the one closest to the fireplace, then he sat in the other. *God, help me,* he prayed silently.

"You're wasting my time, boy. Speak your peace or leave."

Gabe nodded. "I know we parted on hard words last time I was here."

Hudson grunted, a sound of affirmation.

"Look, I know we can't undo the past, but I...*we,*" he amended, glancing at Akira, "hope we can make things better between us in the future." He took hold of her hand. "You know, of course, that Akira and I are married."

"So I heard. What's it to me?"

Akira placed her free hand on Gabe's shoulder. With a slight shake of her head, she stopped him from answering. Then she turned toward Hudson, saying, "Mr. Talmadge, you're going to be a grandfather. Next June. We wanted you to know. We hoped you might—"

"How do we know it's his child?"

Gabe whipped his head toward his father. *"What?"*

"It's a simple question. How do either of us know it's your child? Women throughout the ages have cuckolded their husbands. She could have done it to you." He leaned back on the sofa and crossed one leg over the other. The right corner of his mouth lifted in a self-satisfied smirk.

MOTHER.

One simple word, and yet he understood the meaning. Gabe's anger quieted, calmed by the Spirit's voice speaking to his heart.

"You're talking about my mother, aren't you?"

Hudson's grin vanished.

Gabe stood. "You're talking about me." He spoke softly, wondering why he'd never guessed it before. It explained so much.

A kaleidoscope of memories flashed through his mind, the countless times Hudson had called Max "son," and the endless times he'd called Gabe "boy."

"That's why you've hated me."

Hudson stood. "She lied. Right to the bitter end, she said you were my son. But I knew better. She couldn't fool me with her pious ways. She loved that preacher. I could see it every time she was with him. She loved him, not me."

Gabe felt pity for Hudson Talmadge, a pity so strong he thought it might break his heart.

"I should have put you in an orphanage," his father went on. "Max would still be alive today if I had. You killed my wife, and then you killed my son."

Gabe turned toward Akira. "We should go."

She nodded as she rose from the chair. There were tears on her cheeks.

"You're no good," Hudson ranted, his voice rising. "You're no good. I never should've let you carry my name. I should have let you die with her. You can hide behind religion all you want. Won't change a thing."

Gabe met Hudson's gaze. "You're right. Religion doesn't change a thing. But knowing Christ changes everything." He took hold of Akira's arm and drew her close to his side. "Knowing Jesus saved me from what I was."

Hudson called him a foul name.

"Maybe that's what I was," Gabe answered quietly. "Once. But I've found something better." He extended one hand in a gesture of supplication. "You could know that same peace, if you chose to."

"Get *out!*"

Gabe glanced at Pauline. She was still staring at the floor, her expression taut. "I'm sorry," he said, although he doubted she knew he spoke to her. Then he escorted Akira out of the Talmadge mansion.

Akira prayed in silence for a long while, seeking peace in her spirit. Finally, she looked at her husband, seated beside her in the wagon.

"He loved your mother," she said softly.

"I don't think he knows what love is."

"Not as we know it, no. But as much as he is able." She laid her hand on his forearm. "He loved her, and he was jealous of her devotion to something or someone other than him. It wasn't the preacher who was the problem. It was your mother's love of Christ—that's what he was really jealous of."

Gabe stared into the distance, squinting his eyes against the harsh gray light of a cloudy day. "What if she *was* unfaithful?"

"That's useless speculation. Would it change who you are, either way?" She sighed. "And besides, I don't believe it's true. Like it or not, I can see your father in you."

"No, I'm not sure I like it." His scowl deepened. "There's a part of me that hopes I'm not his son. I'd almost rather believe my mother was an adulteress, that there's another man out there who fathered me."

"Forgive him, Gabe. For today and for all the years gone before."

The silence that followed was punctured only by the creaking of the wagon wheels and the clomping of the horses' hooves against the hard surface of the road.

Father God, only You can heal the hurts life sends our way. Gabe and I have put all our hope in You. If You don't help us, no one can.

"All those years," he said at last. "All those years I wondered why I could never measure up, why I wasn't as good as Max. No matter how hard I tried, no matter what I did, Hud never approved of me, never praised me. Now it begins to make sense." He looked at her, his eyes filled with sorrow. "It even makes a crazy kind of sense why he accused me of murdering my brother, why he wouldn't believe it was an accident."

She nodded, the lump in her throat making it impossible to speak.

"Back there, when we were at the house, I pitied Hud more than any man I've ever known." He cleared his throat. "I've lived with drunks and thieves and men dressed in rags in the dead of winter, but it occurs to me they were all better off than my father. There he is, in that fancy mansion of his, with a fine car and a bank full of money and servants to tend his every need. But all I can feel for him is pity because he's got nothing that matters."

"Nothing," she whispered.

He turned his gaze forward again, saying, "He'd hate being pitied almost as much as he hates me."

Chapter Twenty-Three

A bitter wind bent the tall row of poplars, whistling an eerie melody through the leafless branches. Standing beside Brodie and Gabe near the stack yard, Akira turned up the collar of her coat before stuffing her hands into her pockets.

"Ye'll need to bring the sheep to the feed yard by December, lass. Those lower pastures won't support them until January. The grass is near gone."

"But have we enough hay to see us through to March if we bring them in early?"

"Aye. I believe so."

"How can you tell?" Gabe asked.

Akira answered before Brodie could. "It normally takes six hundred tons of hay to winter feed a band of two thousand before the spring grasses come in. Our alfalfa fields did well this year. We've more than that here."

"'Tis irrigation that saved the crops," Brodie interjected. "Dundreggan's underground springs have never run dry."

Akira continued, "The question is, how much more feed than usual will we need?"

"There's no answer for that, lass. And what choice have ye, enough or not?"

"None, I suppose." She glanced over her shoulder, looking toward the Wickham cottage. "Mrs. Wickham will be glad to have her menfolk at home again."

After turning the bucks loose with the ewes for five weeks after their return from summer range, the band had been driven to the southernmost grazing lands. It wasn't far in terms of miles, but far enough to require the shepherds to live in their sheep wagon.

Akira turned to Gabe. "Maybe you and I should relieve Mr. Wickham and Mark for a week or two."

He looked surprised by her suggestion.

"When I was a girl, I loved to accompany my grandfather. I thought it grand fun, cooking meals in a Dutch oven over a campfire and sleeping on those tick mattresses inside the wagon. Or under the stars when the weather permitted."

"I'd say it's too cold for that now."

She nodded but wasn't dissuaded from her pleasant memories. "I loved walking about with Grandfather's staff in hand, calling commands to the dogs." She grinned. "I even learned to use a slingshot. I'd pretend I was David of the Bible. Sometimes, I'd sit up late into the night, slingshot in hand, waiting for a lioness to attack the sheep so I could slay it with a pebble. It never happened, of course. Grandfather always ended up putting me to bed after I fell asleep."

"Ye'll not be going out with the sheep in your condition, lass. Not with winter hard upon us."

"Lachlan's right," Gabe chimed in. "This isn't the time for that."

She sighed, knowing the men were right. She hadn't gone out with the sheep in years; she'd been too busy with the day-to-day business of running the home farm. And if she were entirely honest, she probably wouldn't find camping in the sheep wagon nearly as comfortable as she had as a child.

She shivered as another gust of wind cut through the fabric of her coat.

"You need to get inside." Gabe settled a protective arm around her shoulders. "I don't want you taking a chill in this weather."

All this coddling was going to spoil her rotten, she thought. Then she smiled, deciding she would enjoy it while it lasted.

Gabe looked at Brodie. "I'm going to ride out to the Jones's place. I'll be passing by the sheep camp. Do you need me to take anything to Charlie? Pass along any news?"

"I'll ride with ye."

Gabe chuckled as he gave Akira's shoulders a squeeze. "He thinks I'll get lost if I go on my own," he confided in a stage whisper, his lips near her ear.

"I know."

Brodie harrumphed.

"Actually, I'd be glad for your company, Lachlan. If the Widow Jones is as strange as folks say, I may be glad for it."

"She'll not shoot ye dead, if that's what ye fear." The Scotsman almost revealed a smile. "But she might wing ye if she gets a chance."

"Why, Brodie Lachlan!" Akira exclaimed, grinning at him. "You're actually teasing my husband."

"Ach! I never *tease*." He said the word with complete distaste. "'Tis a woman's tool, that." Before Akira could respond, he added, "If we're goin', let's be about it. I'll see to the horses." He strode away, only a slight limp evident.

"I knew it would happen," Akira said. "He likes you."

"I wouldn't go that far."

"But he does."

"Well, he won't if I keep him waiting." He gave her a quick kiss. "You get inside out of this wind."

"I will as soon as I've looked in on Mrs. Wickham. She's been rather listless the last week or two. I hope she isn't in for another bad spell."

"Take her some of your stew. It's good enough to cure whatever ails her."

She grinned. "Thank you, sir."

"You're welcome, ma'am." He gave her another quick kiss. "We'll try to be back before dark."

"I'll keep your supper warm."

He started to walk away.

"And Gabe?"

He stopped and looked back at her.

"Be careful."

He smiled, nodded, then headed for the barn.

Danny Peck looked at least a decade older than his twenty-five years, Hudson decided. Hard drinking did that to a man. He was about average in height and weight, probably average in appearance, too, when cleaned up. Right now he wasn't clean. His jaw was covered with dark stubble, and his clothes looked as if he'd been sleeping in them for weeks.

When sober, which he rarely was, he was said to be a skilled carpenter. He'd come to the valley about five years before. No family that anyone knew of. No friends, except the men he drank with in the bar. He was a loner. An angry loner. And a drunk.

"Have a seat, Mr. Peck," Hudson said in a cordial voice while motioning toward a chair.

Danny mumbled an indiscernible reply as he complied.

"I'm glad you came."

"The guy said something 'bout work."

Hudson caught a whiff of cheap alcohol. He wrinkled his nose in distaste. "Yes."

"Here at the mill?"

"Not exactly."

"What, then?" He hiccuped.

Hudson hoped Danny wasn't about to vomit on the Persian rug. "It's a personal matter," he answered.

"Like what?" Danny wiped his mouth with the sleeve of his shirt, then licked his lips. "You wouldn't have somethin' to drink 'round here, would you?"

"No, Mr. Peck," he lied. "I wouldn't." He leaned forward, placing his forearms on his desk. "I understand there's bad blood between you and my...son."

"Hey, listen. It wasn't my fault what happened. He tried to choke me. Should've been arrested, but—"

"Relax, Mr. Peck. I happen to agree with you."

Danny's eyes widened in surprise. "You do?"

"Yes, I do. And that's why I asked you here. I want your help in sending him back to prison where he belongs. The sheriff isn't going to do it, so it's up to law-abiding citizens like yourself to see it gets done."

"What could *I* do?"

Hudson rose from his chair. "I'm not sure. Yet. Nothing difficult. I'll simply let you know when I need some help. Things like keeping an eye on Gabe when he comes to town, trying to provoke him into another fight if possible. And, if I ask...well, to stretch the truth a bit. Would you be willing to do that?"

"I reckon I could." He wiped his mouth again. "If'n the pay was right."

"I assure you, the pay will be right. We'll start you at ten dollars per week."

"Ten?"

"Dollars. Per week."

"Just to pick a fight with your son and lie when you tell me to?"

"Yes." He narrowed his eyes. "Let me make something clear, Peck. If you tell anyone about our little agreement, you *will* regret it." He opened his wallet. "So do we have an agreement?"

Danny stood, rubbing his hands together in anticipation. "I reckon we do."

Looney Lindy and her children lived on a small clearing of land hewn from the side of Bobcat Mountain. Theirs was a hardscrabble existence, judging by the shack that served as a house, the small barn that looked near collapse, and the variety of junk that littered the surrounding area—cars, trucks, wagons, wheelbarrows, a tall stack of bricks, a rusty potbelly stove, a porcelain bathtub with one claw foot missing.

Brodie reined in his horse, and Gabe did likewise.

Cupping his mouth with one hand, the Scotsman shouted, "Hello in the house."

They had a lengthy wait before the door creaked open. A moment more, and a girl of about seven or eight years of age stepped onto the rickety front porch. She was wearing a shapeless dress made from a flour sack. Stringy, unwashed hair hung to her shoulders. Her legs and feet were bare.

"Is yer mother about, lassie?"

"She cain't come out right now. Whatcha want?"

Gabe nudged his mount forward. "I'm interested in buying one of these automobiles."

"Cain't none of 'em run."

"That's all right. I'd at least like to talk to her."

Without a word, the girl slipped back into the house and closed the door.

Gabe looked over his shoulder at Brodie, then dismounted.

After a minute or two—although it seemed longer with the icy wind buffeting him—the door opened and the child reappeared.

"Ma says you kin look if'n you want, but she's not sayin' she'll sell you nothin'."

"Fair enough."

Once again the girl disappeared inside.

"I guess it's okay to look them all over," Gabe said to Brodie. He tethered his horse to a wagon that was missing both of its right wheels, then headed for the nearest Model T Ford.

"You're a blessing," Nora said as Akira stoked the fire in the stove.

"I should have come sooner to check on you. That wind seems to be blowing right through those windowpanes."

"Heavens, girl. I'm not your responsibility."

Akira crossed to the bed. "You are as long as your husband and son are working for me." She tugged at the thick quilt, then tucked it snugly beneath Nora's feet.

Nora sighed. "I'm such a bother."

"Nonsense."

"I was hoping…" She let the words trail into silence.

Akira took hold of her hand. "I know."

"It's been hard on Charlie, having a sickly wife. He's been so good to me. Not a word of complaint. Not ever."

"I'll tell you what would make Mr. Wickham happy if he were here right now—he'd be pleased if you'd eat something."

Nora released a weak laugh. "You don't give up."

"Not easily. No."

"Then I'll eat some of your stew. If you promise to sit and keep me company while I do."

"It would be my pleasure."

Akira grabbed some pillows and placed them behind Nora's back. Going into the kitchen, she dished stew into a large bowl, then sliced the loaf of warm bread she'd brought with her and buttered it. Finally, she filled a glass with milk and carried the tray back to the bedroom.

"Here you go," she said, arriving at the bedside.

The expression on Nora's face clearly said she couldn't eat everything on the tray, but she dutifully lifted the spoon and tested the stew. "It's delicious," she proclaimed.

"Thanks." Akira sat on a nearby straight-backed chair.

"Where's your husband off to? I saw him and Mr. Lachlan ride out awhile ago."

"He hopes to buy an automobile from Mrs. Jones. The widow woman up on Bobcat Mountain."

Nora set down her spoon. "The one they call Looney Lindy?"

"Yes." Akira leaned forward, took the spoon, and placed it in Nora's hand, closing her fingers around the stem, at the same time giving her a stern look. "Eat."

The older woman obediently dipped the spoon into the bowl and brought another bite to her mouth.

"I don't know why they call her such a name," Akira continued. "She's a recluse, but there's plenty of folks who like to keep to themselves. If not for taking part in church services, I'd rarely go into Ransom myself."

"Have you ever met Mrs. Jones?"

Nora shook her head. "Never laid eyes on her. Not once in all these years. Her husband, Ned, died at least five years back. I believe he was a fur trapper by trade. Her oldest boy's been known to come into town now and again for supplies. Guess that's the only way any of us know she and her children are still living up on the mountain."

"Well, I hope Gabe finds what he wants up there. He's determined we won't be without a car."

"It's because he loves you."

Happiness flowed through Akira at her words. "I know."

"Gracious. Look at you blush."

Akira touched her cheeks with her fingertips.

Nora chuckled. "I'd nearly forgotten what it's like to be young and giddy with love."

"I didn't know it would be like this," Akira confessed, feeling her skin growing warmer still.

"It isn't like this for every woman. God has blessed you, my dear. He's showered you with blessings of happiness." Nora shook her head. "I must confess, I had my doubts about the union. I feared you were rushing into it, and…well…with Gabe's history…" Her sentence trailed off, unfinished.

Akira patted the back of Nora's hand, communicating with her touch that she understood. "God has His purpose for bringing Gabe and me together. So we have nothing to fear. Not from the past or from the future."

"I've been a Christian for as long as I can remember," Nora said after a lengthy silence, "and I don't think I've ever known a believer who trusted the Lord the way you do. You're blessed with that childlike faith we're all supposed to have but so few of us do."

Although she could have told the older woman of the many times she'd lacked faith, she decided it was better to let the moment pass. Akira could see Nora was growing tired.

She rose from the chair and took the tray. "You'd better rest. I'll look in on you again at suppertime."

"Thank you, my dear. I am suddenly done in."

"God keep you," Akira whispered as she slipped from the bedroom.

"Mrs. Jones?" Gabe rapped on the door with his bare knuckles.

It opened a few inches, and the same little girl peered out at him.

"I'd like to speak with your mother, please."

"She don't see nobody."

"I'd like to make her an offer on one of the automobiles."

The girl looked over her shoulder. "Ma?"

"Who is he?" came a gravelly voice from inside.

"My name's Gabe Talmadge," he answered without waiting for the child to repeat the question. "My wife owns Dundreggan Ranch. It's about halfway between here and Ransom."

"And who's the fella with ya?"

"That's Brodie Lachlan. My friend. He works with us."

His reply was followed by a lengthy silence. He glanced down at the girl standing just inside the door. She was shivering from the cold draft. He considered telling her to close the door until her mother decided what to do, but before he could act on it, the woman spoke again.

"Ask him in, Fern."

The girl opened the door wider. "Ma says you can come in."

"Thanks."

Gabe removed his hat as he stepped into the dim interior of the shack. He noticed several things: the floor was hard-packed earth, the air was thick with smoke from the wood stove, and something in the room smelled putrid.

It took his eyes a moment to adjust before he was able to locate Lindy Jones. She was seated in a wooden chair near the stove, her right leg—wrapped in a bandage—propped on a barrel. A rifle rested across her lap. Handy if she decided to shoot him, he thought. Her hair was as wild and unwashed as her daughter's. Perhaps it was only the poor lighting, but she seemed to have a wraithlike appearance. Gabe shivered involuntarily.

"If my Ned was livin', he wouldn't sell none of those cars."

"Mrs. Jones, I'll pay you thirty dollars for the green Tudor Sedan." He pointed. "The one over there. And I'd need to take some parts from the black one by the creek. Those would be included in the purchase price."

"Thirty dollars?"

"Yes."

"That'd see my young uns had provisions for the winter. I reckon Ned'd approve o' that." She leaned forward in her chair. "All right, Mr. Talmadge. You bring that money and take what you need. It's yours for the thirty dollars."

He put his hat on his head and turned to go. But something stopped him. He glanced back at the woman. "Mrs. Jones, are you all right?"

"All right?"

"Is there something...*anything*...I can get for you?"

She made an odd, strangled kind of sound in her throat. Then she said, "Ain't nothin' you kin do for me, Mr. Talmadge, but I thank you kindly for askin'." She turned her head, staring into a corner as she released a deep sigh. "Been a long time since anyone cared enough to ask. Long, long time."

The wind never let up throughout the day, continuing its mournful melody long into the moonless night.

Inside the house, in the safety and warmth of their bedroom, Akira lay in bed, listening as Gabe read aloud from the Bible. She supposed she should be concentrating on the words, but instead, she was lost in the pleasant timbre of his voice. It had a soothing quality. It made her forget the brewing storm outside. It almost made her forget there was anything beyond these four walls.

Gabe suddenly closed his Bible and set it on the bedside table. "Akira, I need to find a doctor."

It took a moment for understanding to work through her slumberous thoughts. When it did, she sat up. "Why?" She closed her hand around his arm, trying to quell her alarm. "Are you ill?"

"Not for me. For Mrs. Jones. Something's wrong up there. It's been nagging at me ever since Brodie and I left her place." He narrowed his eyes and shook his head slowly from side to side. "I can't explain it. I just know it's important I get a physician to see her."

"The nearest doctor's over the pass, up in Lovejoy. I don't know his name but George Edwards would know. You could try calling Lovejoy from his place."

Gabe nodded. "I'll ride over at first light."

"There may be snow by morning," she said as she glanced toward the window.

He took both of her hands in his. "Then we'll have to pray hard that it's not so much the doctor can't get through."

Chapter Twenty-Four

"I can't save the leg," Dr. Kirkland told Gabe. "And it's question-able whether or not she'll survive, even after it's amputated."

Gabe glanced toward the cot in the far corner of the cabin where the girl, Fern, sat beside her brother, a boy of about eleven or twelve. Ethan, his mother had called him. The boy had one arm around his sister's shoulders, and Gabe could see he was trying hard to comfort her while pretending he wasn't afraid himself.

"I reckon it's me you oughta be talkin' to, Doc," Lindy Jones said in that gravelly voice of hers.

Dr. Kirkland held Gabe's gaze a moment longer, then nodded, and returned to the woman's bedside. He spoke softly to her, and Gabe knew the physician was doing his best not to be overheard by the children.

Amputation. He shuddered.

He glanced around the one-room shack with its dirt floors and tarpaper walls. He looked at the frightened, unwashed, painfully thin children. Then he turned his eyes upon their mother, lying on her bed, her putrefying leg elevated on a pile of rags.

It had been many weeks since he'd felt the darkness of despair himself, but he still recognized it. He knew it pursued Lindy Jones.

"I cain't leave my young uns. They ain't got nobody 'sides me t'look out for them."

"Mrs. Jones," the doctor said firmly, "if you don't have the operation, having no one is precisely what will happen to them. You *will* die without the surgery."

Fern began to cry. Ethan gathered his little sister in his arms and patted her back.

O God, Gabe prayed, *what would You have me to do?* Instantly, he knew the answer.

"The children can come to Dundreggan. They can stay with my wife and me until you're able to care for them again."

"We don't take charity, Mr. Talmadge. 'Specially not from strangers."

Filled with compassion, Gabe knelt beside the bed. "Mrs. Jones, I *am* a stranger to you. That's true. But I'm no stranger to pain and fear." He hesitated a second before adding, "Maybe that's why God sent me here. Not to buy an automobile but to help you in your time of need."

She closed her eyes and didn't answer.

"I think it was." Gabe tightened his grasp. "Mrs. Jones, I promise you, your children won't be in want. They'll be cared for…no matter what happens."

Tears trickled down her cheeks.

"We don't wanna go with him, Ma," Ethan said with all the belligerence of a boy trying to be a man. "We wanna stay with you. I kin take care o' you. And Fern, too. We been doin' all right up t'now."

"Mrs. Jones?" Gabe whispered.

She opened her eyes. "You've got no reason t'help us, Mr. Talmadge."

He glanced toward the children. He remembered what is was like to be twelve and motherless. He knew the awful feeling of being unloved and unlovable.

Then he thought of Akira, kneeling in the road beside a starving, unwashed tramp. He thought of how she'd reached out to him, even after she knew who and what he was, never judging him, never condemning him. He remembered how she'd shared God's love with him long before she'd learned to love him as a woman loved a man. He thought of how God had used Akira to draw him back into the arms of the Father. He remembered the boundless grace, the unmerited forgiveness, the faithfulness of God despite his own faithlessness.

"You're wrong, ma'am." He leaned toward her. "I have more reasons to help you than anyone will ever know."

Hudson stared at the report with a growing sense of panic. Another bank had closed, and this one had taken a sizable chunk of Talmadge money with it.

"Didn't we have any warning?" he barked at Rupert.

"Yes sir."

"*Well?* Why didn't you *tell* me?" His voice rose with each syllable.

The man blanched. "I did tell you, sir. I cabled you in Washington." He pointed. "And…and I brought that file to your home upon your return. Remember?"

Fury pounded at his temples, nearly blinding him. His world was spiraling out of control.

Everything he'd wanted.

Everything he'd worked for.

It could all be lost.

"Get out," he murmured.

Rupert didn't reply. He just left.

His eyes closed, Hudson rubbed his temples with the tips of his index fingers.

How could so many things go wrong all at once? At the beginning of the summer, all had been well. He had weathered the worst of the Depression. He'd added to his properties. He'd cut jobs, cut salaries, hiked prices in all the stores that belonged to him.

He swiveled his chair around, rose, and stepped to the window, gazing out at the pewter-toned day.

If he owned all the land south of Ransom, if he controlled the water rights to the better part of two counties, then Senator Fortier would start taking his calls again. How dare that sniveling weasel of a man think he could ignore Hudson Talmadge? Hadn't Hudson put him in office? Didn't he *owe* Hudson for his position of power?

He swore violently as he slammed his fist down onto the window sill.

Gabe. Gabe and that Macauley woman. They were the reason for all of this—their stubborn refusal to sell.

He would have that land, and he didn't care what he had to do to get it. He would own Dundreggan, and he would see Gabe back in prison where he belonged.

Hudson Talmadge never lost.

Never.

Akira looked at the two children—the boy sullen, the girl frightened—and her heart went out to them.

"I didn't know what else to do except bring them here," Gabe said softly.

"Of course you brought them home. Poor dears."

"I doubt Ethan'll care much for your sympathy. I get the feeling he's been taking care of his mother and sister for a good share of his life and figures he's man enough to keep right on doing it."

Akira nodded as she looked into the boy's wizened eyes.

She drew in a quick breath, saying a silent prayer for wisdom, then walked slowly toward the children. "I'm Mrs. Talmadge. I'm glad you've come to visit. Would you like something to eat? You must be hungry."

Fern looked at her brother, as if seeking permission.

"I reckon it wouldn't hurt nothin'," Ethan muttered.

Fern looked at Akira again and nodded rapidly.

"Good." Akira smiled. "Come right over to the table. I've got a pork roast, fried potatoes, creamed peas, and fresh baked bread just waiting to fill you up."

Lord, please let me have prepared enough for these extra mouths. I wasn't expecting company. Multiply my loaves and fishes so there's plenty for these hungry children to eat.

"Ethan, why don't you and your sister wash up at the sink and then sit there." She pointed toward two chairs.

The children looked confused by her suggestion. Akira wondered if anyone had ever asked them to wash their hands before eating.

Gabe must have had the same thought. "If you don't mind, I'll wash up first."

He strode to the sink, picked up the bar of soap and, adding a little hot water from the kettle on the stove to the cooler water in the basin, worked it into a lather. After rinsing his hands, he dried them on a towel.

It was obvious to Akira that he did it all slowly so the children would be able to emulate him when he was through.

Glancing over his shoulder at them, he said, "Your turn." Then he looked at Akira. "What can I do to help you?"

She wanted to kiss him for his thoughtfulness. *He's going to make a wonderful father.*

"Akira?" He raised an eyebrow.

"Sorry," she said, smiling at him, loving him more by the minute. "Would you mind taking the roast from the oven? I'll get the vegetables."

Later, as day drew to a close, Akira made beds for the children on the floor of the living room.

"We had a couple of dogs once," Fern said as she was tucked in. "They died."

Akira followed the girl's gaze to where Cam lay on the rug before the front door.

"They was hounds for huntin'." Ethan's tone was derisive. "Workin' dogs."

"Oh, don't let Cam's pretty looks fool you. She's a working dog. She's the best on the ranch. But she's also one of my best friends, so I like to keep her near me."

The boy grunted.

"Well, one thing's for certain." Akira suppressed a smile as she straightened. "Nothing gets in or out of this house without going by Cam. So you two don't have to worry about sleeping in a strange place. Cam will keep you safe."

"Don't need no help from no fancy dog. I kin keep me 'n' Fern plenty safe."

"I'm sure you can, Ethan. I'm sure you've taken great care of both your mother and your sister since your father passed on. But it's okay to accept help now and again too. This is one of those times."

The boy muttered something unintelligible, then turned his back toward Akira and jerked the blankets up over his head.

God, bless them and keep them. And, Lord, keep their mother in Your tender care, as well.

The kerosene lamp on the table near the bedroom door had been turned low. It cast a pale circle of light, enough for Gabe to see the children lying beneath blankets on the floor when he came in from his evening chores.

He gave Cam a pat on the head. "Keep an eye on them, girl," he whispered. Then he walked silently toward the bedroom.

Akira, clad in a white nightgown, was standing before the mirror. She caught sight of his reflection and turned toward him as he closed the door.

"Did they go to bed without trouble?" he asked.

"Yes, but Ethan's angry about being taken from his home. He's trying so hard to prove he's a man. And Fern… Well, she's frightened."

"I doubt she's been off that mountain in her entire life. And from the pallor of her skin, I'd say it's been a long while since she spent much time outside the four walls of the shack they live in."

He shook his head. "Maybe Lindy Jones really is looney. She should've sent for help long before now."

His chest felt heavy as he recalled the squalor he'd seen, as he remembered the look of despair in the woman's pain-filled eyes.

He walked across the room and took the hairbrush from Akira's hand. With a gentle pressure on her shoulder, he turned her away from him. He'd discovered a couple of months ago how much she enjoyed having him brush her hair, but if truth were told, he found equal pleasure in it. It soothed him somehow.

Tonight, he felt a great need to be soothed.

"Don't worry," Akira said softly, closing her eyes as he stroked her cascading tresses. "God will show us what to do."

He pressed his forehead against the back of her head. "I've known that kind of hunger, Akira. I've known that same kind of fear." He released a ragged breath, then straightened and resumed his brushing. "But I wasn't a kid when it happened to me. It's got to be a hundred times worse for them."

"They won't go hungry now."

"No." He sighed a second time.

"You're still worried."

He finally voiced the question that had been nagging him for most of the day. "What if their mother dies? The doctor didn't seem to think—"

"We'll cross that bridge when we come to it, Gabe." She turned toward him, gazing up into his eyes.

"But you didn't bargain for this when I went off to buy an old car. You didn't bargain for two possible orphan kids sleeping on your floor."

"No, I didn't." She smiled gently. "But then, I never bargained on finding a husband when I was out walking last summer either, and yet here we are." She wrapped her arms around him and pressed her cheek against his chest. "For all you know, you've brought home a miracle. Let's trust God and see what happens."

Pauline couldn't sleep. The night seemed too dark and ominous. The house seemed too cold. Her head was too filled with worries and fears.

She reached for her dressing gown, then sat on the side of her bed, sliding her feet into her house slippers before rising. She crossed to the fireplace and, leaning one forearm against the mantelpiece, stared for a short while at the glowing embers.

Hudson had been in a strange mood at supper tonight, she thought. It had been something worse than anger, worse than rage.

Involuntarily, she touched her face where he'd hit her four days before. The bruise had faded enough that she could hide it with the artful application of cosmetics. A few more days and all traces would be gone.

That was a lie. *All* traces would *never* be gone. The bruise would remain on her mind and soul.

"O God," she whispered.

That was it. That was her whole prayer. It was all she could say. She wondered if it was enough.

The Bible, she thought, straightening. *I wonder if we have one in the house.*

She doubted it, knowing the way Hudson felt about religion. But if there was a chance she might find a Bible, to read for herself, if there was a chance she might be able to find some answers...

Akira said a person could always find the answers in God's Word if she looked for it with an open heart.

Taking up the lamp, she hurried out of her room, moving as silently as possible along the corridors and down the staircase. The library was at the back of the house, a room she'd rarely entered since the house was built. There'd been little reason to. She didn't care much for reading.

With the library door closed behind her, Pauline turned up the lamp, throwing its golden light over the dark cherry wood book-cases that lined three walls of the room. She hadn't realized there were so many books. Hundreds of books. Ceiling-to-floor books. Books of all types and sizes.

Where would she begin? Was there any rhyme or reason to their placement? Perhaps it was useless to try.

She gave her head a shake, mentally chastising herself. She was going to look. She *had* to look.

Resolutely, she moved to the nearest bookcase. Holding the lamp in her right hand, she ran the fingertips of her left slowly over the spines of the books, reading the titles. First one shelf. Then another. And then another.

"What are you doing in here?"

She gasped and whirled about. "Hudson!"

"Well?" He stepped into the room.

"I—I was looking for something to read."

"You?"

She stiffened, retorting before she could think better of it. "I *can* read, you know."

"Can you?"

"Yes."

"Perhaps I can help you." He moved closer. "What exactly are you looking for?"

Her mouth was dry. Her knees were weak.

"Pauline?"

"I…I was looking for a Bible."

"A Bible?"

"Yes."

His voice was as cold as the November night. "And why would that be?"

"Well, you see"—she drew back against the bookcase—"Reverend Neville said something the last time I was at church that confused me. I was hoping to look it up for myself."

The lie came to her lips so easily, but on its heels came shame. She wasn't supposed to tell lies. She was sure of that. Lying was wrong. A sin.

"Hudson," she whispered, "that isn't quite the truth." She looked at him, hoping for understanding, for a shred of some sort of caring.

What she found was hatred, loathing, and…

Madness.

Chapter Twenty-Five

George Edwards brought news from Dr. Kirkland on Friday morning, two days after the amputation was performed on Lindy Jones at the small hospital in Lovejoy.

"He says to tell you she came through the operation, but it'll still take a miracle for her to survive."

"I believe in miracles, Mr. Edwards," Akira replied. "We'll keep praying for her. And for her children."

Lord knows, we could use a miracle with those kids, Gabe couldn't help thinking as he watched George drive away from the house a short while later.

Yesterday, Ethan had set out on foot, his little sister in tow, headed back to their home on Bobcat Mountain. Gabe wouldn't soon forget the mixture of anger and relief he'd felt when he found them traipsing along the road, Fern clutching the baby doll Akira had given her. Judging by the boy's unrepentant attitude, both then and since, Ethan was likely to try leaving with his sister again. Next time they might not be so easily found.

How do we get through to him? Gabe wondered as he drove the

team toward Ransom later that morning, a list of items to purchase, written in Akira's neat hand, tucked in his coat pocket. *We're
trying to help, and he's acting like we've kidnapped him and his sister.*

Maybe it was Ethan's age that had Gabe so concerned. He
didn't want to make any mistakes with the boy at this critical stage.
When Gabe was twelve, the choices he'd made had altered the
course of his life forever.

He frowned, thinking of his father—or at least the man he
believed to be his father—and wished he had the answers to all of
life's dilemmas, both large and small.

"Only, if I did," he said aloud, looking up at the wintry sky, "I
guess I wouldn't need faith in You, would I, Lord?"

Thomasina Attebury set a cup of coffee and a piece of gooseberry
pie on the table in front of Jane Sebastian. Other than Thomasina,
Jane was the only person in the River Restaurant.

"I heard Mr. Talmadge plans to close the Logger's Café."
Thomasina sighed before adding, "Maybe it'll help my business
some. Heaven knows I could use a few more customers, or I'll be
forced to close down myself."

Jane searched for something encouraging to say, but she could
think of nothing. The facts echoed in the silence all around her.

"There's even a rumor he's going to shut down the mill."

"Shut it down? *Completely?*"

Thomasina nodded. "Henry Teague told me so when he and Lilybet came for supper last night. Lilybet's afraid they'll have to leave Ransom like the Wickhams did."

"Well, the Wickhams didn't have to go far. Thanks be to God."

"And how many displaced lumbermen do you think Akira Macauley can employ as shepherds?"

"Akira Talmadge."

"Yes. Well. What does it matter? The answer's still the same." Thomasina rose. "Did you know Akira's got that crazy Jones woman's kids staying with her? Her husband brought them home with him earlier in the week. I hear Looney Lindy's dying. Leastwise if George knows what he's talking about, she is." She turned and walked away, mumbling, "So much trouble and heartache. So much trouble."

Jane stared at the slice of pie. Was the mill really going to close? If it did, there'd be more folks than just the Teagues who'd be leaving. Ransom could well become a ghost town in no time at all.

She took a bite of the pastry, but it didn't taste as good as she'd anticipated. Not because there was anything wrong with Thomasina's baking. No, Jane had simply lost her appetite for anything sweet and rich.

O Lord, she's right. There's so much trouble in the town. What can be done?

She didn't have to worry about her own needs. The Sebastian farm wasn't mortgaged, and they raised the majority of their own food. Her brother, Zachary, was a conservative man, and she was no spendthrift herself. They would have ample means to see themselves through leaner times. The same was true of Akira and Gabe and all who worked for them.

But there were many others, already suffering in these hard times, who would be devastated if the mill closed. Where would they go? Men were out of work all over the country. How would her neighbors and friends support their families?

Jane left some coins next to her plate to pay for her coffee and dessert, then rose from her chair. As she turned, the bell above the door tinkled, announcing another customer's arrival. She lifted her gaze to see who it was.

"Gabe," she said with a note of surprise.

"Hi, Miss Jane."

She smiled. "Good to see you."

"I ran into Zach a few minutes ago. He said you were over here, having a bite to eat."

"Come join me." She sank onto the chair. "You can finish my pie."

He crossed the restaurant to the table where Jane was seated. "Wasn't it any good?" he asked softly, looking at the dessert on her plate, then casting a quick glance toward the kitchen.

"It's delicious. I just—" She stopped abruptly. "It doesn't matter. Sit down, please."

He did.

"Is everything all right out at the ranch?"

"George's been talking, hasn't he?"

Jane nodded.

"Everything's fine." A small frown puckered his brow. "But I did come to see you for a reason. I need to ask you something." He dropped his gaze to the table. With his fingers, he turned the pie plate in a slow circle.

"What is it?" she prompted after a lengthy silence.

"You knew my mother. You were her friend." He met her gaze again. "Am I really a Talmadge or the by-blow of some preacher she knew?"

Jane gasped. "Where on earth...?"

But she didn't need to finish her question. She knew where he'd gotten such an idea.

Gabe hadn't meant for the question to come out quite that way. He touched the back of Jane's hand. "It's okay. You don't have to answer if you don't want to."

"Yes, I do. I should have told you long ago why your father acted the way he did toward you. I was wrong not to, but I kept hoping..." She sighed. "Gabe, your mother was not the sort of woman who would break her wedding vows. God alone knows why, but she loved your father. Deeply loved him. It brought her little but grief, far as I could see. Except for you boys." She smiled sadly. "She loved Max, and she loved you before she laid eyes on you."

Questions swirled in Gabe's mind, but he stopped himself

from asking them, believing it better for her to tell the story in her own way and at her own pace.

"Max was a toddler when your folks first arrived in the valley. Ransom wasn't anything more than a few farms and a general store where the old stage stop had been, but it didn't take your father long to start making changes. He worked all the time, seven days a week, from dawn to late into the night, building his mill, creating his empire."

Jane seemed to look at him, but Gabe sensed she was actually staring into the past.

"Hudson built Clarice a beautiful house. Nothing like the mansion he's got now, but beautiful all the same. That's when I came to work for her, doing housework a couple of times a week. She made that house a home, filling it with warmth and love. Never knew another person with a heart so full of love. At least, not until I met Akira." She sighed again. "And like your wife, your mother had a great love for God. Hudson never believed in anything except getting richer and richer."

Gabe nodded.

"There wasn't a church in Ransom back then, but the preacher from over in Lovejoy came to lead services once each month. Your mother offered the use of the Talmadge parlor for those services. Reverend Bell was a handsome man, but what was most noticeable about him was his enormous heart for Jesus. He and Clarice loved to talk about the Lord and about the Bible. She *did* love him, but only as her brother in Christ. Hudson couldn't understand that kind of love. He couldn't 'cause he had no concept of God or what pure love is. He finally told Clarice that if Reverend Bell ever set foot in their house again, he'd kill him. And I think he would have."

Gabe felt a horrible weight on his chest.

"I don't know what your mother wrote to Reverend Bell, but he didn't come back to Ransom again. I heard he got a church up north somewhere the next year." She drew a deep breath and met his gaze. "It wasn't long after that that Clarice told your father she was going to have another baby. She was thrilled. She considered it such a blessing. Max was over two by that time, and she'd feared there wouldn't be any more children." Tears glistened in her eyes. "Only your father accused her of carrying Reverend Bell's child."

Gabe could almost hear Hudson shouting the accusation.

"Clarice told me she and Reverend Bell were never alone together, had never behaved in any way inappropriate. She wouldn't have lied. I knew she wouldn't. She wasn't capable of telling an untruth. But that didn't matter to Hudson. He believed she was unfaithful to him, and as far as he was concerned, that made it true. Clarice prayed that once you were born he would realize his error. She loved your father, despite everything. She prayed and prayed, but…" She fell silent, dabbing her eyes with a napkin.

"But she died," Gabe finished for her.

"Yes."

"And that was my fault too."

Softly, "Yes."

Silence encompassed them.

Maybe Akira's right. Maybe in his own twisted way, Hud loved my mother. The thought brought him little comfort.

"Gabe," Jane said at last, "you are like your mother in so many ways. You inherited her kind heart and her generous nature. You share her faith, too. That would have brought her the greatest joy of all. Remember that."

"I'll remember."

Pauline winced as she stepped from the automobile. Even after three days, it hurt to walk on her ankle.

She noticed Eugene carefully avoided looking in her eyes. Her chauffeur had to know, of course. All the servants had to know what Hudson had done to her in the library the other night. When he hit her the first time, she'd screamed loud enough for anyone in the house to hear. She'd thought someone might come to her aid. No one had. Not any of the times she had screamed.

"I won't be long, Eugene," she said, then walked toward the dry-goods store.

She'd been surprised when Hudson told her she could go shopping. She had thought he meant to keep her locked up. Perhaps forever.

Be careful what you say, Pauline. Cross me again, and you won't live long enough to regret it. Do I make myself clear?

She shivered involuntarily at the memory of his words and drew her coat more closely about her.

Dorothea Baker welcomed her the moment she entered the store.

"I'd like to look at some of your dress patterns," Pauline told the woman.

"We got in a new selection last week, Mrs. Talmadge. You're sure to find something you like."

After she was seated, the pattern book on the table before her, Pauline whispered a soft thanks to Dorothea.

"You're welcome, Mrs. Talmadge. You let me know if I can help you."

"Mrs. Baker, wait." The words escaped her before she could think better of it.

Dorothea looked back.

"Do you sell Bibles here?"

Surprise fluttered across the woman's face. "Yes."

What if Hudson heard what she'd asked? What if Dorothea told him?

"Thank you," she said again, then looked down at the pattern book, pretending to be utterly engrossed.

After a moment or two, more customers entered the store, stomping their feet and talking amongst themselves. Dorothea returned to the front counter to wait on them.

But maybe Mrs. Baker wouldn't tell Hud what I bought. Why should she?

It would be crazy to buy a Bible. Hudson had hurt her for merely looking for one in the library. What would he do if she were to spend his money to buy one?

Gabe noticed the Talmadge automobile parked on the street, so he wasn't surprised when he saw Pauline inside the store. After nodding a greeting at Dorothea, he wended his way through the shelves and display tables to where she was seated.

"Hello, Pauline."

She nearly jumped out of her skin at the sound of his voice. And he knew, as he looked into her wide eyes, it wasn't mere surprise that caused her to start.

It was fear. Real fear.

"What's wrong?" he asked, lowering his voice.

She shook her head, her gaze darting beyond him. He suspected she was checking to see who else was in the store.

"I'm sorry for the scene at your house last Sunday," Gabe began. "Akira and I both hoped it would make things somewhat better between my father and me, finding out he's going to be a grandfather. We were wrong."

"Yes." She rose from her chair. "I...I'm glad for you both. About the baby."

"Thanks."

"I hope she has an easy confinement."

Gabe had often thought the worst of Pauline Talmadge, but now what he felt was an overriding concern. She was nervous as a cat.

"I'd best be going," she said softly. "Do give Akira my best."

She started to walk past him, but he put his hand on her shoulder to stop her. She gasped—an unmistakable sound of pain. He immediately released her, at the same time stepping into her path.

"What happened?" he demanded, again making sure only she could hear.

"Nothing, Gabe. Let me pass."

Then he knew. "He hit you. Didn't he?"

She neither confirmed nor denied it.

Even after all the years, Gabe remembered the feel of the back of his father's hand as it connected with his jaw.

"Don't go back there, Pauline."

"Where else would I go?"

"What about your parents? Aren't they in Boise? You could go to them."

Tears welled in her eyes as she mouthed the word, "No."

"Are you sure?"

This time she nodded.

"I know what Hud's like. He knocked me around plenty when I was a boy. I thought if I took it, if I was strong, if I tried harder to earn his respect or do what he wanted me to do, things would get better. They never did." He moved to one side. "If you need me, all you've got to do is send word and I'll come. All right?"

"All right," she whispered before hurrying away.

He hoped he hadn't made another mistake, letting her go.

"You have no choice, Mr. Talmadge," Rupert said as he placed the open ledger on Hudson's desk. "The mill will have to be closed." He took a step back. "The longer you delay, the worse the end result will be. It will be hard on the remaining employees but—"

"Hang the remaining employees!" Hudson shouted. "Do you think I care about any of them? Do you think I care about *you?*"

Rupert's face was perfectly expressionless.

Hudson slammed the ledger closed, then rose and turned to the window. "Shut down the mill. Send everyone home now."

"Yes sir."

"And, Carruthers…"

"Yes sir?"

"Inform them all the payroll money was lost in the bank closure. There'll be no final paychecks."

"But, sir, it wasn't—"

"I think I made myself clear, Carruthers. See to it."

"Yes sir." The only sound that followed was the soft click of the closing office door.

So much. How had he lost so much?

He was too old to start over. He'd given his life to acquiring his fortune. He'd worked hard. He'd gambled. He'd cheated. The only thing that had mattered to him was his wealth and the power that came with it.

The love of money will destroy you, Hudson. Please. There's a better way.

He placed his fists against the window frame and pressed his forehead against the glass. He closed his eyes, at the same time trying to silence the voice from his past. He hadn't believed Clarice when she'd said those words to him. He wasn't about to believe her now.

Money meant power, and power was everything.

Jesus won't tarry forever. There will be a day of reckoning. Don't wait until it's too late. Please don't wait.

Looking out the window again, Hudson swore at the God he didn't believe in, blaming Him for all that had gone wrong in his life.

CHAPTER TWENTY-SIX

Ten days after the amputation of her leg, Lindy Jones arrived at Dundreggan, brought there by Dr. Kirkland and his wife. Akira and Gabe had prepared the small cabin next to the Wickhams'— the one Gabe had used before their marriage—for the Jones family. It was there Gabe carried Lindy while the doctor spoke to Akira.

"I'm amazed by her progress, Mrs. Talmadge," Dr. Kirkland told her, "but she isn't out of danger yet. She'll need plenty of rest and good nourishment. And exercise. She hates the crutches, but if she wants to return to that mountain home of hers, she'd better learn to use them. Inactivity will only slow the healing process. I can't stress that enough."

"I'll do what I can to encourage her."

"Good." Dr. Kirkland nodded, then glanced at the sky. "We'd better get over the pass before the snow starts to fall again. I'd hate to get caught in a blizzard."

"It was kind of you to bring Mrs. Jones to us. Gabe hoped he'd have the Ford running by now, but—"

"Don't mention it." He opened the automobile door and got

in. "Unless the roads are bad, I'll be over this way next Saturday to look in on her."

"Thanks again, Doctor. Have a happy Thanksgiving."

"The same to all of you." He closed the door, then waved at her through the window before starting the engine and driving away.

Pulling her coat more closely about her, Akira hurried into the cabin. Gabe was standing near the entrance. Lindy was in bed, her back propped with pillows, the children on either side of her, holding her hands.

"Cain't say thanks enough for what you done for me 'n' mine," she said to Akira the instant the door closed. "Like I was tellin' your man here, I ain't been a party to such kindness before. Always made do on my own since Ned passed. Reckon you know how it is. I know it cain't have been easy, takin' in my young uns."

"We were glad to do it."

"They been good, I hope?" Lindy looked from Akira to Fern and then to Ethan, questioning her children with her eyes.

The boy turned his gaze on the floor. His neck flamed beet red.

Gabe stepped to Akira's side. "We got along fine, Mrs. Jones. Ethan's been helping me tend the livestock, and Fern's helped Akira with the cooking."

Lindy touched the boy's shoulder. "That true, Ethan?"

"Mostly, Ma."

"We'll leave the three of you alone," Akira said. "You rest and don't worry about a thing."

Lindy sighed. "I am a mite tuckered out."

"Ethan," Gabe said. "You come for me if your mother needs anything."

"Yes sir." There was less belligerence in his voice than in the past. Perhaps even a note of gratitude.

Snow had begun to fall while they were inside—fat, wet flakes forming a curtain of white in the air, a curtain that would soon become a heavy blanket over the earth.

Akira turned her face upward. "Oh, isn't it beautiful?"

Gabe put his right arm around her shoulders, drawing her close to his side. "Yes," he answered, but he wasn't looking at the snowfall. He was looking at her.

"Listen."

He did. "I don't hear anything."

"Exactly." She grinned at him. "Total and absolute silence. Peace." She closed her eyes, whispering, "Be still, and know that I am God: I will be exalted among the nations, I will be exalted in the earth."

"Amen."

She leaned her head against his chest. "We have so much to be thankful for, Gabriel. So very, very much."

He was unable to reply, suddenly overwhelmed by the magnitude of blessings God had poured out upon him. Unmerited blessings.

There'd been a time, not long ago, that recognizing how unmerited those blessings were would have left him weighed down beneath a heavy load of guilt. But no longer. It only left him rejoicing, amazed at the goodness and mercy of his loving heavenly Father.

The prodigal did come home, didn't he, Lord? I came home to You, and You welcomed me with gifts and celebrations and a Father's love. The love I longed for and couldn't find from my earthly father.

As if reading his thoughts, Akira lifted her head and met his gaze, then nodded in agreement.

They started walking toward the main house, but before they reached the front porch, they heard the telltale sounds of an approaching automobile.

"Two visitors in one day?" Akira peered through the tumbling snowflakes. "And in this weather."

A few moments later, the sheriff's car came into view.

Gabe couldn't help the momentary spark of dread. It was a conditioned response, and one he wasn't particularly proud of. Especially since he now considered the sheriff a friend.

Andy exited the automobile, placing his hat on his head as he straightened. "Afternoon, Gabe. Akira." His breath formed a tiny white cloud before his mouth.

"Afternoon, Sheriff," Akira responded. "You look like you could use some hot coffee. Come inside. I've got a pot on the stove."

"Thanks." He strode forward.

Akira led the way to the house, but Gabe hung back.

"Is something wrong?" he asked in a low voice when the sheriff reached his side.

Andy shook his head. "Nothing out of the ordinary," he answered obliquely.

Gabe gave him a hard stare.

"Three more families left Ransom this week. The Logger's Café is closed, and Mrs. Baker's been told she won't be needed at the dry-goods store after the New Year." Andy shook his head. "Plenty of folks are afraid of what'll happen next. Tempers are flaring. I broke up two fights last night outside the bar. I've got Peck cooling his heels in my jail cell today."

Gabe gritted his teeth. He didn't like Danny Peck and hadn't been able to forgive him for his attack on Akira. Oh, he'd mouthed the words of forgiveness in prayer, but he knew he hadn't released it in his heart. Not yet.

After stepping into the house, the two men shrugged out of their coats and hung them on pegs near the door. The sheriff removed his hat, and Gabe took it from him, setting it on a small table beneath the window.

Akira turned from the stove, steaming mugs of coffee in her hands. "Would you like cream or sugar, Sheriff?"

"No thanks. Black's fine."

They all sat at the table, silently sipping their beverages, listening to the crackling and popping of wood burning in the stove.

Finally, Andy spoke. "You make real good coffee, Akira. Better than my wife, but don't tell her I said so."

Gabe ran out of patience with both the silence and the attempt at small talk. "So what brought you all the way out here, Andy? Wasn't for coffee. Not in weather like this."

"No, it wasn't." The sheriff leaned back in his chair. "I'm on my way down to Boise. A friend of mine's in the hospital there." He gave his head a slight shake. "Nothing serious, but I wanted to talk to him a bit more. He mentioned something when we spoke on the telephone last week that's been bothering me." He looked at Akira. "This friend works for the state government, and he said there's been some sort of talk—nothing official, mind you—about building a dam and flooding this valley to make a reservoir."

"What?" Akira and Gabe exclaimed in unison.

Andy nodded. His gaze dropped to his coffee mug. "Hudson Talmadge has been looking for loopholes that would allow him to take the land from you. You're the only significant holdout. Most others who'd be impacted by a dam have sold to him." He looked up again. "So far, he hasn't succeeded in finding that loophole. He doesn't seem to have much support. But I thought it couldn't hurt to poke around a bit. See what else I can learn."

"Surely he couldn't *take* this land from us?" Akira whispered, looking at Gabe with unbelieving eyes. "We own it, free and clear. It was my grandfather's. Now it's ours."

Gabe held her hand.

He knew his father hated to fail. Hudson would do anything he had to do to get what he wanted. And sometimes men with power twisted the law to suit themselves.

"I'm not saying he'll be able to do it," the sheriff answered. "But forewarned is forearmed, as they say." He took a last gulp of coffee, then set the mug on the table and rose from his chair. "I'd better get back on the road. I don't want to get stuck in this storm."

Gabe and Akira followed Andy to the door where they bid him a safe trip.

As they watched the sheriff walk to his car, Akira said, "Your father won't succeed, will he?"

Gabe pulled her into his embrace. "No, he won't."

He hoped he spoke the truth.

Chapter Twenty-Seven

Danny wanted a drink. He *needed* a drink. When was the last time he'd been sober for four days in a row? Five years? Even more? Too long ago for him to remember, he supposed.

Seated behind his desk, Hudson Talmadge peered at him with disdain, as if he were a bug about to be crushed beneath his shoe. "Do you understand what I'm saying?"

"Sure I do. You bailed me out 'cause you want me t'do your dirty work."

Hudson's eyes narrowed.

The two of them were alone at the mill. Not even that secretary was around today. But why should he be? The lumbermill had shut down completely. Not a single employee left. The place was as quiet as a tomb.

"Look, Peck." Hudson leaned forward on his chair. "This is your opportunity to get even with my son and his wife. No one will notice you as long as you're careful. They'll be too busy with their *Thanksgiving* celebrations." His tone mocked the holiday. "And *if* you succeed, you can get away from Ransom with what I'll pay you. You can go someplace with a warmer climate. You'll have plenty to drink and plenty of friends to drink with."

Danny could use a drink. His mouth was parched, and his hands were trembling. There was liquor in that cabinet against the wall. He knew it was there because he'd seen the fancy crystal decanters last time he was in this office. But Hudson wasn't offering.

What was worse was Danny didn't have the money to buy a drink when he got back to town. He was broke, and unless he accepted Hudson's offer, that condition wasn't likely to change soon. With the close of the Talmadge mill, more folks had left town and others would be leaving soon. There weren't going to be any odd jobs to be had for the asking. Nor would there be many kind souls left who were willing to give a handout to somebody like him.

"Well, Peck?"

Danny's thoughts turned to Akira. She reckoned herself better than him. Holier than thou, as his ma used to say. Akira had never given Danny the time of day, but she'd let that convict move right in. As if Gabe was better than Danny.

He was tired of being looked down on. Tired of everybody's self-righteous attitudes.

Hudson Talmadge wasn't asking him to do more to Akira and Gabe than what they deserved. He wasn't asking him to do more than what Danny wanted to do.

"All right." He stood. "I'll do it."

There were eight of them around the Thanksgiving table this year, and it filled Akira's heart with joy to look at the other seven: Lindy Jones, still pale but growing stronger with each passing day; Lindy's two children, Ethan and Fern; Charlie and Nora Wickham; Brodie Lachlan; and Gabe. Mark Wickham had volunteered to stay with the sheep while the rest partook of the feast the women had prepared. Akira had promised to save him some of everything.

"Heavenly Father," Gabe prayed aloud, all of them standing except for Lindy. "We ask Your blessing upon this food, which has been so lovingly prepared for us. We have countless reasons to be thankful on this day, Lord. We thank You for Your free gift of salvation, for the grace You've poured out upon us, the people You've called unto Yourself. We thank You for this good land, for the crops and the livestock, for the rain and the sun and even this season of snow. May we learn to draw closer to You and be able to say, like the apostle Paul, that we're content, whether we have much or little. In Christ's name we pray, Amen."

"Amen," the others echoed.

They all sat down, and in a matter of seconds, the room grew noisy with several competing conversations, with laughter, and with the clatter of utensils against plates, platters, and serving bowls.

Akira's heart was too full with thanksgiving to stop praying yet.

Thank You, Jesus, for sparing Lindy's life. Thank You for Ethan and Fern. Help heal the wounds in their hearts, O God.

Her gaze moved to the opposite side of the table.

Thank You for Brodie. Lord, You know how stubborn he can be. He has yet to surrender to Your love. Break down those walls, Jesus.

Nora looks better, Lord, and I thank You for that. Continue to strengthen her. Bless Charlie for his hard work here on Dundreggan. Jesus, keep Mark warm out there with the sheep on this cold and windy day.

As she looked toward the opposite end of the table, Gabe glanced up and met her gaze.

Thank You, Father God, for my husband. Thank You for making us one. And thank You for this child, growing inside me, a child fashioned by Your loving hands and loaned to us for a time.

Gabe smiled, and she knew his silent prayers were much the same as her own.

"Ma?" Fern said. "I ain't never seen so much food on one table before. Is this just for us here or is there more comin'?"

"Hush, child," Lindy said, clearly embarrassed.

Akira laughed. "But she's right, Mrs. Jones. It *is* a lot of food. Even for eight of us. Nine, counting Mark."

"And it's all delicious, too," Nora chimed in. "Akira, you must give me your recipe for this dressing."

"I'd be pleased to."

"Miz Talmadge?"

"Yes, Fern."

"Kin I have some of *everythin'*?"

Tears sprang to her eyes, and Akira fought to keep them from falling. "Of course you can." She swallowed the lump in her throat. "You can even have two helpings if you want."

Pauline stood at her bedroom window, staring into the distance without seeing, lost in thought. Her parents would be sitting down to dinner about this time, joined by her cousins from Philadelphia who were visiting for the winter. They would dine on roast turkey and baked ham with a honey glaze and potatoes and gravy and those scrumptious rolls Cook made every year. Oh, and the pies and puddings. How she'd always loved Cook's desserts.

There would be no special Thanksgiving meal in the Talmadge household today. In the past, she and Hudson had entertained to impress or to curry favor from the right people. Things were different this year. Hudson hadn't told her, of course, but she knew he was in trouble. She could see it in his eyes. It was part of his rage. It was part of his madness.

"I should be more afraid."

Odd, that she wasn't. She couldn't say why. It wasn't because she didn't think Hudson capable of striking her again. She knew he might. In fact, she knew he would if she got in his way. And yet, she wasn't afraid.

"Because greater is He that is in me, than he that is in the world."

She pressed the small Bible against her chest, taking comfort in the feel of it.

Amazing.

She looked up at the crystal blue sky. "For the first time in my life," she whispered, "I understand what Thanksgiving is about. For the first time, I'm truly thankful. Because of You, Lord. All because of You."

"I cain't figure you out," Ethan said as he trudged through the snow beside Akira, both of them carrying food for Mark.

"Why's that?"

"I been goin' into town for supplies and such ever since my pa died. I know what most folk think of Ma. Nobody's ever tried helpin' her before. They call her Looney Lindy, you know."

"So I've heard. That's unkind. No one should call another names."

He was silent awhile before saying, "Ma would've died if'n Mr. Talmadge hadn't come."

"That's what the doctor believes." She glanced at the boy. "But God took care of her. And you and your sister, too."

Ethan didn't reply as they continued their climb up a small foothill.

On the path in front of them, Cam came to a sudden halt. The dog lowered her head and growled a warning.

Akira placed a hand on Ethan's shoulder. "Stay here," she whispered as she passed him the plate she carried. She moved cautiously forward, wishing she'd brought her rifle. Heavy snowfall often brought predators down from the high country, looking for an easy kill.

There was no sound as she neared the top of the rise, except for the snow crunching beneath her boots and her collie's persistent growls. Then the valley came into view, and her heart stopped at the sight before her. Dozens of sheep lay scattered across the ground, their blood turning the snow to crimson.

"Mark?" she shouted, not seeing any sign of the young man. *"Mark!"*

No answer.

She looked over her shoulder. "Ethan, get Gabe. Quick!"

The boy dropped the plates of food and took off at a run. Akira didn't watch his race back toward the ranch house. Instead, she hurried down the slope toward the slaughtered sheep.

"Mark!"

No wild animal had done this. Only man was capable of this carnage.

"Mark!"

The cold air stung her lungs. She stumbled more than once in the snow, but caught herself each time before she fell.

O God, help me find him.

"Mark!"

She saw him then, a crumpled form beneath a misshapen Ponderosa pine. For a moment she couldn't move toward him; she seemed to be frozen in place. Then she heard a soft moan. The sound broke the spell of fear.

"I'm here, Mark. It's all right." She made her way to him as fast as she could.

As she fell to her knees on the ground beside him, he touched the back of his head with one gloved hand and groaned again.

"Don't move," she ordered.

His eyelids fluttered, then opened. "What happened?"

"You've been hurt." She leaned forward for a better look. There was a stain of blood on the snow beneath his head. "Someone hit you from behind, I think."

"Hit me?" Mark groaned again as he closed his eyes. "Why would anybody do that?"

"Let me see that wound." She didn't mention the sheep. He would know soon enough.

Before Akira could lift Mark's head for a better look, she heard her name shouted from over the rise. Gabe appeared a moment later, Brodie, Charlie, and Ethan hard on his heels. Relief flooded through her, and her vision blurred with tears.

"Gabe," she whispered, choking on a sob.

It didn't take him long to reach her.

"Are you all right?" he demanded as he took hold of her arms.

"I—I'm fine." She sniffed. "It's Mark who's hurt." She turned to look behind her.

Charlie and Brodie were kneeling on either side of the young man. Charlie was examining the wound on his son's head while Brodie supported Mark.

"Why would anybody do this?" she whispered.

"It wasn't *anybody*," Gabe answered, his voice harsh. "This is Hud's handiwork."

"Oh, Gabe. You don't think he would—"

"I don't have to think. I know. If he can't take your land any other way…" He didn't finish.

Akira pressed her face against his coat. "Mark could've been killed."

"Thank God he wasn't."

"Yes." She took a deep breath and let it out slowly. "Thank God."

Danny felt like puking again. Killing those sheep hadn't made him feel better about himself, hadn't made him feel strong and powerful, the way he'd expected it to. All that blood. All that death.

He swallowed the bile in his throat as he inched toward the ranch house. It was a fool thing to do. Even he knew that. He should have made tracks for town as soon as he'd finished the gruesome job.

But he had to know what Ethan Jones was doing at Dundreggan Ranch.

When Akira found the sheep, the boy had run back to the house for the men. Danny figured the chances were good only womenfolk were left inside.

He sidled up to the window and peeked in.

There was Lindy, looking thin and lots older than when he'd last seen her. She was holding the girl in her lap. He thought her name was Fern. She wasn't a baby no more. Time had a way of doing that with kids. How many years had it been?

Another woman stood at the sink, washing dishes. When she spoke, Lindy twisted to look at her. That's when Danny noticed that the chair she was in had wheels.

You should've known, an accusing voice whispered in his ears. *If you wasn't a worthless drunk, you would've known what'd happened to your own sister and her kids.*

If the Lord had taught him nothing else in recent months, He'd taught Gabe to bridle his anger before acting.

It was a lesson Brodie Lachlan could use right about now.

"I'll see Talmadge hangin' from the nearest tree," the Scotsman vowed as he paced the parlor.

"No, my dear friend." Akira placed a hand on his arm, stopping him. "We mustn't act in hatred, or we're no better than the person who did this. Besides, we have no proof Hudson was behind what happened to Mark and our sheep."

Brodie rolled his eyes.

"She's right," Gabe said, albeit reluctantly. "There's no proof he's involved." He raised a hand to stop Brodie's expected expletive. "Yes, I think he hired someone to do it, but my opinion doesn't count for much. We've got to have solid evidence or a confession. I doubt we'll get the latter, and Andy doesn't seem to think we'll find the former."

"Are ye sayin' ye mean to do nothing? Do ye know what the loss of so many ewes will mean to ye and Akira? 'Tis no small matter. Ye'll feel it for years to come."

Gabe released a deep sigh before answering, "Believe it or not, I *do* realize what it means. But there isn't much else we can do for now. Except forgive whoever did it."

"*Ach!*" Brodie marched across the room and jerked open the door. "I'll never understand ye two. Turnin' the other cheek and prayin' for yer enemies. Daft, the both of ye, and all those who think like ye besides." He stormed out, slamming the door behind him.

"Not daft," Akira said softly. "And it isn't easy, either. To forgive."

Gabe nodded as he placed an arm around her shoulders.

She turned into his embrace, tilting her face up to meet his gaze. "So what are we to do besides pray?"

"I've got to try talking to Hud one more time. Not about what happened with the sheep. About Christ. I feel as if time's running out for him."

"Do you think he'll listen?"

"I don't know. Probably not. But I've got to try. Whether he wants to admit it or not, like it or not, he's my father." He shook his head slowly. "He's trapped in a prison far worse than the one I was in."

They were silent for a while.

Finally Akira said, "I suppose we should go first thing in the morning."

"*We?*"

"You don't think I'd let you go alone, do you?"

"Well, I—"

"We're in this together, Gabriel. You'll need me to pray while you speak, if for nothing else."

"You're right." He leaned down, pressed his forehead against hers, closed his eyes. "What would I do without you?"

"I have no intention of letting you find out, my love."

Chapter Twenty-Eight

The green sedan chugged along Main Street, the sound of the engine disturbing the strange silence of the otherwise deserted streets.

Akira read the signs posted in shop windows and on store doors:

Closed.

Out of business.

Shop for sale. Inquire within.

"Oh, Gabe," she whispered. "It's so awful."

"I've been through a lot of towns between here and Seattle. Ransom hung on a lot longer than some." He shook his head. "It isn't like we didn't know it could happen. With the mill closed…" He didn't finish, and she didn't need him to.

She thought of the Dundreggan sheep that had been needlessly slaughtered. The men had been able to save only a portion of the meat. The remaining carcasses had been burned this morning. What a waste when so many of her neighbors were out of work, some now homeless besides.

It made her want to cry.

Gabe took hold of her hand. "Hud's in worse shape than I thought."

She looked at him.

"He's lost his town. Ransom was his empire. Somebody will have to pay for his losing it."

Something in his tone caused a shiver to run up her spine.

"I know my father. When he doesn't get what he wants, he gets angry, and when he gets angry, he takes it out on those around him."

"Pauline?"

"That's what I'm afraid of."

She looked at the road ahead of them. "Hurry, Gabe."

The Duesenberg was gone, which meant Hudson wasn't at home. Gabe didn't know whether to feel disappointed or relieved.

The moment the Ford stopped, Akira opened the passenger door and got out. She hurried toward the entrance of the Talmadge mansion, not waiting for Gabe nor looking behind to see if he followed.

He caught up with her as she knocked for the second time.

"Where is everyone?" she asked after a lengthy silence.

"I don't know." Gabe frowned. "His butler should have answered by now."

"Maybe he gave the help time off for Thanksgiving, and they haven't returned yet."

"Hud?" He released a humorless laugh. "Not likely." He pounded his fist against the door and shouted, "Is anybody home? Come on. Open up." He pounded again.

Akira took hold of the knob and turned it. The door opened an inch. She stepped back, glancing at Gabe in question.

"We're going in," he said as he pushed it all the way open. "Stay close." He led the way.

All was silent. An unnatural silence, Gabe thought. As if the house was holding its breath.

"Brrr." Akira shuddered. "It's cold in here."

A look in the formal drawing room revealed a dark hearth. The same was true in the dining room. Had it gotten so bad Hudson couldn't afford to build fires to heat his house?

"Who is it?" a female voice called from the second floor. "Who's there?"

"It's us, Pauline," Akira answered, turning toward the stairs. "Gabe and Akira."

A few moments later, Pauline appeared near the ornate railing. The right side of her face was puffy, her eye nearly swollen shut, the skin beginning to discolor.

Akira gasped. Gabe felt a white-hot fury shoot through him. Together they raced up the stairs.

Akira reached Pauline first. "What happened?"

"He was in a horrible temper." Pauline gingerly fingered her cheek, wincing when she touched her cheekbone. "If Carruthers hadn't been here, I don't think he would have stopped this time."

Gabe clenched his hands into fists. "Where is Hud now?"

"They went to the mill. About an hour ago. I suspect Carruthers had more bad news about money." A tear slipped from her left eye. "I'm packing. I'm leaving. I don't care what else happens. I won't stay here."

"Akira, help Pauline get her things together. I'm going to the mill to see Hud. When I get back, we'll take Pauline home with us."

"Don't go, Gabe." Akira took hold of his hand. "Let someone else confront your father. It doesn't have to be you."

He pulled away from her and took a step backward. "Yes, it does. It *has* to be me." He moved to the top of the stairs, distancing himself from Akira, too angry at his father to be near her. "Don't you see? I came crawling back, looking for help, looking for a little human kindness, maybe a little fatherly affection. I let him humiliate me because I didn't think I deserved anything better." He grabbed hold of the banister. "I haven't been turning the other cheek like Brodie thinks. I've been letting Hud kick me. Again and again and again." He looked at Pauline. "And not just me. I've let him do this to you. I knew it was happening. I knew and I didn't try to make sure it didn't happen again."

Pauline shook her head. "I made my own choices. You couldn't—"

"All Hud does is destroy the people around him who aren't what he wants them to be or who don't do what he wants them to do. Anything he can't control, he ruins. He's got to be stopped."

He spun around and descended the stairs, three steps at a time.

"This is your fault, Carruthers." Hudson grabbed the small book from his secretary's hand. "It wouldn't have happened if you'd done your job right."

"My fault, sir?" Rupert stared at him with a bemused expression.

"I should have fired you years ago. You're inept."

"Inept?"

Hudson hurled a curse at his secretary. "Stop repeating my words. You sound like an idiot. Now get out. You're fired."

"Fired?" Rupert didn't move.

"You heard me. Get out."

The small man's eyes nearly bugged out of his head. "I've worked for you for forty-seven years. From the very beginning, I've done anything and everything you needed done. I've doctored papers and documents. I've helped you buy politicians. I've lied whenever you asked me to. I've helped you destroy men who got in the way of your success. I've broken the law in more ways than I can remember. I helped you make your fortune. You couldn't have done it without me. And now you think you can just fire me, tell me to get out, like one of your stupid mill hands?"

"Precisely." Hudson grinned at him. "Get out...*stupid*."

An odd, choked sound escaped Rupert's throat.

Hudson turned away. "Don't let the door hit you on the way."

"You...miserable..."

That was all Hudson heard before pain exploded in his head. He fell face forward onto his desk. Instinct—or perhaps the guttural noises of his assailant—warned him not to stay still. He moved in time to avoid a second crushing blow to his head.

He straightened and whirled about, somehow arriving at the side of his desk. Rupert was holding the brass-and-onyx lamp stand in both hands, ready to take another swing.

"You fool!" Hudson shouted. "Put that down this instant."

"You're not doing to me what you've done to others."

Dizziness caused Hudson to stagger. His knees nearly buckled. Fear sluiced through him as he realized the precariousness of his position. He steadied himself with a hand on his desk and began to inch away.

Rupert followed him.

Hudson tried to move more quickly, but his legs seemed unable to obey. Something trickled down his forehead. He put his fingers on his face and felt a warm stickiness. Blood!

Rupert raised the lamp stand higher above his head. "You're not destroying me like everybody else. Not me."

Hudson leaned to one side. The sharp edge of the stand glanced his temple. At the same moment, his hand fell upon the letter opener.

Instinctively, he closed his fingers around the cold metal handle and lunged toward Rupert before he could lift the stand again. The sharp point of the letter opener slid into Rupert's belly with surprising ease. Hudson's vision began to dim, but he had enough forethought to give the opener an extra thrust and twist before unconsciousness overwhelmed him.

Gabe's fury had spent itself by the time he arrived at the mill. He turned off the Ford's engine and sat there, hands gripping the steering wheel, staring at the Duesenberg parked near the entrance.

God, what am I doing? He's never wanted anything to do with You, and even less to do with me.

He remembered the dying town he and Akira had driven through earlier. He thought of the cold mansion on the hillside and Pauline's bruised and battered face. He thought of the sawmill before him, a business without employees. He remembered the slaughtered sheep.

He's lost it all, hasn't he, Father? He's lost the only thing that ever mattered to him. His money. It's easier for a camel to go through a needle's eye than for a rich man to enter into the kingdom of God.

Gabe sighed. Maybe that was why he was here. If his father had lost his fortune, maybe now he would listen to the truth. More importantly, maybe Hudson would meet Truth.

He got out of the car, took a deep breath, then walked through the snow toward the entrance. The silence that greeted him inside the building seemed eerie. He supposed it was because he'd never been in the mill when machinery wasn't running, creating a never-ending cacophony of noise. He looked up the stairs leading to Hudson's second-story office. He assumed that was where he would find his father and Rupert Carruthers.

Go on. Get it over with, he admonished himself, then headed up the stairway.

He paused in the anteroom. The door to Hudson's office was ajar, but Gabe heard no voices. He hesitated, then said, "Hud?"

There was no reply.

He shivered involuntarily.

"Hud? Carruthers?"

He walked to the door and pushed it open. The scene before him caused his heart to sink, and for a moment, he couldn't think what to do. Hudson lay on the floor beside his desk, a dark pool of blood staining the Persian rug beneath him. Rupert lay on his back about ten feet away from him. He was clutching his stomach with his hands. The lamp stand had been overturned, and items had been swept off the desktop onto the floor. Papers were scattered everywhere.

Reason returned as suddenly as it had vanished.

Gabe went first to his father. Kneeling down, he touched Hudson's throat, feeling for a pulse. It seemed strong, and a cursory glance at the head wound suggested it wasn't life threatening.

Hudson groaned, and his eyelids fluttered, then stilled without opening.

Gabe rose and went to his father's secretary. Again he knelt down and felt for a pulse. It was faint, erratic. His gaze moved to Rupert's belly where blood oozed between the man's fingers. That was when Gabe noticed the end of a knifelike object sticking up. He moved Rupert's hands out of the way for a better look and knew immediately he was too late.

Rupert sucked in a raspy breath. Gabe looked toward his face. The wounded man's eyes were open now. He worked his mouth, as if to say something, but the only sound he made was an ominous death rattle.

And then he was gone.

Still kneeling, Gabe glanced over his shoulder toward his father. Hudson was pulling himself up, hanging on to his desk with one hand while holding his head with the other. Their gazes met for an instant. Then a sound from the outer office drew their attention.

Andy Newton stood in the doorway. "What the—?"

"Arrest him, Sheriff," Hudson cried, pointing an accusing finger at Gabe. "He tried to kill me."

CHAPTER TWENTY-NINE

Gabe couldn't believe what he was hearing. He looked at his father, then back at the sheriff. "That's not true. I didn't—"

"He hit me over the head with that lamp stand," Hudson interrupted, his voice rising. "And when Carruthers tried to stop him, he stabbed him." He took a step toward Gabe. "Is he dead? Did you kill him?"

Gabe raised his hands in a gesture of innocence, only to see they were bloodied from his attempts to help.

"Step over to the window," Andy commanded in a low but firm voice, "and don't move. Talmadge, sit in that chair before you fall down."

When both men had obeyed, the sheriff knelt beside Rupert, checking for a pulse as Gabe had done only minutes before.

"Is he dead?" Hudson demanded.

"Yes." Andy stood. "He's dead." His gaze moved to Gabe.

His father leaned forward in his chair. "You murdering dog. I hope they hang you this time. They will if I have anything to say about it."

It was surreal, the way Gabe seemed to step outside his body and watch from a distance. This wasn't happening to him. It couldn't be. It had to be a nightmare from which he would awaken any moment.

But he didn't awaken.

"I'm afraid I'll have to take you in, Gabe," the sheriff said. "You'll have to come with me, too, Talmadge."

"*Me?* Am *I* under arrest?"

"No sir. But until I can go over things in this office, nobody can be in here. Besides, your head needs to be looked at."

"But this is *my* office," Hudson objected. "You can't lock me out of my own place of business."

The sheriff wasn't dissuaded. "It's a crime scene now, Talmadge. Let's go." He took hold of Gabe's arm above the elbow. "Sorry," he added softly, then sent a pointed look in Hudson's direction. "I'm afraid you'll have to leave everything here until I conclude my investigation."

"I trust I can at least take my suit coat." Even as he spoke, he picked up the article of clothing and slipped his arms into the sleeves. Then he led the way out of the office.

Andy looked at Gabe.

Gabe looked down at Rupert's body. "I didn't kill him. I found them like this."

The sheriff's only reply was to tighten his grip on Gabe's arm and steer him out of the room.

Akira's heart was in her throat as she disembarked from the Talmadge automobile in front of the sheriff's office, not long after Pauline received Andy's phone call.

From the corner of her eye, she saw several people staring out the window of the dry-goods store. Two men stood together in front of the bar and grill down the street, both of them looking in her direction.

She ignored them all as she hurried inside.

"Andy?"

The sheriff rose from his desk chair.

"Where's Gabe? What's happened? I came as soon as I—" She stopped abruptly when she caught sight of Hudson Talmadge, seated in a far corner. Wallis Greer was stitching a wound in his head.

"Come with me," Andy said.

He led her through a doorway to the back of the building. It was chilly back there, and the air smelled of stale sweat and alcohol. Gabe was locked in one of the two cells.

"What on earth?" She looked from Gabe to Andy to Gabe again.

He stared back at her. His eyes reminded her of a wounded animal—caged, hurting, confused.

"O God," she breathed. "Help us."

"Carruthers is dead," the sheriff said, not hearing her soft prayer, "and Hudson Talmadge has been injured. He says Gabe did it." He paused before saying, "I found Gabe kneeling over the body. His hands were bloody."

Akira reached for one of the bars to steady herself. "But he didn't do it. Gabe wouldn't—"

"You're the one who called me and told me to get up to the mill." Andy cleared his throat. "You said you were afraid because he was so angry."

Gabe winced visibly, as if the sheriff's words had struck him. Did he think she'd betrayed him? Then he dropped his gaze to the floor.

"I'll give you two some time alone." Andy touched her shoulder. When she didn't respond, he turned and walked back to the front office.

"Gabe?" Akira gripped another bar and pressed in against the cold steel, trying to draw closer to her husband. "I didn't call Andy because I thought you would hurt anyone. I wanted to protect you, not your father."

"I'd rather you didn't see me like this. You should go back to the ranch." He spoke in a lifeless monotone.

"I'm not leaving you in this place. I know you didn't kill Mr. Carruthers."

Gabe met her gaze again. "But I *look* guilty, Akira. That's all Hud needs to make the charges stick." He closed his eyes. "Just like last time."

"But it isn't like the last time." She blinked away the tears that threatened to blind her. "Last time you didn't have me on your side. And you didn't know God was there with you too. We're here, Gabriel. You aren't alone."

He rose from the cot, then came slowly toward her. He searched her face with his eyes. Then he reached through the bars and touched her cheek.

"Then why do I *feel* alone?" he asked in a hoarse whisper.

An hour later, Akira knelt at the prayer altar at the front of the church's sanctuary. Tears ran unchecked down her cheeks as she rested her forehead against her clenched hands. Tears she hadn't allowed herself to shed in front of Gabe.

"O God. Help us…O God…O God…"

She swallowed the lump in her throat as she lifted her head to look at the cross on the wall.

"Calm my spirit, Jesus," she pleaded in a whisper. "I can't think. I can't pray. It's not right, what's happening. When will it end? What can I do? Why? Why?" She knew asking why of the Almighty was never the proper question, but she asked it again anyway. "Why?"

At first the silence in the sanctuary seemed cold and desolate. But slowly it seemed to envelop her, began to quiet her, little by little, began to bring order to her chaotic thoughts.

Do I truly believe God is sovereign? she asked herself after a brief time.

"Yes," she answered aloud.

And do I believe He cares for me and for Gabe? Do I really believe He loves me?

"Yes."

And do I believe His will is perfect?

"Yes." Her voice broke on the word.

THEN TRUST ME, BELOVED.

She drew a ragged breath. "I'm trying, Lord. I'm trying."

TRUST ME.

A sob escaped her, torn unwillingly from her chest. "Have mercy, God. Have mercy. I don't know how much more he can take." She covered her face with her hands. "No, it's me who can't take much more. Father God, I'm empty. I haven't any strength left."

BELOVED, IT WAS I WHO BEGAN THE GOOD WORK. IT IS I WHO WILL COMPLETE IT. WILL YOU TRUST ME?

Shortly after Andy Newton returned from observing the undertaker's removal of Rupert Carruthers's body and conducting a more thorough investigation of the crime scene, Pauline Talmadge arrived at the sheriff's office. She stood on the opposite side of his desk, looking beautiful and elegant despite the ugly bruise on the side of her face.

"You know Gabe is innocent, Sheriff Newton," she said, not bothering with pleasantries. "I don't know what *did* happen at the mill, but I certainly know what *didn't* happen."

"Shut up, Pauline," Hudson growled from his chair in the corner.

There was a momentary flash of surprise when she heard her husband's voice. Andy thought she paled slightly, although it could have been the poor light in the room playing tricks on his eyes.

"Gabe may have been angry when he left my home," she continued with obvious determination, "but he isn't capable of killing a man."

"He killed his brother." Hudson shot to his feet, his voice raised in anger. "He killed my firstborn son. They never should have let him out of prison. They should have thrown away the key and let him rot."

Pauline didn't look behind her. She kept her gaze fastened on Andy, pleading with him with her eyes.

Andy wanted to say he agreed with her. Problem was, the evidence seemed to suggest otherwise. That evidence, coupled with his prior conviction, meant Gabe was in serious trouble.

The office door opened again, and Jane Sebastian, followed by her brother, Zachary, entered the office.

"Sheriff Newton," Jane said as she marched toward Andy with all the bravado of a drill sergeant, "I certainly hope the gossips in this town are spreading untruths. In the name of all that's good, tell me you haven't arrested Gabe Talmadge."

"Well, I—"

"You know that young man didn't kill Mr. Carruthers. His father twisted the truth once and saw him convicted unjustly. Don't let him get away with it again."

"I'm afraid I—"

She placed her hands, palms down, on his desktop and leaned toward him. "Don't be fooled by the wiles of a snake, Sheriff. He's crafty, but he's still a liar. That's a perfect description of Hudson Talmadge."

Andy leaned to one side and looked behind Jane. Hudson's face was beet red. He looked about ready to explode.

Once more the door opened. This time it was Simon and Violet Neville who entered.

"Sheriff, is it true?" the reverend asked.

The chair creaked as Andy leaned back. As he nodded his reply, he released a silent sigh. This was going to be a long afternoon.

Through the closed door separating the jail cells from the front office, Gabe heard voices, though he could rarely make out what was being said.

The voice he heard most, however, was the one in his head.

Akira's voice, reminding him of the truth: *But it isn't like the last time. Last time you didn't have me on your side. And you didn't know God was there with you too. We're here, Gabriel. You aren't alone.*

He leaned his head against the wall and closed his eyes. "I can do all things through Christ who strengthens me."

He wondered if those words were true. *Could* he do all things? Could he lean on Christ and trust in His strength, no matter what the circumstances?

Even being sent back to prison?

He remembered the night, more than fourteen years before, when he'd sat in this very same cell, scared and alone. He'd known Max was dead. He'd even known the accident was his fault. He'd been drunk and acting irresponsibly. He'd known his father would hate him more than ever.

He remembered his trial, the way everybody in town thought he was the bad seed. He'd seen his guilt in their eyes, those people who had come to view the trial, those men who'd sat on the jury.

Scared and alone.

We're here, Gabriel. You aren't alone.

"Gabe?"

He opened his eyes to see Andy's approach.

"I think you'd better come up front."

"What now?" He stood reluctantly.

Andy shook his head as he put the key in the lock and turned it. "You'll see for yourself." He yanked open the cell door, then motioned for Gabe to follow him.

The buzz of many voices grew louder as he approached the office, but the moment Gabe stepped through the doorway, all became still. Confused, he looked around the room.

Akira had returned. When their gazes met, she offered a brief smile of encouragement.

She was standing between Miss Jane on her left and Brodie Lachlan on her right. Behind them were Zachary, Reverend Neville and his wife, and Pauline Talmadge. Near the outside door was the Wickham family, Nora framed by her husband and son. Ethan Jones was with them. On the bench behind the sheriff's desk, closest to the wood stove, were Thomasina Attebury and Dorothea Baker. Next to them stood Henry Teague, Andy's sometime deputy.

And even though he didn't look in that direction, Gabe knew precisely where his father was seated.

Akira crossed to stand beside him. She took his hand, squeezing his fingers, telling him with her eyes how much she loved him, how much she believed in him.

"They've all stepped forward as character witnesses," she said softly.

Gabe glanced at the sheriff.

"You heard right. Not only that, they've all offered to pool their money to post bail for you. To a person, they swear there's no way you could commit murder."

We're here, Gabriel. You aren't alone.

He returned his gaze to Akira. He tried to think of something to say, but his heart was too full, his emotions too strong.

The door opened again, and along with a blast of cold winter air came George Edwards and Dr. Kirkland from over in Lovejoy. Seeing the crowded office, the two men hesitated before the doctor closed the door.

"Sheriff," George said as he removed his hat, "we've come to talk to you about Gabe Talmadge."

Several people actually chuckled.

A roar of outrage silenced them all. En masse they looked toward the corner where Hudson was now on his feet, glaring at them.

"What's happened to this town? A man's dead, and you're all speaking up for his killer. Doesn't anyone care what he did?" Hudson pointed at Gabe. "He's murdered before, and now he's murdered again."

In that instant, God spoke to Gabe's heart: WHAT MEN HAVE MEANT FOR EVIL, I MEAN FOR GOOD. The last vestiges of his disquiet and despair vanished, as if excised by a surgeon's scalpel.

"You know I didn't do it." He looked at his father, calm and unafraid. "You know I didn't kill him, Father."

Hudson called him a foul name.

"Gabe's telling the truth," a man said from the open doorway. "I was there. I saw what happened."

George and Dr. Kirkland stepped aside and allowed Danny Peck to enter the deathly quiet sheriff's office.

Chapter Thirty

Akira didn't know what to think as Danny Peck moved to the center of the room. Especially when it appeared he was sober. She didn't think she'd seen him that way before.

"Peck—" Hudson began.

"Sit down and shut up, Talmadge," the sheriff ordered. "Danny, you were at the mill?"

"I was there." He looked at Gabe. "I was hiding in the closet in his office."

Hudson made a rude noise. "Sleeping off a drunk, no doubt."

"No," Danny responded without looking away from Gabe. "I was stone cold sober. By choice. I went to the mill to tell your father I wasn't doin' no more of his dirty work. He paid me to kill your sheep."

Akira pressed a hand against her chest.

"I felt like you and your missus owed me somethin'. I was glad to get paid t'try and hurt you. Then I saw the boy there." He pointed. "Ethan's my nephew. Ain't that true, boy?"

Several people in the room muttered words of surprise as Ethan nodded.

"Looney Lindy's my sister, and I know now what you done for her. You took in my kin when it shoulda been me doin' it. You and Akira cared for them when they didn't have nobody else. They sure didn't have me. Lindy washed her hands of me a long time ago 'cause of my drinkin'."

Hudson stood again. "What does this have to do with Carruthers's murder and the attempt on my life?"

"I told you to be quiet, Talmadge," Andy responded, "and I meant it. Don't interrupt again, or I'll put you in one of the cells in the back."

Danny took a step closer to Gabe. "I went to the mill to give your old man back what money I had left. I didn't want it. Not no more. I was sick of what I done." Now he turned his gaze toward the sheriff. "When Talmadge and Carruthers got there, they was arguing, and I thought it'd be better if I saw Talmadge alone. So I slipped into the closet, leaving the door open a bit so's I wouldn't get locked in."

When Danny paused, every person in the room—Akira included—seemed to stop breathing, waiting until he continued.

"Carruthers told Talmadge he's ruined. That he'd shut things down too late. The banks're gonna take everything he's got left."

Several gasps punctuated the air.

"Carruthers showed him something written in a little book he always carried. That's when Talmadge told him it was his fault and called him stupid. He told Carruthers he was fired and to get out. Talmadge turned his back. Carruthers hit him over the head with that brass lamp stand. I thought sure he'd kill him. When he came at him again, Talmadge stabbed him in the gut with somethin' he grabbed off his desk. Carruthers, he was bleedin' like a stuck pig when he went down. Then Talmadge passed out."

Akira glanced up at Gabe, but she couldn't tell what he was thinking. Did he realize this proved his innocence? The sheriff hadn't told anyone how Carruthers had died. There was no other way Danny could have known all this. He must have been present, just as he said.

Andy rubbed his jaw thoughtfully. "Were you still in the closet when Gabe arrived?"

"No sir. I was gettin' outta there as quick as I could. But I only made it down the stairs before I heard Gabe comin' in. So I hid in the boiler room. He went up the stairs and about five or so minutes later, you arrived. I laid low until you took Gabe and Talmadge away in your car, then I skedaddled."

"That's a fine story, Mr. Peck," Hudson said, disdain riddling his words. "But it's the word of the town drunk against mine."

Fourteen years before, all that had been needed was Hudson Talmadge's word. His word had been enough to send Gabe to prison for ten years. But looking around her at the faces of those in this room, Akira knew Hudson's word was no longer enough.

"It ain't just my word," Danny insisted. "You don't believe me, sheriff, take a look at that little book he's got in his coat pocket. I can tell you what some of those entries is about 'cause I heard Carruthers readin' from it. Talmadge took it before he told him he was fired."

Hudson rose from the chair and strode toward the door. "I've listened to all of this I can stand. I'm leaving." But instead of parting before him, the onlookers tightened their ranks, impeding his departure.

"I don't think you're going anywhere, Mr. Talmadge," Andy said.

Hudson whirled about. "You have no right to keep me here. If what that little weasel says is true, then I acted in self defense. And if he's lying, then I'm still the victim of an attempted murder." He glared at Gabe. "And you," he said with loathing, "I let you wear my name, even though you're no son of mine, and look how you've repaid me. I should have strangled you the night you were born. You came back to Ransom to get your hands on my money, but you'll get nothing." His voice rose to a crescendo. "You'll get nothing. Do you hear me? Nothing!"

The sheriff's office was quiet now, all of Gabe's supporters returned to their homes except Akira and Brodie.

"I won't be long," Gabe told his wife as he touched her cheek with his fingertips. Then he turned and walked toward the back of the building, toward the cell that held his father.

At the sound of his footsteps, Hudson glanced up. Hatred twisted his expression into a grotesque mask.

Gabe prayed for wisdom.

"Get out," his father growled. "Do your gloating elsewhere. They won't be able to keep me in here for long. My attorneys will see to that."

"I didn't come to gloat." He stopped about a foot away from the bars.

"Then why did you come?"

It was a fair question, Gabe thought. If only he had an answer.

"You know the money is gone, and what there is the attorneys will take. You'll inherit nothing from me. You won't get a cent." Hudson's eyes blazed with an almost gleeful lunacy. "Not a red cent."

"Listen to me a moment, Father."

"Don't call me that. I didn't sire you. You're not mine."

Gabe stepped up to the bars, gripping them with both hands, staring hard into the other man's eyes. "Listen to me and try to understand something. It doesn't matter if you believe I'm your son or not. It doesn't matter if I inherit anything from you or not. In fact, the *last* thing I wanted was your money." He leaned forward. "My inheritance is in heaven, and it's far better than all the riches you ever had or might have again."

Hudson growled something unintelligible.

"That's why I came back to Ransom, though I didn't know it at the time. I was returning to Jesus, not to this town and not to you. Oh, I wanted your love and approval. I've wanted it since I was a boy. But God chose me for another purpose. He chose me to receive *His* riches. I'm His rightful heir, no matter what the circumstances of my birth. I'm an heir to the King." He paused, impacted by the truth of his own words. Softly, he added, "Hard to believe, isn't it?"

"You're as crazy as your mother. There is no God."

"I feel sorry for you."

Hudson glared at him.

"I feel sorry for you, because if there is no God, then this life, the best you've ever had, is as good as it gets. And no matter how rich you are, what good will your wealth do when you're dead and buried?"

A look of dread crossed his father's face. For an instant, Hudson seemed to hear what Gabe was saying. Then the moment passed.

"Go away." Hudson turned his back. "Go away and take your God with you."

Gabe was surprised by the lump in his throat. He hadn't known it was possible he might still hurt for his father.

"All right. I'll go. But like it or not, God will be here, giving you another chance."

He waited a short while, hoping for the man who had no hope, but Hudson didn't move.

"Goodbye, Father," Gabe said at last. "I'll keep praying for you. Remember that when things are at their darkest. Remember that I'll be praying for you."

EPILOGUE

May 1935

MacRae Gabriel Talmadge entered the world just before dawn three weeks after the Basque sheepshearers had completed their annual visit to Dundreggan.

Ahead of schedule and in a hurry—as would prove true for much of his life—MacRae Talmadge gave little warning of his imminent arrival. So it was that Gabe delivered his son and held him as he drew his first breath. A moment later, the room was filled with the lusty wail of new life.

Gabe grinned, then whispered, "Hello, Mac. Welcome to the world."

"Is the baby all right?" Akira asked.

"He's perfect." He moved to the side of the bed. "Listen to him."

She held out her arms, and Gabe placed the baby in them, watching as she drew the child to her breast.

"MacRae," he said, "meaning a son of grace."

Akira smiled, her misty-eyed gaze caressing their firstborn son. "Gabriel, meaning a strong man of God. Like his father before him."

He leaned forward and kissed Akira's forehead. "I love you," he whispered. Then he kissed the top of the baby's head. "And you, my son."

As he straightened, joy unspeakable filled his heart. There were no words to describe what he felt. That this small life was blood of his blood. That he was responsible for raising him up in the way he should go.

But what if he wasn't a good father? What if he failed his son? What if he—?

BEFORE I FORMED THEE IN THE BELLY I KNEW THEE.

Gabe didn't know what lay ahead, what the future held. Not for his son. Not for his wife. Not for himself. So many things could go wrong. So many ills could befall them.

BEFORE THOU CAMEST FORTH OUT OF THE WOMB I SANCTIFIED THEE.

Once Gabe had tried to run, tried to hide, from the Savior he'd rejected. Once he'd been pursued by darkness, hopelessness, and fear. But he hadn't been able to run far enough, climb high enough, or sink low enough to escape the love of Christ. He'd learned, as well as any man who'd lived, the abounding grace of God.

FOR I KNOW THE THOUGHTS THAT I THINK TOWARD YOU, SAITH THE LORD, THOUGHTS OF PEACE, AND NOT OF EVIL, TO GIVE YOU AN EXPECTED END.

An expected end.

Comfort warmed him.

The end won't be a surprise to our Father. It's expected.

And with that knowledge planted in his heart, Gabriel—a strong man of God, an heir to the King—faced the future unafraid.

Dear Reader,

The Shepherd's Voice was born out of the desire to remind believers that God's forgiveness isn't just for the moment a person is born again. Christ died for all sins, including those that happen after we come to know Him as Savior and Lord.

In my own Christian walk, I've fallen flat on my face whenever I've chosen to pursue my own will over the Father's. Afterward, I've discovered how hard it is to forgive myself for my willfulness. I have no problem accepting God's forgiveness after I've confessed my sin, but forgiving myself is something else entirely. Then the Holy Spirit revealed to me that I am actually giving victory to the enemy when I cling to the guilt. I don't want to do that.

God has a plan for each and every one of His children, and He is speaking to each of us all the time. When we listen to Him, He keeps us from chasing after our own will. When we obey, He keeps us from stumbling. If I had to name one desire I have for my novels, it would be that they serve as an encouragement for readers to listen and hear the Shepherd's voice.

In His grip,
Robin Lee Hatcher

If you enjoyed *The Shepherd's Voice*, look for…

THE FORGIVING HOUR

by Robin Lee Hatcher

IS HER SON'S ENGAGEMENT A DREAM…OR A NIGHTMARE?

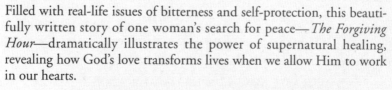

Though Claire Conway's life hasn't turned out exactly as she had planned, she has much to be thankful for: She has raised a fine son, Dakota. Her career is going well. And for the first time since her divorce, she's met a man who stirs romantic feelings in her broken heart.

Then Dakota brings home his fiancée, Sara Jennings, and for the second time in Claire's life, her world crumbles. By what seems to be a cruel twist of fate, Dakota has fallen in love with the woman who was involved in the destruction of his parents' marriage. The ramifications of this discovery threaten to destroy the lives of all involved. Claire wishes she could forgive Sara. But this seems impossible. Yet only in that hour of forgiveness can the three of them be truly set free…

Filled with real-life issues of bitterness and self-protection, this beautifully written story of one woman's search for peace—*The Forgiving Hour*—dramatically illustrates the power of supernatural healing, revealing how God's love transforms lives when we allow Him to work in our hearts.

AVAILABLE NOW AT YOUR LOCAL BOOKSTORE.

"Break out the tissues. I loved *The Forgiving Hour*, and so will you. Robin Lee Hatcher shows God's grace and mercy in bringing healing into the most painful of circumstances. This book cuts through the darkness of betrayal and brings in the miraculous light of Jesus Christ."
— FRANCINE RIVERS, best-selling author

If you enjoyed *The Shepherd's Voice,* also look for...

WHISPERS FROM YESTERDAY

by Robin Lee Hatcher

A SPELLBINDING TAPESTRY OF
DISCOVERY, DELIVERANCE, AND
ROMANCE ON AN IDAHO RANCH

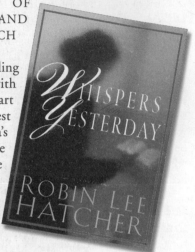

The author of the powerful, best-selling
novel *The Forgiving Hour* is back with
another stirring journey into the heart
of a woman. As the reluctant newest
resident of her grandmother Sophia's
Golden T ranch, pampered socialite
Karen Butler wants nothing more
than to return to L.A. But there's no
going back to the past. Her father is
dead. Her family home has been
sold. Her finances and options are
exhausted. And her hope is gone.

Also living at the broken-down ranch is Dusty Stoddard, who operates a
summer camp for troubled teens there. In this strange setting, far from
everything familiar, Karen is surrounded by people who love God and
seek to serve Him. She yearns to escape, to return to her old way of life.
Yet the call to her heart is unmistakable. And in the diaries of a woman
who died twenty-eight years before Karen was born, Karen discovers
secrets and amazing truths that cause her to finally find a way to the
greatest love of all.

Powerfully illustrating that God does have a plan for each person's life and
can use every individual to fulfill His purposes, *Whispers from Yesterday*
offers a dramatic story of healing, hope, and God's glorious compassion.

AVAILABLE NOW AT YOUR LOCAL BOOKSTORE.

"*Whispers from Yesterday* moved me to tears, again and again. How
like Karen I once was...and how like Esther I long to be! This
remarkable love story glows with the light of truth and grace.
Another winner for Robin Lee Hatcher. I loved it!"

—LIZ CURTIS HIGGS, best-selling author

ROBIN LEE HATCHER

Robin Lee Hatcher is the author of more than thirty novels with over four million books in print and is a past president of Romance Writers of America. Her books have won numerous awards, including the Romance Writers of America RITA Award for Best Inspirational Romance, the Heart of Romance Readers' Choice Award for Best Historical, a Career Achievement Award for Americana Romance from *Romantic Times*, and the Favorite Historical Author Award from *Affaire de Coeur*. For her efforts on behalf of literacy, Laubach Literacy International named their romance award "The Robin." Robin, a mother of two and grandmother of three, and her husband, Jerry, live in Boise, Idaho.

Readers may write to her at
P.O. Box 4722, Boise, ID 83711-4722
or visit her Web site:
<http://www.robinleehatcher.com>